Passing strange

Passing strange

short stories

Bill Reed

First published in 2015
Published independently by Reed Independent
Melbourne, Australia
brrrreed@gmail.com

Printed by CreateSpace, an Amazon.com company

Available from Amazon.com, CreateSpace.com, and other retail outlets

This book is available in print-on-demand and ebook formats:
paperback: ISBN13-9780994239921
ebook: ISBN13-9780994239938

This book contains works of fiction. The incidents, dialogue and plot are the products of the author's imagination or are used fictitiously. Any coincidence to actual events is purely coincidental.

National Library of Australia Cataloguing-in-Publication entry:
(paperback)
Author: Reed, Bill, 1939 - author.
Title: Passing Strange / Bill Reed
ISBN: 9780994239921 (paperback)
Subjects: Australia—Fiction/short stories
Dewey Number: A823.3
(ebook)
Author: Reed, Bill, 1939 - author.
Title: Passing Strange/ Bill Reed
ISBN: 9780994239938 (ebook)
Subjects: Australia—Fiction/short stories
Dewey Number: A823.3

Contents

To the memory of Charlie
and his soft laying off the batting the breeze.

Extinction is forever, give or take a day.
And there's always Redemption trying to take that precious minute of
your time.

The inclusions

I don't know whether the few stories which I've included in this collection without them gaining national short-story-competition recognition would have been up to the same award/recommended standards as the others. I think they might well have, though, and have made that the judgment to include them.

For one thing, the years 2006 and 2007 weren't the only years I've had the pleasure of writing short stories as might seem from the list of awards or recommends I list below. It is just being an Australian ex-pat writer most often, if not now mostly always, disqualifies one from entering Australian short-fiction competitions for which, for some reason, residence seems to be more important than citizenship... even though a story is set in Australia or revolves around Australians.

For another thing, few serious short-story wroughters would argue against the seeming fact that the major international short story competitions, as truly grand as they are and wonderful to lottery-win, struggle to be fair and open given either their tens of thousands of submissions or their profit-making structures, or both.

The stories that have the 'award' right to be included are given that inclusion on the basis of:

As 'The Case Inside', the inclusion here of 'The Meat Axe Hanging on the Kitchen Door' won the national 2007 Katherine Susannah Pritchard Award.

Messman on C.E.'s Altar' was first published in *Expressway* (Penguin Books Australia, 1989) with the subtitle 'Twenty-nine Australian writers respond to Helen Daniel's invitation: stories based on Jeffrey Smart's painting "Cahill Expressway"'.

The twosome of 'Blind Freddie' came about like this: 'Blind Freddie Purblinded' won the 2006 National Short Story Competition of the Canberra University. It then morphed into 'Blind Freddie at the End of the Cord' which was commended in the 2007 Bauhinia Literary

1

Awards which, in turn, morphed into the short play 'Blind Freddie Living on Mars' which morphed into the full-length play 'The Relic Holding the Pickle Jars'. This last was officially entered in the MTC's so-called 'long list' for the 2007 season but sadly that short listing proved as drop-to-ocean as the company's other promissory 'long lists'.

'Those 250-year-old Feet Being Bought Out From Under Me' started existence as 'Those 250-year-old Feet' and was awarded second prize at the 2004 Ames Greater Dandenong Literary Award.

The short play 'I Don't Know What To Do With You' was published in the 'Australian Theatre Workshop' series, Heinemann Educational 1979, and has been reprinted seven times. And the short play 'I Know' was shortlisted by the Short and Sweet awards organised by the Victorian Arts Centre in 2006.

Under the early title of 'Shades of You, My Dandenong', the piece 'Dandenong Ladies and Their All' won the Australia-wide 2007 Ames Greater Dandenong Literary Award, which remained one of the richest short story competitions in Australia until it was stopped in 2008.

'The Last of Her Tribe' went out to the 2006 Ames Greater Dandenong Literary Award under the title of 'Look Out, World, Madam Mountain Coming Through' and gained the Highly Recommended recognition.

'Sticking the Boot into Charlie' was also place in the Highly Recommended category of the 2006 Ames Greater Dandenong Literary Award.

'No Better than the Kids' started out as 'The Old Serviceman' and was winner of the DVA Story Competition 2006.

At the 2007 Bauhinia National Literary Awards, both 'The Councillor' shorties included here were given special commendations.

The meat axe on the kitchen door

'HEY! HEY! THE CHURCH BUS FLOAT BY?'

He feels like chuckling that she doesn't know she is only asking something sent to try him. This old bird Violet, all dolled up in cardie and cock-eyed hat and shiny-white Adidas runners at this time of night. He doesn't chuckle out loud, because he has to be careful. He's been lying doggo all day out in the open on the couch in the TV lounge in the oldies' Home making like all he's doing is watching the box and here it is coming up Wednesday midnight and she's asking did the Sunday-morning church bus come. He has stopped himself from chuckling, remembering not to muck up, but just think how he did it last time. He thinks how the man in the black cloak keeps telling him that… that it will come back to him. So now David is answering her craftily, cunningly seeing where this could all lead:

'It's Wednesday, not Sunday, dopey'.

But would she move? No, she won't move. She is waiting for him to muck up, but he at least remembers he's been through this before. He knows the Americans ruined him the last time. He doesn't bother to tell the old girl he's left her now to grope his way along the pitch-black corridor to that full-of-pong old Mumpsie to get out here and get old Vie back into bed. Already, yes, he can see where this could all lead. And at her door and after it's opened, he tries to explain like any reasonable man, but this Mumpsie is always shouting at him:

'I'M A MARRIED WOMAN!'

His face boils. Why she is yelling at him again just because he's at her door coming on midnight sort of? What his father said: just relax and it'll come back to you how you did it last time. But she has already slammed her door in his face and is waddling off into the dark in her greasy old nightie, going for the TV glow back down the corridor. He can't let her get away with shouting at him all the time:

3

'YOU'RE NOT MARRIED!'

'I AM!'

'YOU'RE NOT! HE'S DEAD!'

'SO WHAT? I'M STILL MARRIED!'

Following her sick-making powder trail, David sees clearly the meat axe hanging on the kitchen door. It's not much of an image; he only sees it momentarily, how it suddenly was hanging there on account of the new cook saying how she always does that, that's her thing. He doesn't know what she means by that, but it doesn't matter. He nearly has the meat axe in his hand as he squashes himself against the wall to let the two old ladies pass him by. Mumpsie pushes old Violet deliberately into him as they go, take that you, as if I didn't know what you're doing, you stink. She is lucky he doesn't use the meat axe then and there; what with half the night lights still working he couldn't miss.

David holds the meat axe out and up and lets it waggle playfully in the moonshine of the TV just reaching there, seeing how its edge thrills in and shimmers with the strobing colours of some dance light he knows he must have seen once. He can chuckle now, but only to himself. This is definitely a pointer as to how he did it last time. He sees the colours collect themselves for him and how they are letting him see again the image of his kitbag, in which lies waiting the most precious thing of all his born days that has been promised.

The kitbag hums to him as he hides in the night shadows outside Mumpsie's room there. It brings tears to his eyes what he has been made to bear all those born days. He recalls the man in the black cloak telling him your mother left you at birth for the State he has come to realize has to mean the States, and how the judge must have told the Americans to lock his childhood away in the kitbag for safekeeping until he was ready to collect it. You will know when you are ready from the last time, the man in the black cloak has said the judge has said to tell him. The thing is just relax and it'll come back to you, how you did it last time. .

4

Outside Mumpsie's room, covered by night, he looks down at the meat axe in his hand.

Well, it doesn't matter if it isn't there. The man in the black cloak knows where everything is.

Mumpsie bumps and gropes her way with old Violet back to the old lady's room. They just grunt at the effort of making clear way in the night's dark side of the Home. They wouldn't think to speak in such blackness with those few pins of lights up ahead, fearful for all women. She holds old Violet ahead of her like a sort of protection you ought never to forget you need. Watchit; don't let the old legs go or they all try to climb all over you. Mumpsie thinks of the man in the black cloak somewhere near and relaxes somewhat. She rehearses how to get him to put that dirty cheeky David in his place. Ash all over him and how he stinks. How would you be, mothering that? She doesn't care why he thinks he can shout at her all the time; she won't lie down to abuse like that. That trying to shout her down, on about her poor husband; she's never let anyone climb all over her and she's not starting now. They let them in out of the gutter these days.

I shouldn't, she thinks as she stops with a sudden fear outside the kitchen, I shouldn't have come to this at my age. Thank the Lord my God I've got my legs and know where the new cook hangs that vicious-looking thing on the kitchen door.

She waves the meat axe before her for protection as a lady can never forget she needs if they won't fix at least half the night lights.

Mumpsie stumbles a bit onwards. She continues to grope the walls to feel her way in the dark. Why am I always the one they come to when someone's in strife? The trouble is how can anyone get some shuteye with that filthy reeking David and his television going all hours of the night? The man in the black cloak promised something was going to be done about it. She thinks. She knows she needs to piddle. I've got a right to. Even so she is wary of hurrying on. She knows she can expect to see David crouching in TV-glow opposite her door. She knows he

5

will have the meat axe dangling at his side, as if he was all innocence. She is not scared of him, but knows how her legs can go first and then they start trying to climb all over you. Again, hanging back as much as she can there, she shudders to think what would happen if anyone found out that the most precious things in her whole life are safe and sound in her wedding travelling case in her room. They'll be okay as long as her legs hold out. So she forces herself on, backing up to her door, snorting bravely, raising the meat axe threateningly towards the darkness there she knows he is lurking in. She is suddenly maddened again how he intends to find out what's preciously hers in her wedding travelling case, and keeps reminding her about what he intends.

David snorts and is raising the meat axe threateningly towards the darkness he knows she is backing into. Again, he feels the blind fury about how she intends to stop him from getting back what's preciously his childhood in his old kitbag, and keeps reminding him about what she intends.

It's as usual, that they can't stop shouting at each other:

'DON'T YOU TRY AND CLIMB ALL OVER ME!'

'YOUR FAMILY WON'T EVEN LOOK AT YOU, OLD LADY!'

'I'LL CLOCK YOU ONE!'

'THEY'RE NOT STUPID. THEY WON'T HAVE A BAR OF YOU!'

'THEN WHY DO THEY STILL WANT TO LIVE WITH ME?!'

'BULLSHIT!'

At least they know the man in the black cloak will be waiting nearby to keep the peace. He claps his hands to announce it is so, but not alarmingly. It's as usual; that they both recognize his kindly voice kindly come and not a moment too soon:

'Ssh. Go to bed.'

They each bow their heads to the soothing presence somewhere nearby of the man in the black cloak, each smug in the knowledge he cannot be heard by the other. David hides the meat axe behind his back knowing it's not there anymore. Mumpsie hides the meat axe behind her back knowing it's not there anymore. They both hide the meat axe still hanging on the kitchen door and return to their rooms feeling they haven't mucked up.

The meat axe has gone missing from the kitchen door. The management raises the alarm with the police. The new cook is now not the most popular person. All staff has to be more alert these days with this new rehab thing they call family-recouping. They should know it's become the correct opinion to let the mentally-disabled, make that nutters, take up vacancies in the state-funded infirmaries, make that among defenceless old ladies. Like, which brain-dead's opinion?

Mumpsie knows who the thief is. David knows who the thief is. They sit, each, with their backs to the walls. Across the sitting room they eye each other furtively. They are sweating so much the chairs next to them are even vacant. They know what they must have the courage to face in the depth of tonight.

When the police have finally checked all the rooms and got around to the sitting room, Mumpsie lets them search under and around her, barely containing herself from confiding in them what she deep down knows:

'If you don't keep a lookout, your legs go first and then they start having a go at climbing all over you!'

As they search around and under him, David wants to confide in them what he deep down knows:

'I only have to think how I did it last time, don't I?'

Somewhere around them, the police with long looks let the management get back to work. The meat axe has been found somewhere in the kitchen. The new cook, no, is now not the most popular person. The residents file in for lunch and nobody notices that both Mumpsie and David would rather be eating with them than transfixed there where they have to be. They remain seated in the sitting room staring madly at the meat axe spinning in the air between them. It spins and thrums like a whirling dervish, like a wild diamond in the sky.

Mumpsie knows he is circling, ducking, slinking somewhere near just waiting for her to leave her room unguarded. She herself circles in the mid-night there. She herself ducks when she hears a shuffle in any of the shadows anywhere near. She herself slinks from unlit doorway to unlit doorway in the soft and dark corridor some-parts hued blue from the TV left on by him, the dirty b. The crutch of his slaggy tracksuit down around his knees; half his bare bum dirty-filthy hanging out. She can smell the soak down of his tobacco reek. At least it's the night now, when he can be avoided. She chuckles to herself, knowing he is too stupid to know she knows what his game is.

Watchit, keep the old legs going. They go first, and then they all think they got some right to try climbing all over you. As usual, she moves down the long vague corridor, herself circling, ducking, slinking in the throbbing of deep-night electricity somewhere, until she can let herself see the Border Collie of her younger time sweeping its lovely golden-browns across the sweeping green of the cricket field to explode all the skies in and around her with the purity veil of the dancing gulls. In that moment, she knows she is in sweet drench, as it always will so wonderfully be for her live-long, as ever long as she has legs to reach it, her wedding travelling case. In it, in her wedding case, the most precious things of her life live safe; they are quiet and still; they are smiling at her as the purity veil comes down.

After the meat axe was stolen, she has heard the kitchen door is locked night and day. Mumpsie nods to her dark-orange reflection in the night opacity of one of the garden windows. Maybe now she doesn't need to worry so much about that dirty cheeky David circling, ducking, slinking around her. But she keeps the meat axe readied before her, just in case.

8

Just after midnight, this one night of other nights, when the TV dims any plain light, the man in the black cloak moves and shifts and carefully approaches in a calming way. In that way, he speaks in his usual soft way:

'David.'

'I only have to think how I did it last time, don't I?'

'Yes.'

'The Americans ruined me last time. See, everyone knows me, so I can't muck up.'

'Your father's coming to see you pretty soon, I promise.'

'I don't want to let him down. He'll want to know what happened about my kitbag.'

'Ssh. Go to bed.'

And while this is going on, the man in the black cloak watches the Border Collie of Mumpsie's younger time sweep its lovely colours across the cricketing greens to douse Mumpsie's mind with the purity veil of the exploding gulls and, as the high night wanes, he speaks softly in the way he usually does, as is his way:

'Mumpsie.'

'You have to watch it or your legs go first.'

'Yes.'

'Keep a secret about what the best medicine is?'

'Okay.'

'If it wasn't for my wedding travelling case, I'd be flat out on my back

9

long ago with 'em trying to make my legs go first.'

'Ssh. Go to bed.'

Now David is feeling the thrill of a cunning that is panning out.

'Did the church bus float by?'

There it goes again; and see how by setting up something as routine he
has manoeuvred old Vi to have been there, madly crashing around in
the dark... there once more in her Sunday best when it's another black-
as-spades Wednesday night outside... to be that old bird Mumpsie's
responsibility. Who didn't want to but had to get out of her room and
get old Violet back to the cot.

Now, in that glow of cunning, David has gained his kitbag at last.
While she blindly steers old Vi back to bed, he has successfully turned
the key he has found unimaginatively in the lock through something he
must have done equally as cleverly, and has barged sensationally into
that Mumpsie's room. He does not need light. He has always known
where his kitbag of his childhood would exactly be.

He feels, yes, the thrill of kneeling at his own wanted place at last.

The kitbag is locked but with the thrill at first he does not panic that it
resists the point of the meat axe in his hand. Straining and gouging with
it, he tries hard to remember, yet still cannot think, how some other
screwdriver or other has already gouged and clawed the locks until he
realizes there must have been some other last time. In the panic come
now, he strikes with the meat axe. He bashed blindly at the kitbag with
the meat axe. At the kitbag, he strikes out again and again with the
meat axe, until he has found unimaginatively that he has burst the old
leather through. The thrill he can feel. He pushes his wanting hand in
through the leather of it; he gropes for what has been in promise of
safe-keeping for him from his best young days for all of his born days.
What the judge said. What the judge promised all those thirsting years
ago when he told the Americans to lock his childhood away in the
kitbag for safekeeping until he was ready to collect it. You will know

10

when you are ready from the last time, the man in the black cloak had whispered that the judge had said to tell him personally.

David has to try again. He is beholden to himself. Again, he has to try. He tries again, grabbing around the sides, around the ups and downs of it.

There is nothing in there. He cannot feel where they have locked his whole childhood away for safekeeping. It is not there. In there, is nothing.

He screams up from his kitbag where Mumpsie is now come and is screaming up from not his childhood kit bag at all, no, but her own cherished wedding case trying now to wrench it from him.

Mumpsie lets the hot intimacy of her own blood rive down her cheeks. She tastes much of it and finds it warmly her own and not so good. It is strange how her meat axe is in his meat axe and how it is swinging against herself in heavy chunks and against his head in heavy chunks and he lets the hot intimacy of his own blood roll down his cheeks and tastes much of it and finds it warm and not so good. She finds it strange to be looking at last down into her secret wedding case, in which has always kept safe and sound her dear husband and dear children and yet, after all the wait for her waking and wedding dream, they are not bursting into the purity veil of the exploding gulls she is offering from all her skies. They are not. In there, they have gone missing. In there, is nothing.

Confused, David stares down at the empty space of his childhood they had promised would be in keepsake. Confused, Mumpsie stares down at the empty space where she had secretly kept her family safe and sound and in purity veil.

'YOU'VE KILLED ME!'

They think they themselves have shrieked this first.

In the fading light of the next evening, the man in the black cloak, the

11

Night Nurse, is the single soft voice that is softly rebuking them:

'You know it's a no go running around at night trying to spook each other out. It's not how a mother and son behave.'

'SHE AIN'T MY MOTHER!'

'HE'S NOT MY SON!'

'Oh, you big kidders, you. What we want both of you to do is relax and let it come back to you, how you did it last time, hmm?'

'HEY! HEY! THE CHURCH BUS FLOAT BY?'

goes again old Violet, blessing herself and floating by on top of her red-and-blue Adidas runners. She is somewhere around.

Messman on C.E.'s altar

When all was said and done, it should have been said that Messman would have said he was shocked to see himself painted into a painting by an artist he might have admired if he had ever met him or even seen any of his works before. Hadn't at all.

Is this what was 'likeness'? A stranger plucks an image out of the air and he's got no idea who it is because it's me and I haven't ever met the sod (Messman amusing himself with bravura there in front of the painting), yet he'd have no idea how my life's been bound up with the building of the Cahill Expressway long before this one J. Smart (the moniker at the bottom left hand corner of the painting, so Messman knew, didn't he ever) even thought of immortalising me'n'it in paint. If only that J. Smart knew.

Standing there, with the polished wood of the gallery floor between the painting and him, Messman wasn't all that surprised to see himself immortalised with the Cahill Expressway of that time like that. When all's said and done.

For one thing it was the first art exhibition he had ever been to, so you tell him how it was, other than destiny, that Messman found himself there just because there were too many sorts of shirleys waiting back at his Ex-servicemen's Club to pick a bone with him, so he had to give the usual civilising jars a miss that Sunday. For a week, say. They tend to quieten down in a week. They get other bones to pick at, Messman guessed. Someonething like that had directed his slow loafers into here for to gander at his own mug immortalised on this wall there. Obvious. It was never much Messman's lot to reason n' wonder why.

He'd never had much call for a deep blue-grey suit either, ever in his life, but what the hell, must be what they call artistic licensing, like bottle licensing and where would a man be without that? (Well, certainly not standing on the side of a deserted expressway in a deserted landscape in a painting, no way.) Gotta be the destiny thing. Destiny. J. Smart being given the insight of me maybe being more than the warehouseman I've only thought I ever wanted to be in my life. He and destiny must know better. Such must make art.

13

Gave me a blue-grey suit; takes my hair away. Fair enough, frug it. Who can argue with an artistic swop when it comes your way? And where's this J. Smart to argue the toss with anyway?

Outside, on the bus bench, not waiting for a bus which could not have come anyway. Messman wondered whether the artist J. Smart really knew how he, Messman, had had his life shoved in hock to what he called his C.E. that long day ago. Since he had never told anybody about it, Messman presumed that only God, C.E. and himself knew the sacred part that existed between Messman, the mess up, and the Cahill Expressway, whoever the frig Cahill was. He preferred it as his C.E. Now that J. Smart obviously knew about the secret relationship existing between Messman and C.E... obvious again or you don't go sticking it all around arty walls... Messman wondered whether God had blabbed through, what do they call it?, that inspiration destiny thing, or whether J. Smart was in God's pocket and got leaked the gen when the penny dropped. They say you get some artists who paint divinely, ha ha. Waiting there at that non-existent bus stop.

But Messman knew naught about all that shoot-on-the-shiggery stuff between man and God when it comes to laying down brush strokes. Strokes, plain and simple, I'm in the know a bit with. Keeping the old fingers crossed.

Nor did Messman know, sitting there, immortalised now in paint upon the dark tunnel opening of Sydney's Cahill Expressway, that the sacred pact between him and his tied-in destiny with C.E. (it hums, still, ever, in his ear even now, not far off) only had two more days to run. Two more days only. What an artistic stroke of luck. After twenty years. Goes to show foot-directing destiny ain't dumb. Nor J. Smart. Nor the old femmes back at the club on for his bones for to pick. Must've known something in their bones too. One of two with a few strokes left in 'em too.

So Messman sat there musing on the yesterday, twenty years ago, when became inextricably linked his own destiny with that of C.E., inhockingly. N' this much he also knew, oh yes: that every day of the last twenty years was an extra day he should never had had if it wasn't for C.E. and getting to sort of stand there looking into the dark tunnel opening like J. Smart had painted him. Did Messman know. C.E. hath given and C.E. would taketh away. That much was painted in the caves of J. Smart's art. No wonder they call them art works.

Messman. That day long ago Messman. That day, then, remembering that day long ago, while the Sunday-dressed C.E/. hums as-ever nearby him as-ever, empty as ever and always in his mind.

He had his job in North Sydney. They hadn't as yet by then torn down the working-class cottages to upchuck the North Sydney business district. And he had his one-bedroom 'roach-cage' on the other side of the northern reaches of the Cahill Expressway they were in the processes, then, of building. And in between the work plan and his fleapit, divided by the rising his-C.E., Messman had his routine, too. He had his own processes.

Yes, and that day long ago, at 7.30 out of the apartment block, going steadily for a 7.30 arrival at the freeway's ongoing construction. Along which would he walk, the Harbour Bridge before him, not to mention a 7.48 arrival at his warehouse laid out before him in his, oh yes, mind.

Down by there where the flyover in Alfred Street North is now, Messman cuts across the freeway construction, feeling it sweeping down upon his right as it whooshed on to the Bridge, or would soon, and thereuntosodoing enter North Sydney itself.

This was one of those days when the blue of the sky twinkle-twines with the blue of the Harbour waters and they tingle with clashing acts of coruscatings n' pervading blues that even J. Smart'd go green with envy about. Even Messman too, as he walks and walked that day around 7.42 a.m. upon the inchoate C.E. there, wasn't feeling lonely after all. Meaning Messman and even probably C.E. itself if you took J. Smart at his brush-word.

Shows you how much of a sparkling morning it was. Just as J. Smart has it painterly.

And since there wasn't another human creature in sight nor any fired-up machinery pumppumppumping there, Messman was feeling even less lonely humming along.

Shows you how much more of a sparkling morning you might've at first thought it was.

But you ask Messman how everything became hitched up so just about then, and, blowed, he wouldn't be able to tell you. It just did, says he. One minute, Messman was mentally stepping out of the cesspool of his miserable shitfaced existence for a few unlonely moments, the next thing there's this electric jarring of all his nerve ends. At least those that hadn't already jumped outa his body were on the jar end. Christ. He is turning; Messman has begun the act of turning in alarm and even thinking expletive. There is this truck sweeping down the expressway construction. Okay. But the heavy metal road roller it is towing is going something funny otherwise to it. This is a tarmac compacter that is definitely out of its fucking mind and jerking and breaking loose from round the back of the truck and bearing down on Messman with that single intent that rollers get on with. It is no good the truck driver breaking hard; this thing just continues its thunderous bouncing down the sweep of the half-formed expressway with a completeness that is definitely standing out. A huge metal lard of flotsam jack-knifing over and over, gaining messman-immolating momentum. Like, watch out the whole of Sydney...

after it deals with Messman.

Messman stands transfixed; he does not move, even did not move. The only human being in a vast concrete compound wasteland and, sure-sighted along Fate's barrel with a vindictiveness that's going: 'Okay, if you're the only sucker around, then don't bother hitching up any wagon, guy!'

And in that instant, Messman knew the Cahill Expressway would claim him forever, since subjectivity wasn't in it. And that roller was less than twenty yards, even by pre-metric standards, from the Messman dead centre when it veritably leapt into jumping-bean mode, whatever

16

that is, and flew high and turtle'd into the air. It did. And it did what Messman would later come to recognise as a two-and-a-half somersault with full twist and double-pike in the air space above Messman – smuchasif it had long been starved of applause – and cannoned to earth on the other concreted side of him. Where it hit a retaining wall some one hundred pre-metric yards down the construction site and came top-spinningly, disappointedly really, to rest in a harmless sort of fashion, smuchasif to say retaining walls ain't any fun at all and shouldn't be erected around road rollers.

But in the tiny time of high-falutinery, Messman had come to understand what it was all about: C.E. not only would claim him, but it now had claimed him, and nothing could be as scary or gentle as that.

Oh, sure, he was alive if you took the vibrancy of the deep blue-grey of his suit but not even he could overlook the fact he had just been singled out for dead. N' every day after that, of course, just a wonderful bonus given to him by that living Messman-minded entity he thereafter knew in the most intimate terms as C.E. N' what C.E. gaveth it would taketh away one day, sure as Messman was sure of anything which he always otherwise avoiding claiming to be.

That same, that very same day, that the one J. Smart got through to Messman, through the obviously oracle'd nature of dipping brushes into oily concoctions, the days among that day that C.E. still remembered him (Messman) by how it inspired him (J. Smart) – no borrower a pawnbroker forgets to be, nor lender bethinks – Messman was able to arise from that there bus bench outside the gallery and find a very special, of course, St Vincent de Paul's op shop open. Both of which, the bus-stop bench and the op shop J. Smart seems to have missed or deliberately left out.

It was a very special op shop because not only was it open on a Sunday (which would otherwise have been straining fiction were it not, in Messman's mind, only natural now that C.E. directed human feet as well as human brushes in oily hands, but mainly because hanging newly dry-cleaned there was not just a blue suit but in the very same deep blue-grey depicted by J. Smart, if not the very same suit depicted

17

by J. Smart. Messman traded in his own clothes there and then for the deep blue-grey suit C.E. had undressed another creature Messman's size for the dress Messman expressly as in the one J. Smart's painting, as no one could deny. Go ask the nearest road roller.

And Messman wore this suit from then until bedtime, then all the next day, which was a Monday until Messman's bedtime, and then the next day until it happened at 12.56 in the early afternoon when he was wide awake.

This made it undeniable that Messman wore the J. Smart blue-grey suit until C.E. came for him like he knew it hadta. He did not go to work. This was palpably a deeply-royal blue-grey too good for any warehouse. Instead, he hung around the Cahill Expressway on the southern side as possibly depicted by the one J. Smart, like one waits on a church to open and not too patiently at that, either, and certainly with a cocky air of one who knew he was required to be there.

And he did with a b'jesus mien, a mind-your-own-business, as captured so totemically by the native artist J. Smart. There he was and is, Messman, eagle-eye'd locked-on if you dared move an inch, proud and *in,* and cocky, yes, with it, likeasif he was posing in a studio you-know-where.

No, a better 'likeasif' would be like it was really: likeasif the newly-anointed warehouseman of the C.E.

When it hit the left-hand bend on the southern side of the Cahill Expressway, about half-a-mile, whatever metrics might say, along from where J. Smart depicted, the oil tanker flipped as neatly as an greasy baby in the hands of a Collingwood centre-half-forward and dumped itself n' its load upon the west-going lanes and the east-going lanes of C.E. Like, splat all over, adding pile-up to an unholy fucking mess.

This was at 9.53 on the Tuesday morning in Messman question, just after the rush hour but in good time to immediately clog up the whole universe of Sydney road driving, nerve ganglions and nerve ends, human and otherwise.

From this bottleneck, and within the hour, there was not a hiway or byway, a road or lane that came in or went out of this major hustling gogogogo city of the world that was not jammed. Not hustling so much now. No flow, no go, no way. The entire centre of Sydney completely, dangerously over-cholesteroling.

Nor was it any consolation to the tens of thousands of motorists gorped in this vehicular gloop that military strategists were already seeing the bright side of being able to redefine modern urban warfare – eg, forget the Buzzes from Above, stall the drones, just get an old oil tanker and some mad hatter of a brain-dead driver and paralyse the bastards, meaning anybody from civilian to enemy impertinent enough to be living right where you wanted to drop a dirty bomb.

Nor was it any consolation unto the drivers wherein the gloop that the reasons why they had to stay stuck in that vehicular quag for the ensuing seven hours of mire were only a matter of logistics, is all, with all the lanes of C.E. having had to judder to an outward and inward form of a traffic jam halt; after which the cops n' others had buckleys in being able to get any winch-bearing truck to the site to right the tanker or any sand'n'foam etceteras that might help to clean away the slick. Which was worse? The military strategists were not helping by being stuck on that question before they could round out their strategic responses.

No help, either, that the Army was promising to come to the rescue with one of its helicopters swinging a red traffic emergency truck beneath its belly astho mighty proud of the equipment God had given it at birth, and being so heavily delayed while its emergency taskforce crews had their photographs taken. Not that few didn't understand. That Army helicopter was housed in South Australia and if you have to wait until an *Adelaide Advertiser* photo guy turned up... well, turn out Maintenance first.

And talking of no driver consolations, you only had to look at the first five cars stuck at the head of the east-going lanes. Been there since one micro of a second, even by imperial time, after 9.53 in the morning when the tanker did its flip. The burning rubber from their own screeching tyres still in their nostrils; money down the drain for a start. As if that was the only thing making their nostrils flare.

The driver of the first car would now miss forever the business meeting that would have set him up on easy street for life. He was a business convenor and had put years into setting up this meeting of his industry's leaders, so impressive since not one of them had any intention of ever being convened... indeed, so impressed each had sent his open cheque book along in his place so he would not be seen being convened. Pity that driver of that first car to the oil spill was one loser in a million.

The second car's driver was going for an interview to become a senior editor she always wanted to be and now never would. It was for a magazine called 'Women in Control', which was appropriate before the tanker flipped, but was incongruous after it had, because she had lost her one-hour's head start over the other interviewees by sleeping with the interviewer the night before. Given her performance she knew even that one hour was stretching things even if things were going right.

The third car's driver was stuck with his wife and three kids in one overheated interior which would have turned anyone suicidal, especially if you knew how bad his brood was, what with that restraining order that he couldn't come within striking distance of them. That order even included his wife, who not only got in the family way but kept getting in every bastard's way, meaning if anyone deserved restraining it was her not him, so much resentment did he have in him. He didn't even know what they were doing in his car anyway.

The fourth car contained a human creature who missed a flight on which was a beautiful nympho (not to put too fine a point on her) he had lined up to accompany him on his roundaworld business trip in order to show his overseas potential partners that he was such a go-getter that he never missed out *getting*. Now he had to sit there, stuck by oil smuchas Messman was stuck in J. Smart's painting, knowing she would go on the ticket he had dopily handed over to her and he would be paying for each'n'every one of his overseas potential overseas partners to *get* at the flick of her fingers. No credit to him.

The fifth car on the rack there was the owner of a human creature on her way to hospital for a therapy stay because of her mass of named and unnamed phobias that mostly remains a mystery to this day onaccounta, after Messman and the C.E. altar incident yet to come up but not ere long, they all simply disappeared. She started appearing around the social traps of Sydney as the life of any party or any other starting position you wanted to throw at her as in perfectly-cured all of a sudden, invitation or no invitation. She was to create a small piece of medical history of becoming the woman who got cured of her named and unnamed phobias before she could be analysed as having them.

And these individual furies comprised the accreted and mounting murderous fury in only the first five cars banked up on the east-going and the west-going lanes of C.E. Backed up by banks of other furies in cars stretching in all ways as far as the I could see and as far as unending rages could stretch beyond known horizons.

And it was no consolation either that at 12.37 that early afternoon and precisely on the knocker of 1237 hours, Messman had turned to the C.E.'s neighbourhood be-blue-grey-suited n' all, and had spotted this unholy muck-up upon the altar that was his C.E. there and was racing to the rescue as fast as his legs could carry him across the open warehouse to his prescribed destiny.

Forgive him; he knows not why.

Messman appalled by what he sees when he mounts the small barrier along from the NSW Conservatorium of Music. He fell to his knees appropriately and religiously upon the oil slick of the C.E. there, before climbing back up to the full height of his J. Smart regally blue-grey suit pose and ploughing forward with high attitude of heywhatgoes whazfrigginghellsgoing and so forth on. Crossing past the overturned oil tanker and past the cops and past the DMR employees standing around in the same place the last two hours of looking down at everything and everyone and shaking their heads, smuchasif to say real hard luck, all this from the top right, say, of J. Smart's painting.

On past all, Messman still ploughing on with that attitude. To the crux of the matter. Never mind the tanker. Never mind the oil spill. This is C.E. It's human creatures that matter and missing their heads with road rollers. Don't I know it, twenty years ago. Is what C.E. called me for through J. Smart; obvious. To calm n' soothe with the telling now to all furies in all human creatures in cars of my own experience. Have faith in C.E. and how it makes even the run-away tonnages flip cartwheels over your head unpummellingly, brothers and sisters, bros'n'sis's, while any's in the palm of C.E.

Messman the humanist on the spouting.

Thus did Messman arrive at the five lead cars aforementioned. In fury and in swelter there. And, not unlike Moses knee deep in waters, or coming to depending on the tide of things, held up his J.-Smart immortalised hands, smuchasif to say, 'Hey, guysangals, no sweat'.

But already the one of the first car and the one of the second car and the ones of the third, fourth and fifth cars were out of their buckets off their rockets and were thrusting their furious blood-rushed faces towards Messman, smuchasif to say back, 'Could this fucker be the driver of that fucker truck tanker thing; jesus, if I could just get my hands on him if fuckers would just stand still n' die the way I want!'

And it is not recorded as anywhere near certain whether Messman ever actually heard (when all was said and done) the question or the statement which followed being thrown at him – or, indeed, if he heard the next question thrown at him, this time by the driver of the first car, being something like viz: 'Are you the absolute arsehole that ruined my whole life from here on end just because you're the stupid fucking idiot fucking cunt who deliberately overturned his dumb-arsed stupid fucking truck out of nothing more than seeing my whole life going down the plughole in front of your stupid fucking eyes and now you've got the fuckingarsehole nerve to stand up in front of me and putting a laugh into some sort of dumb-arsed hallelujah about it right to me face?' With the emphasized question mark thrown in as well without smuchas a second thought.

Tis known that Messman didn't hear that at all if you count every syllable, no. Nfact, he wasn't actually certain if the human creature was

22

calling him or calling him something. Takes some time to work out. All he registered at that particular moment was a slightly reverent awe of hearing himself answering in some third party's voice that would never have C.E. so rudely spiked by the tongue of some human creature, going: 'So who the effery cares about you. Look at this spill! Whothefugg's gonna clean it up? Get a mop or all of youse go root your mother's boot'.

At least it didn't seem his voice, not beyond his voice box it didn't. Instead it seemed to Messman a voice somewhat dark, that is to say blackish, that is to say gravelly, that is to say Macadamize-ish, that is to say as smooth and as anonymous as a highway road strip, make that any expressway you might know intimately, scrubbed'n'polished to look its best.

And, yes, for that moment he stayed stock still in wonder at ways and expressway to behold. What J. Smart had done for him!

And for that moment, as well, it was enough time for the drivers of the second etcetera cars to hear and for to understand that this smuck standing before them was the rightful object of their highly righteous manic furies that God would certainly recognise, right then and there beyond the sleepy eyes (all still yawning in their sockets) of the cops n' road workers nearby, but could be concepts away, like.

Before he or Messman knew it, the driver of the first car had rammed his vehicle in reverse and stamped anger at the accelerator. The accelerator stamped fury at the car mass n' the car mass stamped screeling rage upon the Messman destiny by brutishly jamming Messman's mass between its back bumper bar and the front bumper bar of the second car. When at which time it could be said, when all's said and done, that everything of a Messman nature went a quite euphonic *squelch*. Save yourself the attempt at trying to recognise how it came across, at least; it was just one of those sounds that stick.

Whenthenceupon, the driver of the second car, being fed like a slavering dog that cry of released pent-up fury-unto-joy emanating from the driver of the first car, jealously screamed a better scream of thank-chrissakes relief unpented, and did shove her vehicle into first and ploughed deliciously over that spreading squelch that was Messman once upon a time before he started spreading like a chestnut tree. And him (Messman) not even having time to cry out, 'Hey, watch the blue-grey serge, willya!'

Whenthusupon the driver of the first car cropped up again with fury screamingly unpented again, and reversed back of the squelchier remains. Whenthereunto did the driver of the second car drive forward once more with added fury over the now squizzy mess of Messman. All very delicious from a furied pent-up position behind the wheel. Better out than in.

And before the cops n' other jokers there even noticed a thing, each driver of the first five cars aforementioned had already got in for their coupla bucks' worth of sanity-regaining releases of pent-up furies by joining into a dodge'em-car push'n'shove like sort of thing, back and forward and sideway slides on'n'over Messman in all his gory. Move over; it's my turn.

He might have appeared ghostly in that deep-mysterious blue-grey swatch but that didn't mean Messman made less of a smear. Nfact, it is also said around the world of great squelches that the word of fury, while it was travelling faster than the unblocking of the jam, had at least the next fifteen other vehicles stop on that smear, reverse on that smear, do smoking wheelies on that smear, screamed n' screeched (both man n' machine) revenge on that poor Messy smear before moving on. Much relieved. A bit of a smear always helps the tension.

Having knelled n' nailed on that altar there of C.E. And then knelled n' nailed Messman all over again, again.

Kill, kill, kill. Thrill rills ill.

You could taste the ex-pulsed catharsis in the C.E. air there, so thick it was. With a palate knife, you could have cut it.

And did they ever. Never mind the deeply-royal blue-grey suit in all its serge. How life's-a-jungle-in-a-big-city delicious can you get out of one oil spill?

He might not even remember now, but the one J. Smart, painter, was one of the thousands caught in the citywide traffic jam for hours that day, and who would've given their eye-teeth to get that fuckwit said to have started it all too. Hope his smear boils in the midday sun. First five cars off the rank get all the luck.

It doesn't matter whether J. Smart remembers or not because he could never have known what an oil smear of a killing his oil painting had caused which in turn would have been very inappropriate to his famous hard-edged painterly style verging on the serge surreal. Well, that is put down here as reported without really being positive that he wasn't one of those people in the first five lucky cars.

Say he was the driver or the passenger of the hundredth or the fiftieth or even only the tenth car to flow over that spot after the total of seven hours it took to clear that tanker and that oil away... he might have felt a slight bump as he went over that strange smear, really Messy, which the road people didn't seem to have strong enough solvent for.

Oh, he might have noticed a peek of imperial blue-grey serge sticking out of it, smuchlike the colour of the suit he later, and rather strangely, couldn't resist using for the suit he wanted to put baldy into on canvas. But, even if this were true, J. Smart would have only thought at the time of smear-passing upon, viz: 'Yuk, some dead cat really spilled its guts all over the place'.

Mr Smart, that cat was Messman, man. And if you didn't know that, C.E., which directed your brush, did.

At least what you obviously *do* know about art when it comes to the serges of courtly blue-greys is that they might come across a bit cocky as suits but could never really be said to represent anything as *real*.

25

Blind Freddie purblinded.

... Girlie, it's Dad! Is that you breathing? A breath of you and it's bish-bash to some satellite, ha ha. Not ridiculing; just nerves. What I wondered: did you ever know they used to call me the Nabokov of the South Seas? One Mister-Spot-on once said in literature I spun the spillages. Also, I wanted to ask: has there been another anniversary for us not speaking to each other? If I had fingers to count them, I'd be in one of famous Daddy's pickle jars, right? Tiny infant you with that hole in the heart, and me born with a big hole in commitment. See how early on we were tagged for a two-way bypass? But I won't keep you in suspense. Here's the word inheritance. I did; I said inheritance. I take your silence for the sound of ears-pricking-up. Regrettably, I have nothing, except a Centrelink card which wouldn't bring in much over there in Pommyland. The trouble is my figurative caught up with my realisable. There is, of course, all your professor-granddaddy's stuff, all his famous pickle jars of tribal bits'n'pieces. They'd still be pawnable if you find a pawn shop I never stopped looking for. You give the bits'n'pieces back and fame and fortune will await you back here in the Antipodes. But a fig for inheritance! I wanted to tell you how I loved your mother! Leaving her with a 'see-you-later-Alligator' was really off, I agree. It came out wrongly. Tell her she couldn't have lived with my sulkiness, anyway. .I believe Vladimir Nabokov had the same weakness. Not that you can compare your mother's stalag to his Stalin, ha ha. Incidentally, I've gone totally blind since we last had the little chat we never had. But then, what's sight but yesterday's tears, ha ha? Tell your mother, will you? She deserves a little comeback laugh on me. And tell her she came first out of three, and that, yes, I did end up in drift. Hello? Girlie? You know, just to see your face. Just to run my fingertips across your cheek. Just to see you against a dawn's slow brightening to rose. Just to have your little breath gentle against my cheek once more. Girlie! You write to me about your life! Forget thinking braille! Write to your old Dad! And I'll promise I'll kiss the cheek of my darlin' girl, and so I will!

Hello? Did I tell you how I donated my last eye to the developing-world's marble stocks? It was my one'n'only bluey too and it was in

27

Sri Lanka. Well, when I say donated, I mean I said they could keepsake it if they ever fished it out of the operating drain it'd rolled down into. They said oops, fumble fingers. I said easy-come-easy-go yourselves, you rotten shits. I said, when you airmail my last good cat's-eye back to me, I might consider returning your famous grand pop's pickle jars. Hey, I've got some sum part to bury with dignity, too. Pickle jars? Girlie: inheritance, thy name is pickle jars! There's eyes here *glazed cherry*. There's toeses'n'noses and cancer blobs that've fallen off tribal generations! You'll find in one a Pitjantjatjara fingernail an imperial yard long and grown after-death. They don't make formaldehyde fertilizer like that anymore. There's a six-week-old foetus floating in its own dream world. There's Squatter's pot-shot up through Four-year-old's mouth and out the cranium, a tollable tunnel, clean as a whistle. One you'll like is a penis said to be King Billy's, the last of the Tasmanians. Poor K.B., even his dick got lopped. Return all of it and they'll give you your own name plaques beneath exhibition cases. But not me. I'm not returning famous daddy's stuff until they dredge out the cesspool my eye splashed down in. You tell me how can I give them back without showing what a shocking bloody kleptomaniac of a grave-robbing prick your famous Grand-dads actually was? He's family blood, you might be thinking?! He's the old razor I'm attached to! Should I mind, all my life, he'd just snort like a hog whenever he deigned to look at me, and think it a great joke? I'm talking a *father* here. But hey, we shared the genes of glandular secretions, and are or aren't glandular secretions the glue of the universe? I mated, he gave his best shot. I oozed; he oozed. I cried; he cried. We're one *secretion*. He's who I'm stuck with, and if that's the way it is, that's the way it is, even if I never knew him from a bar of soap. So, no eye, no pickle jars. They can all go root my boot.

… Girlie? Ah, my little girl, if there was one thing out of the millions of words I ever wrote, there's one passage that sticks with me as being worth all the swim. It was written for you my darling Juliet my Brenda my Caz my Sandy my Sophie my Angela my Mary my Elizabeth my other Sandra my Tessie my Lolly… and there has just got to be an Ann in there somewhere. Only for you. It was my dedication to you. Listen:
'…oh, twill triluna trystful while the trust whimsies true…'
Jesus H., I can't remember it! Excusee. It's just that I get this heavy

feeling at the thought of you all. Each and every one of you always gave me the acceleration but kept the brakes to yourselves. When I went to say No, it came out I Want. When I went to say I Wanted, it still came out I Want. Look, Girlie: you tell your mother and all of the others of her, I might have been a disaster BUT I WAS NEVER INTELLIGENT!

Sssh. Sssh. I just think I'm really hurting now. I think this growth behind my eye might've slipped its bonds. I just rang to tell you... when they took Caesar's knife to your mother, what a father I would have been if you had only lived.

Blind Freddie at the end of the cord.

The world he knows now is only his chair and its side table, his telephone and his radio and their cords tailing off beyond arms-reach. Where these lead he can never see again, and the silences that come to him these last days pulse to overwhelming. In the hot twilight, in his dimming of dreams, in his eyes out of the blank, in his phone off and on the speaker:

1. Blind Freddie talking to a wife
Hey!

CLARISSA? MY PEE AND YOUR LEG, CLARISSA!

Clarissa?

Look, don't go yet.

No?

You're a stubborn woman, Clarissa. I know you're thinking there he is trying to be all fanny uptight again. I do not think you climaxing throughout the whole house is funny in any fanny way. You try laughing at your witching-hour caterwauls, Clarissa. You've always confused passion with breaking wind. Am I so pathetic? If you think acting out Vladimir Nabokov's Laughter in the Dark is funny, who's pathetic? D'uh, you're the wife and that bugger you've got there is the lover, and you're having a real giggle slurping just out of blind-man's-bluff-reach of poor old blind cuckold blind-freddie hubby me. Jesus H., Clarissa, get an imagination.

CLARISSA?, YOU THINK YOU'VE GOT TITS BUT THEY'RE PAINT JOBS!

You say you're really taking off this time but that could just mean you're growing mould. I don't deserve that... *slurping* noise. Look, if you're going, take my father's books. Shit, don't keep saying you don't want them; it's his fortieth again soon. You know they'll be lashing out with some other bloody medal called the Cranium Callipers or fart-what and, if I don't get rid of them, how can I claim I wouldn't lower myself to read a word of them? But leave his pickle jars. Promise me you won't take his pickle jars!

'Shall I leave the door a-jar?'

Ho ho, Clarissa. What's that perfume, anyway? Verde de gris. Nice-to-be-alive day outside, is it, or just trying to hide your athlete's foot? And don't think I can't smell testosterone when it's passing. Tell the bloody man he's too near! You know I'm not a brave man, *Clarissa!*

'Henry, you'd hear footsteps if you was drowning.'

That all the bloody man's got, Clarissa? Clarissa's dead right there, old sausage. Yes, I'm speaking to you, you bloody man, whoever you are. No, *wherever* you are... so take that as a verbal coup de grace, old juice! You can go pop-goes-the-weasel with my wife, but I maintain the pretence that any author can remain dignified. They called me the Nabokov of the South Seas. Regrettably it was a once-only. My moniker was exam-set once, too. O levels and we're not speaking of bloody Clarissa's pop-spot, either. Real O levels. Son of a very glitterati professor-bodybag-artist makes good in his own right. Okay, you bloody man, maybe just once, also. So, well, that's me; nice t'meetcha. Oo, but where's me manners what's left over from being unmanned? Perhaps you haven't been formally introduced to my wife you are screwing? She is issa-to-us-all, old sauce. Light and creamy is she. Succulent as any Eurasian should be. Oft, I call her Big Mac, more than a mouthful no matter how little you can stomach. Poor she was, but sumptuous at pretending. Straight-off, we recognised our mutual penchant for promising outrageous lies.

'Then you went blind.'

Oh, ha ha, Clarissa. Very spicy. See, old cock, how my wife aims for brutal honesty too, but not above the belt. So now it's your turn for having to keep your guts protected from her garters, old sausage.
Careful what you wash for, ha ha. It's only fair. Step outside the script, bloody Clarissa.

'I'm stepping outside alright.'

CLARISSA!

'What?'

Don't go; I'll miss your bald bits.

'That's feeble, that is.'

Clarissa, promise you won't leave me alone with my thoughts!

'I'm done with promising you anything anymore, Henry.'

Look, okay, my mind might be so surge incontinent, I can't stop hearing you, bloody Clarissa and then wanting to run for the dunny, but then, I gave you no Taj Mahal, did I? But you, you see, you never were one to realise there could only be one real Queen Mumtaz and you were way too slack, even giving her fourteen kids start. And, I know, I know, poor me, eyeless now, I never looked at you, did I? I should regret that now, though not really. How many of our six dog years would you allow as good, Clarissa?

'Five.'

There you go, then.

'Months.'

No, no, no, Clarissa. My father used to drain his corpses into gutters alongside the dissecting table. All the cockroaches had to wait outside by the open drain. Outside. You send your cockroachy bloody man you've got there outside my house, Clarissa.

'Don't you go upsetting him.'

Jesus H., Clarissa. I'm only ancient old fart starring in some dodgy real-time remake of that Nabokov film as Dirk Bogarde as the blind old guy. Just keep the bloody man away from the pickle jars! There's half of the central Australian tribes in those bottles. The famous half. They used to keep screaming at famous Pops to return them for burial, but he says they're snugger with him. Why not me, then, did someone ask? Why thank you. I do not return them either. They're family. They're science, bloody Clarissa. And if you're worried about your money, don't. It's too late.

'What money?'

You cheated me, Clarissa.

'As my tongue laps here, I did not!'

I don't know how, but you did, bloody Clarissa, and I've had my gumption of it. And then what do you do? You only start going I gave up my eyes just to spite taking you to Australia.

'I wouldn't put it past you.'

What's that tooting? What's that honking?

'The taxi, thank God.'

Don't leave me alone with myself, Clarry! I'm an old man! Jesus H., I've spent my whole life trying to get someone else lumbered with me! Be fair, Clarissa!

'See you in the formaldehyde, Henry.'

All right, so go, Clarissa! Flit off, you and your bloody man of a fink flitter. You think I'm going to miss you? Trying to engage your mind was like free-falling over Disneyland. Your body no longer by my side? Shee, I would've needed a penile engorgement science wasn't capable of. You slack? What's limp like melting plastic, Clarissa? You forget my father left me with body parts here that I was getting stuck with before you were born. I got aboriginal 200-year-old bits'n'pieces with makeovers that'd make your mirror want to defect. And another thing, Clarissa. You weigh any DVD you like, and then write even a thousandth of what I wrote on it, and weigh it again, and what have you got? I'll tell you what you've got, bloody Clarissa. You've got the biggest weight difference in the world, that's all. It's called literature, Clarissa. It's uplifting. It's not your sag, Clarissa. Jesus H., in a few years your crutch will be dragging lower than Skippy-the-Kangaroo's grandmother's.

CLARISSA, I'VE BOTTOMED OUT, BUT YOUR LARDS BEAT ME BY A MILE!

You there, Clarissa...?

Who's there?

Don't hurt me, okay? Do anything with the mind but leave the body alone, 'kay? 'Kay? *Who's...?*

CLARISSA, YOU STOP THAT PANTING. IT'S LIKE HAVING TO LISTEN TO A CRACK IN THE GUTTER.

2. Blind Freddie talking to The Other
I'll be honest, old custard... apart from Nabokov of the South Seas, they sometimes used to call me Gutsache. But it wasn't often as you'd like me to think. What I've been thinking is: for how long would I have to hold my breath before I heard you breathing? Past my lively time of death, ha ha? Oh yes, you'd like me to admit you're an improvement on Clarissa, I dare say, what with her inner thigh needing pest control. Of course, you're an improvement. So what do we do now we're stuck with each other? Do I get some sign now? I'll wait. No rush...

No?

Blind Man's Bluff your thing? Spin me around and hoick and honk me, is it? All I ask is you tell me if they get too near! Sorry, sorry. Don't mind me; somebody once said I'd hear footsteps if I was drowning. Oh, that you? Everybody wants to get in on the act! So, old sauce, it's you'n'me in the swim, is it? Don't mind the questions. I'm far too

dumb to ask anything awkward. One thing, though... why the big phfutt of phfutts, old custard, when Clarissa and I, we were going along pretty good there? Put it this way: why did old Henry-me suddenly find he couldn't lift blocks of concrete on the strength of the squinty eye of his penis anymore? At least, not without string. It was the bathos not the pathos of the thing, you see, old pie-and-peas. Are you going to say you reached down and touched me? Could you do me a favour and not touch me again? Another thing I'm asking here, old fried egg, is had you always written in I should go blind? Where you there in Sri Lanka with Clarissa's fellow-local surgeon chum when I said to him what're you done to my eye, you prick? And he replied, 'Go back to Australia, sir; you're not long-suffering enough to live here anymore'. Cheeky bugger shoots me down with logic after giving my eye the barbeque fork. Were you there? I mean, shrapnel with the first, and then a fucking unknown surgeon's rapier-wit with the second? It was the most cerulean sapphire of the two too. Twas my light, old can-of-worms. I canst make light of it nor, now, light work. See how your imagery can survive dawn's light uptight? Your poesy should purge, after all. Many pieces immortalized upon the toilet roll and before applied to bot. Vladimir Nabokov was my king of spending a penny over a rhyming couplet or two. A good farter loudspeaks literary talent. But you know all this. So, shall I endeavour to wax lyrical too?:
  'I looked upon seeing the light-gravure/
  the altar candles were lights-out but the callow lit the lit-erature.'
Perhaps needs a touch working on by someone cheeky enough to try. But then, that's my point: as a poet, I'd rather you just look upon me as a really dirty old man. Call me Tiresias or call me a horse's arse. Neigh, neigh. The thing is, as you keep showing, one cannot check anything in before the check-out. This is blindness, and don't think I don't appreciate your metaphor. We can have the smarts, but life we can't see through, right? It's very polished. But, see, you are scaring me witless here! I want to scream my fear every minute of my waking day! I want to screech fright at even the thought of falling asleep! I could break down and bawl my eyes out with such self-pity that I shock myself! This is the thing, see. This is gone-to-shit blindness. Worse, it's added-on bathos. The Evil Eye didn't do him. Rat fleas didn't end it. Malaria didn't put his nuts in a vice. Not Dengue or TB or the great naughty pretender of diseases. It wasn't even the bloody prickly heat. Only you know, old custard, and you're not saying.

Say, did I do something to you? And you were right about Job. I haven't got one memory left that's worth the pain either, anyway. Call me Brer Rabbit and life the tar baby, and I'll call you right. Except, all I'm asking is why you make us think thinking maketh the man? All thinking ever did was invent you don't screw granny. I know that's me being what makes Clarissa want to tear her hair out. But, likewise, I know you and your compensating look on the bright side. Like, cancer's just an opportunity of losing weight. Right? And AIDS was nature's way of cleaning up the world's needle industry. And every jihadist beheading makes us better at the geography of the Middle East. Oh, and it ain't death; it's just changing-places while there's still room, right?

Look, I'm still shaking with fear here!

Sorry, sorry, old cork. My poofy streak. Yellow doesn't fade. Just wondering, though: you ever put one human thought on the shelf of the Great Scheme of Things? Or is it better we stick with the idea of you sort of knocking something off the sideboard and oops, sorry, crash-tinkle big big Bang. Sure, we get all that, but what's the big mystery? What's the why?; or are you saying it actually was all just a case of Misguided Elbow? Oops, how did that get there?, is it? I mean, look at this dump. Is this a real shithouse or what? Is that what your gift is, that I can't see how much of a shithouse it is? You can tell me what a shithouse it is. I won't mind. Anyway, any last requests on, old son?

I take that silence as a maybe. Well, I mentioned about the dirty old man, not the poet… but I'd really like to add… forget about my obsession with hormones and birth canals; just don't forget how my given eyes never missed fixing upon one of your world's wondrous dancing nates. Not once. My missing orb's probably there staring up skirts from some gutter right now.

Hey, Hughie, with all your great gift entailings, at least it's a comfort knowing you have done it unto others.

So send her down, Hughie!

Just knock two times first, okay?, so I know when to trip daintily out of the way.

3. Blind Freddie talking to a daughter

... Girlie, it's Dad! Is that you breathing? A breath of you and it's bish-bash to some satellite, ha ha. Not ridiculing; just nerves. What I wondered: did you ever know they used to call me the Nabokov of the South Seas? One Mister-Spot-on once said in literature I spun the spillages. Also, I wanted to ask: has there been another anniversary for us not speaking to each other? If I had fingers to count them, I'd be in one of famous Daddy's pickle jars, right? Tiny infant you with that hole in the heart, and me born with a big hole in commitment. See how early on we were tagged for a two-way bypass? But I won't keep you in suspense. Here's the word inheritance. I did; I said inheritance. I take your silence for the sound of ears-pricking-up. Regrettably, I have nothing, except a Centrelink card which wouldn't bring in much over there in Pommyland. The trouble is my figurative caught up with my realisable. There is, of course, all your professor-granddaddy's stuff, all his famous pickle jars of tribal bits'n'pieces. They'd still be pawnable if you find a pawn shop I never stopped looking for. You give the bits'n'pieces back and fame and fortune will await you back here in the Antipodes. But a fig for inheritance! I wanted to tell you how I loved your mother! Leaving her with a 'see-you-later-Alligator' was really off, I agree. It came out wrongly. Tell her she couldn't have lived with my sulkiness, anyway. .I believe Vladimir Nabokov had the same weakness Not that you can compare your mother's stalag to his Stalin, ha ha. Incidentally, I've gone totally blind since we last had the little chat we never had. But then, what's sight but yesterday's tears, ha ha? Tell your mother, will you? She deserves a little comeback laugh on me. And tell her she came first out of three, and that, yes, I did end up in drift. Hello? Girlie? You know, just to see your face. Just to run my fingertips across your cheek. Just to see you against a dawn's slow brightening to rose. Just to have your little breath gentle against my cheek once more. Girlie! You write to me about your life! Forget thinking braille! Write to your old Dad! And I'll promise I'll kiss the cheek of my darlin' girl, and so I will!

Hello?

Did I tell you how I donated my last eye to the developing-world's marble stocks? It was my one'n'only bluey too and it was in Sri Lanka. Well, when I say donated, I mean I said they could keepsake it if they ever fished it out of the operating drain it'd rolled down into. They said oops, fumble fingers. I said easy-come-easy-go yourselves, you rotten shits. I said, when you airmail my last good cat's-eye back to me, I might consider returning your famous grand pop's pickle jars. Hey, I've got some sum part to bury with dignity, too. Pickle jars? Girlie: inheritance, thy name is pickle jars! There's eyes here *glazed cherry*. There's toeses'n'noses and cancer blobs that've fallen off tribal generations! You'll find in one a Pitjantjatjara fingernail an imperial yard long and grown after-death. They don't make formaldehyde fertilizer like that anymore. There's a six-week-old foetus floating in its own dream world. There's Squatter's potshot up through Four-year-old's mouth and out the cranium, a tollable tunnel, clean as a whistle. One you'll like is a penis said to be King Billy's, the last of the Tasmanians. Poor K.B., even his dick got lopped. Return all of it and they'll give you your own name plaques beneath exhibition cases. But not me. I'm not returning famous daddy's stuff until they dredge out the cesspool my eye splashed down in. You tell me how can I give them back without showing what a shocking bloody kleptomaniac of a grave-robbing prick your famous Grand-dads actually was? He's family blood, you might be thinking?! He's the old razor I'm attached to! Should I mind, all my life, he'd just snort like a hog whenever he deigned to look at me, and think it a great joke? I'm talking a *father* here. But hey, we shared the genes of glandular secretions, and are or aren't glandular secretions the glue of the universe? I mated, he gave his best shot. I oozed; he oozed. I cried; he cried. We're one *secretion*. He's who I'm stuck with, and if that's the way it is, that's the way it is, even if I never knew him from a bar of soap. So, no eye, no pickle jars. They can all go root my boot.

Girlie...?

Ah, my little girl, if there was one thing out of the millions of words I ever wrote, there's one passage that sticks with me as being worth all the swim. It was written for you my darling Juliet my Brenda my Caz my Sandy my Sophie my Angela my Mary my Elizabeth my other

Sandra my Tessie my Lolly… and there has just got to be an Ann in there somewhere. Only for you. It was my dedication to you. Listen: '*…oh, twill triluna trystful while the trust whimsies true…*' Jesus H., I can't remember it! Excusee. It's just that I get this heavy feeling at the thought of you all. Each and every one of you always gave me the acceleration but kept the brakes to yourselves. When I went to say No, it came out I Want. When I went to say I Wanted, it still came out I Want. Look, Girlie: you tell your mother and all of the others of her, I might have been a disaster BUT I WAS NEVER INTELLIGENT!

Sssh. Sssh.

I just think I'm really hurting now. I think this growth behind my eye might've slipped its bonds. I just rang to tell you… when they took Caesar's knife to your mother, what a father I would have been if you had only lived.

When they found him amongst the tethers that bind, there was not a battery which was not leaking nor a cord not nibbled into. The phone in particular was dead off the hook.

Those 250-year-old feet being bought out from under me

I wouldn't blame you if thought me weird for rolling up to St Mary's Stations-of-the-Cross in Dandenong Park last Easter pushing an iceberg up the last little incline.

Those gloves I was wearing were for frostbite, and that iceberg was my wife even though summer itself hadn't even started to wan.

Why did I bother even rolling up? Well, she didn't actually become an iceberg until we were halfway there, you see. And when it happened, I couldn't think of anyone I could turn to who might have had experience with what to do with icebergs in Dandenong being seen in the open street in summertime.

Then again, you could only say it was all for the good. If I had turned us back home after she had *plopped*, I wouldn't have been witness to the miracle I am just starting to think of as The 15th Station Miracle.

But before others start arguing about that name, perhaps I should take you back to the beginning, so that you can understand that I am new to your Australia by only four months and that my dear wife is newer than me by two months. This was because I came earlier so I could organize some roof over the head and all that.

I had planned it so I would migrate from Sri Lanka in midsummer given that the reputation of the winters of Melbourne, let alone Greater Dandenong, was so anti-everything, save anti-freeze. Midsummer, I thought, would be easier for her blood to thicken before the mercury fell in on her.

I should have felt in my water that it wasn't going to be as easy as all that right from the moment I picked her up at Tullarmarine.

She came out of the Customs area looking so lost, yet such a smile she gave me! Looking back on it, such a *warm* smile she gave me!

I held her in my arms. I kissed her. I had trouble locking onto her lips.

41

Her lips were like cold piano wires in vibrato. I thought it was just trembling with excitement.

I didn't realize it was a shaking from the knees -- already, the first rumblings of a shiver

This was, yes, in January itself.

'Dear,' she whispered, her breath condensing, 'the pilot said it was 12 degrees outside. I thought he meant up *there,* not down *here.*'

Had things got a bit better by, say, the next morning, it would have been the happiest of arrivals, but they hadn't. She woke up in absolute distress at not being able to fight her own way out of the three blankets she had somehow pulled on during one of the warmest midsummer nights on record. Nor did she seem able to raise herself to more than a walking crouch under those flannelette and wool T-shirt, jarmies, cardie, my old footy socks, and a scarf she had found somewhere.

Worst of all came to be her feet. Though I just couldn't bring myself to justify any electric fire in mid-January, I did spend all that first morning on my knees before her massaging those blocks of ice beneath my old footy socks.

Not that I was worried at that stage. You had to expect those feet of hers to play up like that.

They were, after all, 250 years old.

I am not joking. I knew that for a fact. Her mother had told me.

'She got it from me', she had told me. 'All of our side of the family's feet are 250 year old, give or take a day or two. They died *ages* ago.'

Back there in the tropics of Sri Lanka, you can live with feet like that. In fact, they were quite nicely like esky coolers that relieved the extremes of that heat and humidity considerably. Back there in Colombo, it wasn't unusual for people to actually *huddle* around her.

However, here in midsummer, you would have started to worry too if, after three days, your wife hadn't got out from under those flannelette and wool layers, not for one moment of the day or night. And I am talking here about one of the most fastidious women you'd ever come across. She hadn't even stopped 'brrrr'ing or 'grrrr'ing or whatever it was in between. Neither had she stood up straight from her hunched-shouldered stoop, or even looked like evolving out of those stiff-legged shuffling steps that made moving off the carpet onto the lino areas of the kitchen and the loo look like Shackleton going on a suicidal walk around the outside the tent.

It wasn't so much, either, not being able to get food past her throat, but the piteous way she was coming to bend in obeisance (let's not just say sip) over the occasional cup of soup or tea I managed to get her to take. She would hold those cups in such clutch of those mitten'd claws, bending her dear face over the steam rising from that warming surface and blowing as to blow Shackleton out of the tent, then being able to do nothing about the icicles melting from her nose and dropping into and pretty much freeze-drying the precious liquid before she could hardly get at it. Surely even Shackleton's heart would have produced a piteous diary entry of that.

I found it best to hold her in one arm while she blew and slurped and time my tapping of her dear head so the icicles fell to one side. Then one day, on a particularly vigorous tap I really hadn't meant, fell from her a clump of thin ice molded in the shape of her dear forehead!

You can imagine my alarm. All that time I had thought her brow was sweating with the blessed glow of Continental-and-Bushel's cups of soup'n'tea mercy. It hadn't occurred to me that that external heating was making her ice-sheet over like one of Shackleton's base's windows. For some reason, I had the instinct of diving for her lower half to pull her woollie jarmie legs out from my old footy socks. As soon as I did so, a waterfall of thawed ice poured from out of each leg like they say Antarctica's glaziers are giving up the ghost. Whoa!, I went, but her poor dear mouth was still trying for the now luke-warm-only soup!

It was piteous to see. God love her.

I dwell on this shock of a moment not because it was more shocking than other moments but merely to illustrate how this was the first time I witnessed the true nature of those 250-year-old feet of hers and how dangerous the side effects were if one attempted to thaw them. They simply would not be contained. Despite those suddenly-breached waterfalls, those feet remained as dry as dry-ice.

And I remembered, then, the words of my mother-in-law going on: 'Our blood's frozen up in them long ago. It's the same blood that tried to get through 250 years ago'.

After that, events and affairs started to become blurs of antarctic proportions even as the temperature of Greater Dandenong rose to historically-high heights that summertime, or so the Met Bureau kept saying.

I seemed to register vaguely how the apartment was becoming more and more subarctic, midsummer or no midsummer. Halfway up to the ceiling, the air came to be hanging like a curtain of fog. Somewhere along the line, her breath had become as visible as Puffing Billy's. I vaguely came to understand that, whenever I went outside, I was stopping outside the front door to remove my fibre-wool parka. Likewise, whenever I was coming back inside, I found myself stopping outside that front door to put back on my fibre-wool parka. Inside I even started to feel a bit envious that she had commandeered my old footie socks.

Then again, there was the bed business. I do remember that it was early on that I tried to get her up and at 'em, whoever ''em' is, but presumably somebody or something warm-footed. Get up occasionally, go outside and meet your friendly new people; there's a history-making heat wave out there and umbrellas are all out giving shade all over the streets. Shops are throwing air conditioning for free. Go, my dear wife; make a small effort to go out and meet the over-heated with smiles of welcome on their faces, the warm-blooded complaining about the heat, the happy-go-lucky glistening with sweat. Australia is your new country and it's waiting to warm to you.

Well, I mean, we live in a block of twenty-four other apartments, so how hard can it be for a normally chatty little darling of a wife to make a friend or two? At least wave them in as they go by.

But, 'I try', she answered in chilling anguish, 'but they run away'.

I hardened my heart. Show me, I said. I went outside and walked up and down past our apartment like, say, one of our friendly neighbours looking for a bit of a chin wag might've. Oh, I could hear her knocking 'to' me at the glass pane by the front door all right as if, sure, she'd love to talk. And I could see her vague outline maybe waving away in there come-in, come-in. But it was like trying to look in at the label of a McCann's frozen pizza packet all iced over. From the outside, she was just a below-zero blue-ish blur. You could see how she was trying to wipe a seeing circle on the window with her layers of sleeves as if she were trying to see out of a sauna, but anything but since it just kept frosting back over on her.

You didn't have to ask any neighbourly lady that I was trying to be. Anybody's reaction would have been, 'Woo, no even peeking sideways at the creepie in number 7. What's she doing in there, making ice blocks?'

Frankly, all round it wasn't getting any better. Even as that mercury kept rising to those record-breaking heights, she just seemed to be getting colder and colder. Oh, she changed each morning from night attire to day attire, but this was only from flannelette and wool T-shirt under jarmies under pullover tucked into gloves and my old footy socks to flannelette and wool T-shirt under jarmies under pullover tucked into gloves and my old footy socks. And the red scarf over all. With that shuffling stoop and everything else making her look all baggy-knees, the two blankets and the doona sort of followed her around like torn Sweet's ice-cream wrappings.

But it was the changing of her colour that became really alarming.

I noticed her starting to go from coloured-tropical to coloured-hypothermic. I am not kidding. Oh, straight off, she still remained that

45

lovely dusky hue I had married. Then, even as I blinked, she had somehow gone a bread-crusty brown. Then somehow she seemed to be creamy eggshell. Then the next blink of an eye, there she was with pale pink skin with those blue jellyfish veins. Then, seemingly at the next glance, pale blue skin with those pink jellyfish veins. Next time you looked she was somehow as white as true-blue Australians boast to be before they beach themselves trying not to be. Then, somehow or other, I was staring across the way at a deadly blue – more deadly ice-blue than any Eskimo-Inuit in the nude would ever look outside the igloo. Or Shackleton. But there wasn't even any rumour he ever got in the nude.

And following on from the change of colour was the most alarming of all: the poor love's loss of her true identity. God love her.

Week after week, you only had to be a reader of the *Dandenong Examiner* to have followed what I am talking about re that colour-changing time and that resultant loss of true identity.

Undoubtedly, the worst headline was the first:
'**Aboriginal woman goes loco on red lights**'
and all just because some motorist didn't slow down for a look when he saw my wife rubbing herself up against the sun-kissed pedestrian light before he careened in front of 15 other vehicles just before I made good our escape, not stopping to get his mistake about her ethnicity put right.

Then, out of our next excursion out came:
'**Lebanese lady upsets lunchers! Middle Easterner sucks warmth from hardworking doughnut-making machine before others**'; and then:
'**Punjabi mama runs a riot! Peak-hour chaos as expressway woman chases break in cloud**';
and then:
'**Vietnamese unidentified frozen object. UFO??? Safeway's trolley cart turmoil as customers flee mysterious icy pole on collision path**';
then:
'**Scotswoman causes cold-shouldering. Stampede as highland-type**

jumps Myer winter-jumper fashion queue, blue veins sticking out seem the go';
and then:
'Albanian blonde bombshells steam laundry. Wannabe-albino promotes public panic with indelible pink veins sticking out';
and:
'Eskimo Inuit raises hell at Christian blockbuster showing. Dash for exits when Christ flings icy daggers into Village auditorium'.

Yes, loss of her true identity, I said and I meant it. Just as curious to me was: since when does every other nationality rate a mention in the guessing stakes but Sri Lankans?

Not that you could accuse the dear love of my life of not trying. She had to try to cope with those feet. Do you know how hard it must have been for her to even get nail polish to show off over purple finger- and toenails, especially when it freezes on first contact? And how hard was it to get tidy hair when she really needed an ice-pick to comb it? How difficult to live with would have been ears looking like learn-to-swim floaters? Who can even think glamour-pussing around when, even in bed, under all that flannelette and wool and blankets and doona, when you're still shaking and hissing like a batter banana in boiling fat down at your local fish'n'chipper? Without the heat, of course. Well, there was the dry-ice heat of course.

We talked about it; we discussed it; we saw specialists who were more worried, I think, about what those feet of hers were doing to their nice carpets. We read and we listened. But all she could come up with – I could come up with nothing at all – was that she was suffering from the effect of her feet because she had come to Australia and left behind her Lord Jesus. She thought so; she was sure of it.

'I have', she uttered, 'come into the limbo of the lost Lord'.

If I was a religious man, I might have been able to help her. As it was...

As it was, yes, I was useless.

I mean, you'd have to be blind not to see that in church. Had the God of her beloved Sri Lanka – He of the palm trees and whirring cool fans and mosquito coils -- not abandoned her here in Australia, or so she somehow thought, her thoughts and prayers would surely not have frozen above her dear bowed head the way they did each and every Sunday now, the pews around her all empty. Nor would those selfsame thoughts and prayers fallen like arctic hail upon the rest of the congregation suddenly doing the umbrella thing inside the nave. The church's ladies' group even started handing out umbrellas and plastic rain ponchos at the entrance, but still I refused the priest's offer of separate Mass specially for her simply because he said he had a beaut heater in his manse.

Again and again, I asked that dear thing of mine: How can you keep saying you have lost your Lord and here is limbo here?

She quivered her answer with a crying shame of a humble shiver that sent small stalagmites and stalactites raining to the floor beneath her, but by then our own carpets were ruined anyway and she went:

'But don't you see, dear, how my heart's has gone cold?'

I could only weep with her. I didn't know what she meant. I could only wrap my arms around the flannelette-and-wool swaddling that had become my once-sunny and open and tropical wife.

What else could I do but wait and pray for some miracle? Was that silly-incongruous for a self-confessed non-religious man? I don't think so. Wasn't coming to Australia in the first place looking for a miracle?

And so, with that, I guess I have finally come full circle to my wheeling that iceberg up to last Easter's Station of the Cross in Dandenong Park there.

Not ten minutes before, we had been travelling okay on our own four feet until we got to that corner of Thomas and the other street, when a northerly zephyr that was nothing less than a cowardly arctic blast from the south struck her without warning.

Immediately, where she had been, I heard a PLOP! I did. I've told you before. A PLOP! I think it was followed by a piteous sigh out of her ice flows, but can't swear on it. The next thing I know, I'm holding the hand of an iceberg. I know that doesn't sound right, but it's true.

I can barely remember how we made it to the Stations of the Cross. Oh yes, there was a lot of skating on ice the rest of the way. And then, somehow, I am standing on the stage of the sound shell there, and all the congregation sort of down there below, now coming to the 14th Station, the last, right by us, and there is my beloved the iceberg kneeling down beside me, impacted with prayer, And, there, I noticed, standing in front of her was, yes, a small boy, no more than maybe four years old... you know, of that cannot-quite-stand-without-swaying and am-I-in-your-face-or-what? age...

... and he was staring with those unashamedly wide unwavering peepers into her eyes from no more than a metre away, and he wasn't moving even though I was trying furtively to wave him away without attracting attention to us during the 14th Station, like.

What was striking about him was he had such wide brown limpid pools of eyes, warm and somehow soaking-up. And whenever she attempted to rise at the Service's invocations, those eternally-patient, somehow, eyes of that lad followed her skywards. And whenever she managed to kneel back on the priest's instructions, they followed her back to his eye level.

I didn't know how my love might be taking it. But what could I do anyway? He was locked on. I wasn't there essentially. That boy was totally and unyieldingly glued to her. His battery-lit little shoes looked like two lighthouses striking against the vapours, promising refuge. I fancied he stood there rooted in a frosty landscape of some sea. A little stone of rock proportions.

And then, suddenly, it was all over.

Above us, that humming April sun made a hot shot tower of the great tree of acorns -- and there was sudden shade. Shade. There was! *Cool* shade. Blessedly *cool* shade. And a breeze. A breeze you unbutton to.

And there was come back to us the thrummings of midsummer and how it hums along, with people laughing like rejuvenated Christians do and leaving with good hearts with their boys and girls wishing they could really do some damage pinging those acorns onto instead of mostly missing the oldies.

I just stood there, stopped, worshipping warmth again.

It was only getting damp socks that bought me back to reality. It couldn't have been as long as it seemed. The boy was departing, hand in hand with his Dad. I remain certain I heard him giggle as he went, and why not? For, there she was, my dear wife, still kneeling, yes, but now instantly thawed, even miraculously unswaddled from flannelette and wool, knee-deep in a whole pond of melting ice. Those feet somehow firmly back in their icy place ending at the ankles.

I touched the top of her head and raised her up. She was warm and cuddly once more. She was my beloved returned to me, with, for that moment of our lives together, that tinge of rose to her cheeks and how it faintly glows with pleasure and love, and love and pleasure. She really was a dear.

We walked home in the warm sunlight. This was no wintry day but the humming of Easter in Dandenong. We frolicked, going, in the soft cool shades and the autumny zephyrs from the north.

She had truly migrated to Australia at last. That 's what I was thinking.

When I was quite sure the blankets were folded well away, marked 'Unpack in June', later I broached the subject of what happened with her.

'It was finding your good Lord out of limbo again, wasn't it?', I asked.

She gave me that small secretive grin of hers.

'It was that boy, wasn't it?', I pressed further.

She gave me that, yes, small secretive grin of hers.

'But how come? Did that kid, say, warm the cockles of your heart or something?', I asked.

She gave me that, yes, small secretive grin of hers.

And during that time it wasn't beyond her to go around positively glowing most of the time. She might have still had those ice blocks at her ends but she was no longer a walking fridge self-frosting.

You might ask did I really believe about the boy? Well, yes and no. I certainly believe those eyes of his under the nudging of the 14th Station of the Cross had some gosh-almighty warming effect. But I'm just as inclined to think a mathematical error was to blame that, finally, couldn't sustain itself under the New Testament rod of Dandenong Park.

By that I mean, it just wasn't reasonable to think that any little angel of a lad could warm the cockles of any heart belonging to feet that were more than 100 or so years old. Not even in Australia. Eighty, sure. Even, maybe, 103 or 104, like, but nothing over that.

To me that meant either my dear one's mother was wrong and the family feet were only 100 or so years older than the rest of their bodies, or my dear wife still had as much as another 150 years of those feet of hers to go.

Another way I like to put it is: even with the boy thrown in, those feet of my beloved were still at least 150 years old.

It wasn't my fault that I didn't have much further to say in the matter for any older than that.

At least I hope it wasn't my fault.

It's fair to say it wasn't until glaciology came into the picture that we got to the root of the matter. By that time... seeing what a glaciologist could do.... my dear one had gotten a job at the local plant nursery. 'Gotten' may be too strong a word for it. They jumped out and grabbed her to sign on one day she was walking past the place during the drought and high water restrictions on account of her being, I suppose, one great big walking drip.

As I said, I'm still new to Australia so I wouldn't pretend to understand why the country has so many glaciologists when, I think, it's got no glaciers. Is it a cultural thing? Is it simply an industry wish-fulfilment of living in the driest continent on earth? One of my divorce support group maintained that it was because Australians were tired of looking at their native oily plants and were trying to give future tourists something nicer to look at when Climate Change really kicks in and ruins the place. He said the modern Australian authorities were trying for all edelweiss plants everywhere.

Now, I cannot know about that, but I know now that edelweiss means alpine plants and if you're going to try to get rid of all your dry water guzzlers of native Australian plants, it sounds a nice name to begin with. 'Edelweiss' certainly also fitted nicely with my dear wife's feet.

I mean by not knowing about anything about Australian glaciologists all the glaciologists Australia had. It turns out there are thousands and thousands of them to go around, so much so that no plant nursery could claim to be a proper plant nursery unless it had a glaciologist on its books. Of course, the plant nursery that snapped up my wife's feet and put her on the payroll as a damp squid was a proper business, and so had its own glaciologist in attendance whenever he wasn't off in Iceland or some place.

The nursery mostly used her as someone customers could relate to by standing next to in order to keep cool by while eating their ice creams and buying stuff from its plant shop. That was in summertime, of course. When it got really hot, people were simply content to follow her around, even if it meant she kept coming back to the best buy of the day and it cost them. When the water bill started shooting up or there were water restrictions on, the owners had her stand around anywhere needing watering until the ground there got soaked to soggy and she could move on to the next plant or plants needing watering. When the weather turned winter-wise, they used her in the hot house to save water. They seemed to have hit on the water-bill-saving system of spinning her around on some sort platform contraption and, providing she hadn't blown her nose of the sniffles too much beforehand, she would be even better than a sprinkler, with more reliable moving parts. The only complaints she ever got was from people having their glasses fogged up around her.

The owners of that nursery kept saying it was a marriage made in heaven. I don't know about that but our own marriage started to get frosty. This I have to freely admit. The main trouble was, with those feet of hers working overtime, I had to get kitted out like Shackleton himself before I even entered our apartment. You can imagine what problems the conjugal bed presented. Pretty soon it was either the headache of the chill. I even began to have trouble seeing those feet of hers for all the steam that started to come off her.

Yes, I said steam. It was those droplets of sweat from the recovered rest of her that were beginning to freeze instantly on from about the midcalf region downwards and forming glazier delta run-offs from her shins over the top of her feet, down between her toes and out into a melting world... and all hissing evaporations while on the glacial march not unlike the latest pictures of the landscape of Mars or Titan, on which they arguably could have walked in the 200-year period before becoming attached to her.

Apparently those delta markings were important for the glaciologist when he came along.

For along he did come, back from Iceland or wherever, and he needed only to take one glance at those feet of hers to cry out:

'Those aren't feet! Any Subcontinental geologist would tell you those are cryogenetically-tried'n'tested tree roots gone petrified!'

As, apparently she virtually fell at his feet in relief at the truth at last, he (also apparently) started explaining to her those marking on her feet weren't bands of frozen wrinkles or leftovers from some prehistoric cave, but sap growth rings. As I understand it, he explained they were in fact tree sap-growth rings frozen over – that is, they weren't of living frozen flesh at all but indicative of where her sap had stopped rising at various stages of her real botanical growth -- namely, and most traumatically, during the great South Asian drought of 1789 -- the year Australia was so-called founded -- the year being his best guess without taking her back to the laboratory which the nursery's owners wouldn't allow while she was on duty. What was certain was those feet had become frozen in time.

'Madam,' he was reported to have declared to her, 'I am no tree surgeon but you are certainly of a tree rather than of any human being!'

She hardly needed the telling, either. Even as he spoke, yet another anonymous customer was rubbing against her trunk, thinking about whether she was the tree he wanted or not, and whether she would wrap in paper well enough for him to get her home by cab.

The glaciologist was far too quick for that, so it was said. Before the other fellow could ask her if she came with shade, he had assured her all she needed was a shady and moist place to put herself to get back to being her true self again at last – and immediately was declaring that he had just the spot in the garden of his own apartment block.

Now, I don't know how much my dear one hesitated. I know she answered both men with a boastfulness hardly to be credited of her:
'I supply full shade coverage'
before the glaciologist got in the killer blow. This was:

'I got dogs'.

And before anyone knew, the love of my life had cried out in joy:
'They won't have to look past me!'
and apparently she was already wrapping herself up in moist top soil and readying to go in a pot. Ringing herself up, was the last I heard.

After that I pretty much lost touch with my dear wife, which included her feet. I couldn't even go visit her unless I was trespassing on the glaciologist's garden, but I heard she was growing into a fine edelweiss specimen without a single canine neurosis in the whole neighbourhood.

My consolation is I know she hasn't forgotten me, for she returned my old footie socks, washed and neatly rolled-up.

I look at them. I look at them. I look at them. Oh. But what use do I have for them now? I don't care how cold my dear wife's feet got, that cold's not the cold my bed gets now.

Stint in a biblical land

Dear Dad,

Well, here I am in the land of the Bible. It feels strange. It doesn't seem like right. Anyway, this shot shows Greg and Chook and Lofty on the LRPV with me. Greg's on the Browning M2 and Lofty's on the MAG-58 machine gun. It's taken at the same place as last week's car bomb, Dad. An Iraqi civvy collared one from a sniper right in the middle of the intersection you see here off to the right. You should have seen Chook; he didn't bat an eyelid but ran out and dragged a woman to safety. He'd fire, drag her, fire again, drag a bit more, fire again... until he got her behind our LPRV. To answer your question Dad that means a long range patrol vehicle which is a sort of Land Rover but not like yours ha ha. We tried to give that woman first aid but she'd had it. Strange how Chook was all cut up about it after all his time over here. It's his second tour. I'm telling you sometimes it's hard when you're a constant target but then you also get to start feeling a bit sorry for what they're going through too. You just can't afford to shed too many tears that's all

This patrol was sort of average, five stinking days all over 44C moving east then going south. Got all the trouble though from the town called Hit near the Euphrates. See how there's not a sand dune in sight. No trees. No shade except our patrol vehicle. Dunno why the lens don't pick up the mirages or the flies, ha ha. Here's also a shot of my new mate. Said his name was Joe -- probably Mohammed like they all are. Joe and his friends took our last cherry ripe. There goes our main diet out on patrol! They look like dog kakk by the time they get to us oozing out of their wrappers but who cares like? See Joe's chocolate lips I thought I'd practise my Arabic on him with marhaban shismeck meaning I think hello what's your name and he waves me off with hey mister you got sister like he's all of ten. If all the Iraqis didn't want to gut you you'd have to like the stuffers, pardon Mum. It's surprising how beautiful a lot of their houses are inside. Like we did a house search a few weeks ago kicking in gates and bashing down doors. The poor buggers were being dragged out of their bed mats. In one house this old codger comes to the door bowing away sir please come in sir so I gave him a chocmint and say go back to sleep Pops. The Yanks thought I was nuts. As if he's harbouring Osama Shit Bin he'd be saying sir please come in sir look-see home my house sir

By the way thanks for the snap of Nathan in his soccer getup Dad. God willing I'll be seeing him going off the school soon. I email my darling Franny everyday so don't worry Mum. I know you guys prefer letters and the writing. I took this other shot cos at dawn it's mostly I think of you all. In the land of the Bible it's like praying I guess. It helps push all the brain storms you wake up with for a bit, but don't worry we've got the best equipment and we're the troopers one, two, three so look out Osama Bin Dirtbag!! Maybe by the time Nathan grows up I can look him in the eye and say your Daddy helped make a difference. Hey, tomorrow's my 100th patrol!!! My, how time flies when you're having fun ha ha. I look at my guys and think where have you come from, am I good enough to look after you and things like that.

This one's a typical sunset I guess. Greg's got a flute he plays to it see those browns those yellows those crimsons from left to right from top to bottom Greg says these sunsets are the unstruck music of God you should hear the flute at sunset it seems to cry sad and cry sweet not as good as a good old rollicking Waltzing Matilda though ha ha you can just see the Euphrates in the background it's the mother-of-pearl strip in the background it shines its water of life they say there's giant water lilies there being in the middle of the Promised Land makes you want to stop and think of the bible and little Moses floating along in a basket and how lucky we are back home and that's the thing see.

Lastly this shot may look like the lazy sods we are, but it's last Australia Day. Some sleep in or take in a barbie and down a few frothies or swim just to cool off. No complaints, Mum, but pls remember to send enough for me to pass around otherwise I'll get the big flick from my mates. So here's a few dos-and-don'ts thanks. First the cherry ripes and chocomints, keep 'em coming -- and soda water. They keep us going during the days on patrol but remember it's like over 100 every day and they can arrive like used nappies ha ha. The RSL biscuits were ok but we get issued stuff like that anyway. Tea, great thanks, but don't send the herbal stuff in the fancypansy tins; a bloke just gets laughed at. Mainly though keep the gossip rags coming there'd be nothing to yak about without a bit of fruity gossip like one of those Kardashians on the box, just joking Mum. All virgins, eh?

I reckon you'll scream with laughter when you hear this one Mum. When the incoming siren went the other week and they started shouting to evacuate the mess tent, no problems there. But do you know we all still scrapped our food into the bins and stacked our trays like good little soldier boys before bolting for cover like maniacs. It was like staying working at your desk in the World Trade Centre during 9/11!! Sorry, don't mean that crudely. Anyway, stacking all the trays first. Are we trained or what?!! Going down saluting ha ha. Yesterday there was a bombing in a petrol station up at the pet market right near here. They say the fire was so intense, mothers were throwing their babies out of the window to save them from burning alive too. This is not soldiering; this is misery and death while you stand by and watch an enemy that's just animals without pity for their own kind doing their dirty worst. Sorry about getting all maudlin. Anyway, I don't know if we Aussie're a bit dopey but we don't talk about why we're doing this so-and-so or that-such-a-thing. Oh, sure, we have a go at each other or rattle on about getting right up the Poms at the MCG you beauty but we've got no worries about being here.

After I got your photo of little Nathan, now when I see some Iraqi coming towards me maybe going to blow me up I want to shout hey wait-up, mate, I want to see my boy playing soccer. Please make sure to tell my darling Franny, she and our little boy are the beat of my heart, the soul in my body. Without them, what am I?

To: Manager, Secretariat
Action: typing asap → next-of-kin pro forma → return for signing

Dear 1. [title > Mr and Mrs]/ [last name > Nyugen]
I/We/ Myself and all of the officers who knew your son wish to express my/our sincere sympathy for your great loss. Your son was killed on 18 July last while courageously trying to defend his wounded comrades from enemy rocket fire in the [town of/battle of/region called > Epehy].

He was always cheerful and enthusiastic. He never shirked his duty and never flinched to face down any danger. Indeed, I have often heard

his men saying they would follow him anywhere. I/~~We~~ regret his ~~kit~~/personal effects ~~was~~/were destroyed during a fire/~~accident~~ here at the ~~office~~/barracks/~~garrison~~ here so I/~~we~~ cannot return ~~it~~/them to you.
Yours sincerely,
[sender full name/rank > Ryman C. Gasser, Capt.]

Judas acting as Jesus Christ

Look at him.

You wouldn't think he's just killed me.

Just because I've always admitted I'm neurotic and anaemic, what right did he think he had to go and do that? It's me who's got to cart this sickly nature around. What was his burden compared to that?

If only for thinking he had the right to kill me, he's a fink of the finkiest order in my books.

In other words, you can call this thing right now a vacuum I'm in, but I don't care. Who cares what's past tense or present tense. I'm glad it's a vacuum.

Vacuum claque room
Lah di dah. Lah di dah lee.

Look at him. Being my husband has nothing to do with it. Fink. He sits there looking like he deserves a medal for dropping in on me after finishing his damn hospital rounds. Smug and smirk; smirk and smug; sitting there saying sad, sad but, like, rotten things happen. I'm full of beans, me the doctor. Pity about you, the patient. To some is born… whatever… you name it. The absolute murder, _butchery_, of me and he just keeps sitting over there all smirk and smug convinced he's done everything that could be done. That's what he's thinking. I know him. I swear to you that's what's going on in that thick fink skull of his. He's thinking put on the old bedside manner and nothing but blue skies all day long. Fink. _Fink._ Someone get in here and tell the fink to drop in somewhere else, bastard, or just drop off.

Slop off flop off droff
Lah di dah. Lah di dah lee.
Lah di dah la. Lah di dah lo.

Don't try telling me what he is. I know what he is. He's disgusting. Just don't call him my husband any more. That's no husband over there. That's a dirty low down fink of a quack smug and smirked, reckoning he's done all medical science he finkly could, so it's all jake then, isn't it? How could I have contemplated spending my whole life with a man sitting there fink-like like that, like the chair is trying to force its way up into his body. If you know chairs, with that fink chairs wouldn't bother. I hate it how he keeps his hands in his pockets like that, even sitting like that. When we first met, it wouldn't matter if we were in the middle of Collins Street, he'd still be standing there playing... not playing, rolling them around like ball-bearings... pocket billiards. He still does it but see how now he's more like stroking than rolling. I see how he does it around the nursie I've got. Ha, as if he's got anything there to pocket, billiard-wise. And that other bouncing up and down as though he's come to introduce me to some archangel of mercy. He needn't introduce me to her; he's going to need her himself by the time I get through with him.

Him dim sim ho
Lah di dah. Lah di dah lee.
Lah di dah la. Lah di dah lo.
I have a baby my mother said to me.

You take that bald head for a start. That's no fashion statement. That's no Mister Mountain Rocky High. That's no World Wrestling Federation there. That's the great-sahara-desert real thing. With knobs on. They make fortunes in TV land drumming up comedies about heads like that. They say the Nazis made lampshades out of human skin; with his head of skin they could cover the MCG at night. Ever since we got married, God help me, he'll be sitting down, say, and let's say I'd be walking past, he'll whip his hand up to cover that greasy noggin of his and he'll come out with don't look at my bald spots or you'll be tempted into eroding the respect a marriage demands and the next thing you'll be doing is laughing about it with your friends and that'll then lead you on to deriding your choice of husbands. *'Deride my choice of husbands'* – you point and I'll laugh!

Husbands hush beens waste bins.
Lah di dah la. Lah di dah lo.
What do I say when it's all over
Except sing the song with lah-dee-dahs

62

Anyway, why wouldn't a normal person laugh about it? That's a dead-set serious blowflies' skating rink, that skull of his is. My grandmother's knee looks better – and she's ninety if she's a day and still cutting-and-polishing floorboards. He waves it off as just a bit of bone with skin stopping his brains from flying out. If I had a baseball bat, I'd show him how really flying out they could be.

Supercilious. That's what my old gran would say looking at that smug and smirk mug of his. He actually thinks he's gotten away with killing me. Wouldn't it make you want to heave your breakfast up?

Okay, being the Ugly Duckling, maybe I had no right to crave being pregnant all my life. I always thought it was just part of me being a bit bolshy, that's all, but he's suddenly in my life telling me don't use that word. Bolshy is for Bolshevik is for anti-Semites. You get an inkling there of the nerve of the man. He only became a convert as late as late medical school just so he could marry into our money and yet he turned out a more fanatic Jew-boned than any of us. The first time I took him home to meet my parents he'd been to the synagogue for two whole lessons, but he still instructed my father that his hat really should be put on before going out the front door and not put on only halfway to the synagogue, and there's my Dad only descendant from long lines of rabbis! Is that finkness or what? What my father said afterwards, was that ever spot on; Daddy sat me down and asked me what good was ever going to come out of that piece of turdwork of a guy? But, at that time, I just put it down as Daddy always having a bit of a thing about people walking around with bodies the shape of an S. He used to say they had bums like hyenas and snouts to go with them, and that was all you needed to know about them. How can you trust a goyim-always-a-goyim whose chest is sunk behind a backbone that it looks like our dog humping your leg? I should have listened to my Dads, but who thought of crystal balls then, even watching this fink here pocket-billiarding himself?

From the start, this Judas of a fink worse-than-a-fink decided it was his right to completely take over my pregnancy. Oh, my bubba, my little coming one! How did I get to know that? I'll tell you how I got to know that. I go in to the kitchen to start dinner one night and there on the draining board is sheet of paper with a yellow PostIt thing stuck on it going in his handwriting: *For yr info.* For my info! The draining board, I'm not kidding. And meanwhile, like, where's he? He's only upstairs having his pre-prandial bath he calls it up-himself. And what's on the draining board? It's only a copy of a letter he had written to my gynaecologist informing the poor guy that he, said fink, was going to take over all 'duties' himself from then on. Like 'duties' meaning me. What was I, a latrine digger from the army? He had 'kindly' signed it for me on my behalf with one of those ripped-out 'pp's next to my typed name. So big and unanimous, like.

But still, dummy me, lah de dah dee, did I suspect anything? Call me Pollyanna. Call me gullible. Call me Missy Allinnocent. No, really. He was the man I loved. He was supposed to be my mate

Great pate clean slate
Lah di dah. Lah di dah lee.
I have a baby my mother said to me.
Take it and be swan of it, my mother sang to me.
Take this, all of you, and drink in it, my mother swanned to me.

Oh, and on that letter to my gynaecologist on that draining board, I remember was stuck the second of the first PostIts to come. It was at the bottom of the letter, hanging off. It was meant for me personally. Get this. He had written on it: *For the best. Health of the mother, etc. Yrs.* 'Yours.' *Yours*!, he signed off with! That passion of the fink is overwhelming; you'll find it in the deep freeze compartment.

You just look at that face he's got on now. I presume that's supposed to be some sort of look to express husbandy-fatherly concern tinged with moral superiority. With that great head looking like a plasticine likeness of Bruce Willis by the Third Reich, how does he think he can get away with an expression like that that's supposed to at least look like grief? I'm his wife. Yeah, sure, because I'm his wife what would I observe about him... but you'd think everybody else would see how artificial he's putting it all on, wouldn't you? Yeah, well, fink, if only my Daddy was here now.

Big (well, in a manner of tiny speaking) with my little Bubba coming, I

64

felt so good. I loved being preggers. From the start, it was like her little fingers were tickling my deepest me, yoo-hoo out there, coming ready or not.

On the spot
For once in my life I have someone who needs me
Someone I've needed so long
Take it in your arms, my mother said and stop
Throwing it up into the air as in the soooong.

For once in my life, when I got up the duff well'n'good all the loose ends seem to have come together in order to work as hum. Oh, didn't I hum, too! I hummed to the humming and it was the humming of me. Me. My preggery proved something better was at the core. Wasn't that amazing? Even my morning upchucks, I exalted as getting rid of all the unwanted rubbish no longer needed for paving the way for my little Bubba coming. My coming little Bubba wasn't going to come out covered in spew, nuhuh. Little Bubba and me; I felt us both growing. I was giving birth as much to me, myself, as to Bubba closing. We both were petals.

Petals specials hmm-hmm hum-hum
For once in my life I won't let sorrow hurt me
I might be de-flowered by I got de petal, babe

To all of that joy busting out in me, what do you think this fink person said? This bloody man said: *Careful*. He did. Careful! He said, take it easy. Don't get worked up. Don't get those expanding titties in a knot before you'll need two knots. It's only early euphoria and it could really, he said, drop you one right in the stook. This, the fink said, was not to be seen so much my husband as my controlling gyno guy from then on, remember? The big worry, this great frig of a fink here went on, was not to let myself go and get all nerve-thrombic. *Nerve-thrombic!* What's that when it's home? That's how the fink coined it. He wrote it down to remind himself to use it in his lectures. No, really; I wish I *was* joking! He made me stay where I was while he found his pen and lecture notes and wrote down: '*Thrombosis of the nerves*'. And waving me to be silent while he was doing it. You heard about throwing a mattress over a match on fire? That's what he did to all that preggerly joy that was bursting about in me before his *thrombosis of the nerves*. He threw a mattress all over my lovely feelings of growing me and my little coming Bubba as though I was going to burn the whole house down.

This man. This absolute dork of a fink.

This rat-fink so-called man here in this vacuum with me. With him, enthusiasm is putting your finger in a light socket.

Lah di dah la. Lah di dah locket.
I have a baby my mother said to me.
Take it and be swan of it, my mother sang to me.
Take this, all of you, and drink in it, my mother sang to me.
Here, the chalice I licked and sipped with him.
He took me for a ride in the desert and he stove me there.
He seemed etched-set in stone to kingdom come.
Lah di dah la. Lah di dah locket turns the sprocket

Oh, did I say enthusiasm? There was no stopping this character here once I started to show. He personally administered pills for my nerve-thrombic 'explosions' – four tablets of them two times a day. How can I say that many twice a day with such certainty? How else other than he told me not to argue? Once when he had to leave the tablet bottle because he was interstate, he'd stuck on one of his PostIts saying, '*These tablets are prophylactic ONLY*'. What? *What?* You tell me what. Tipped out into the palm of that lily-white palm of his, like I was poor little Oliver having the nerve-thrombic gall to ask for another hit. I can still see clearly what he wrote on the actual prescription too: *1 mane, 1 nocte, 1 b.d. prn.* For the whole seven months after that, I never worked out what that meant and, in hindsight, probably didn't want to risk the putdown if I asked, but, see, it somehow got more and more important I should know. So I plucked up the courage to ask him. Silly me. He threw his fink eyes up to heaven; he sighed like he knew the burdens God had to suffer. He answered it was '4 x 2 x 1x 1 x 1 of course' and he left it at that, left me standing in the hallway while he went back out into the world to tell it all about thrombic nerves in gynaecology with that fink smirk you can see on his moosh now. What was that answer supposed to *mean*?

Obscene so lean lah di dah reen.

I needn't have bothered to tax my brain. Looking back at those ever-flowing pills from this vacuum now, I see they were just re-packeted placebos from the hospital's Research Dept. The only thing they made your body do was peel back their labels. What a fink!

See? There it still is, unmoving, frozen in time, that dirty look on his face. Concern? You'd have to be joking. All these years, did he show me one flea's poop of concern? Or, make that any love and passion, as in marriage-ration? A ha and a ho on that. Lah-lah-lah-lo. He has this towel he keeps in his side of the wardrobe. It's got the monogram of that hotel from our honeymoon on it. It was probably one honeymoon in the world that could've made do with one Home-Brand tissues rather than towels. He'd never admitted he stole it, that towel, would he? No, that'd be too beneath the fink. I don't know what your one does, but with this fink of mine, if you're getting ready for bed, and you see he's folded that towel, oh so meticulously like here come de Host, over the edge of his side of the bed, look out. It means passion's been chalked in on the schedule. Whoopee. Get ready for the dry rub. Just don't blink or you'll miss the summer swallows. Don't look at the calendar either for the time's-right-for-nookie either, unless it's one of those multi-year ones. The biggest jolt of passion I ever finkwise got was a night he suddenly jumped onto the bed and shouted, 'Are you ever going to cop a *feel!*', and scared me shitless. Not that I ever knew much better, you know. You are a goose for what you get. And why the towel? I'll tell you for why's the towel...

Lah di dah, lah di dah wow
Did he sound as from the Mount kingdom come?
He seemed etched-set in stone at heaven's gate.
He lodged me in and I stood dumbly caressed like silk.
These are the untold steps that we can rate.
I flowed through his hands like spilling milk dead spilt

The towel's to wipe himself with, that's what. Don't think it's there to be put to any joint use; it's just for his wipe. My bet is what keys him on to the love-making bit is the word *towel*. He doesn't like the word sex; it's what Germaine Greer does; is what he says over and over like one of those old broken records. I bet it's nostalgia; like, he remembers the honeymoon by the towel, and by the towel remembers the verb *try*. Talk about your vicious circle. On top of that, I think the word 'towel' or the word 'try' pops up onto the schedule whenever he gets the urge to wipe himself. It's a sorry thing to say and I don't want you should get it wrong, 'kay? All I can say is you *can* hold your breath when he leaps on you Even if you've got advanced asthma he's going to finish before you have to draw the next breath. In this vacuum. Oo, I float on the ceiling.

Healing reeling feeling yearling
If you knew Susie
Like I knew Susie
Oh, oh what a girl whose steps're uncensored!

I'm not that stupid. One time I did get up the thrombic nerve to ask the king fink about those pills he was popping me. He mouthed something about diazepams and sartans and some other stuff and then loudly so all the dinner guests could hear that I'd drunk enough in his humble opinion, going, would you believe*?: 'With her heart condition, and her enceinte condition and her thrombic-nerve condition... and the subsequent storms of imploding euphoria... well, you know, how many times does one have to pick her up off the floor before polite company?'* Oh, didn't they all nod their rotten heads and put their smug-fink medically-qualified eyes down to lemon meringue with olive-cream... his special recipe, wouldn't you know. Even I did. With the eyes. Then really hit the bottle later after the smug finks had all left. But I never ever did implode with euphoria like he said. It was the first inkling I had that he might be wrong, or worse. In fact, euphoria never left me, because I wouldn't let it, never once. My little coming Bubba and my little coming me, we were both belting down the highway of sap uprising. Oh, I could feel how we were coming up exploding. If my nerves wanted to go thrombic, stuff all the dinner guesty smug finks in the universe. It's a free world. It's my Show of the Petal.

Pearled hurled curled unfurled world
For once in my life I won't let sorrow hurt me
Not like it hurt me before

68

Lah-lah-lah franny on the sea shore

Fink-wise, I have loved this man I can slowly circle now. I bowed to his superior knowledge of me. It wasn't his lofty postgrad med school to my plain sociology; it was when we took vows. I just took his greater sense as read since it was obvious he could have done better than ugly-duckers me. To forget about all the money I brought into the arrangement took him about five minutes flat. Now, all right, I know I'm not the only Jewish little-lady in the world to give way like that, but I felt I was. As my father used to say: *'Pay your dues or deuce it, honey. Or dry bread. Who?'*

All right. Where were we? But, even so, I've always found it beyond belief that this finko man wouldn't even let his own wife touch his handkerchiefs. I mean, we're only talking snot rags here. It was the same with his underps, too. He's got to wash and iron them himself. That'd be terrific, if it wasn't for why he wants to. It's like this: he says one's 'remainderings' are to be confronted and then addressed by ones own self. They should not be flopped against rocks down by any metaphoric riverside of the wider community, namely anybody else. The fink spouts on: One's partner, once seeing her mate as altogether *too* human, soon loses the magic of The Other. This man. So dust your hands. You've just heard Mankind's last words of wisdom on snot rags and underps.

Look at him but keep your eye out for the little corrosions. That's what he's always going on about, the little corrosions. Talk about fink. It's the little corrosions -- the oxidants this fink here calls them -- that keep on eating and eating away until they all join up and grow into one great big bog hole of rust-distrust in the fabric of marital respect. What normal human can makes sense of that, I ask you?

Respect neglect reject
Hey jude, don't make it bad.
Take a sad song and make it better
Put a little coming One into your belly buttor
And make like the Show-Wonder, lah-de-frutter

It's even more than that according to the Gospel of Fink. It's the small things of a marriage that rust proofs such spreading corrosions, so he kept finkly saying. So, with the nose, that ski-jump for drunken silverfish, and the little corrosions and the imploding eu-bloody-phorias, lah di dah da, and the thrombic nerves... you get the message: don't go near his hankies or his Y-fronts not even in this vacuum. With the underpants side of the equation, once when he went away, he stuck a PostIt on the front of their shelf: '*Careful, they might bite*'

You'd be lucky.

Stucky sticky licky
For once, I can say, this is mine, you can't take it
For once in my life, it was me not fakin' it

Outside this vacuum here, just down the corridor, in the next ward, on that examination table there, not even putting me under any sheet like he'd accord to any other of his rotten patients, this man used to hold that stethoscope upon my little coming Bubba. He would drum on my belly and her with his forefingers, one hand on each side, like he was thrumping out the bass for the drum band of 'Coming around the Mountain' in some roll call. What else could I do but just lay there... what did I know?... looking along my newborn hill of a belly feeling so proud at being able to show how large I could get. How catching up with the rest of the world I was. Who said I wouldn't be up to it? We were coming, my little coming Bubba and me. Stand aside, all you unfructed! And, oh, the Show-Wonder and wasn't I showing it!

She and me free and see
Lah-do-dah-dee, lah-o-dah-dee
At first I was afraid; I was petrified,
I held onto the song while I multiplied

Finally he relented as much as any fink like him can. Just before he finally bent over me with that ultrasound fink machine thing, to signal that, he'd wave to the nurse to pull the sheet up to cover my crutch in a manner that said he was aware of doing the world a favour. I just knew that if he could've stuck a PostIt on my twinky, it would have read something like: *Incontinence is a state of mind.* Week after week on that table under that ultra-sound, month after month, there he used to

70

be, drumming away on the pigs-skin of my coming little Bubba's kettle drum, *dum de dum de dum dum dum,* saying ha ha to the rhythm of Bubba's little pulse in there. *Comin' round the mountain when she comes.* Making that plunging neck-line nursie laugh her horse's laugh. And rictus-grinning, that skeleton of a fink head turned sideways to me, beaver-teething, getting jollier as my weeks rolled by and nursie's neck-line plunged, as the months rolled on. As I sped on to our petalling, little coming Bubba's and mine. Never tell me that wasn't the happiest time of my life. And then that last time, this man turned to nursie and he said to her show-of-leg: *'She's wearing well'.* Wearing well. What am I? Sandpaper?

Admit a bit a sit a twit
Did you think I crumble?
Did you think I'd lay down and die?
Go forth and fribberty and fructify
Hum de dah, lah de hum the guy

I'll go another circle around this man in this vacuum, this vacuum. I'll flutter like a moth about him. I can tell you it's no different with those teeth than any other sorry part of his sorry arse fink self, I'm not being hypercritical, believe me. Wouldn't you be thinking those teeth are like tombstones in a bucktooth'd wombat's graveyard too? Don't blame yourself for thinking about him badly. He's not another human being. He's another *fink.* Personally, I've always thought of those fangs of his as some kind of hand-me-downs from a kind uncle of a caveman. Some Neanderthal in a skullcap. Yet if I laugh and, say, throw my head back to let it out, he turns away in disgust. Why? I'll tell you why. Because he goes on insisting there's nothing worse than someone so insensitive as to willingly show her or his cavities and fillings to the wide world during the act of outright laughing? No, really, I'm serious! According to his finkdom, throwing one's head back with mouth open, showing the inner dental workings of the mouth, is the ultimate degenerative act on the degrading scale of worldly things, like. It's on the fink's Tablet from the Mount writ in stone again. You think it's only laughing openly? Wrong! It's more sinister that that. Outright laughing, the fink says, shows you are wantonly in disregard of the underlining processes of decay which threatens all marriages. Cuckoo, cuckoo, ding-dong dell.

71

Pussy's in the well
I will survive. Hey hey.
Give me some hey and I'll give you a neigh
Lah-de-doh, lah-de-peas in a puddened shell

That leads me onto the crime of handing toothbrushes. This is possibly the biggest crime of all in all finkdom. Taking into account all the times he's gone away, the place where you're likely to find the greatest number of PostIts is around his toothbrush. Here's one: '*It's the thought not the deed'*. Here's another you'd find outa him: *Kindly put me down*. And his fang scrubber has always got to be blue. He'll tell you why too, don't you worry about that. As long as his toothbrush remains blue, see, one can be confident the balance is still being weighed between a man and a woman and her pink brush. No bull! But that's not the worst of it. The worst of it is given on PostIt too; apparently it is the *erosion of individuality*. You do not just walk in when one is using one's toothbrush; you do not treat the brushing of the teeth as nothing-doing. These are actually sacred moments of oneself with oneself in the individual colour that you're brushing with. If not, next stop before you know it, apparently, is the Family Law court. And if he can't make it he'll send along his toothbrush.

Blue hue blew you
Cha cha cha and a bit aslike you too
If he thought this gal was gonna fall apart
Wait til he feels her squeeze on his tenderest part

This man here, this fink, remember when he grew a beard once when he found a few strands of my armpit on his razor? He said he hated beards but I'd ruined his razor, he said, for all time to come. Is there a greater putz? You're thinking it's all very well, but where's the ultrasound in all this? He gave me two final goes on it. The first one was at week twelve, the second at week thirteen. He decided to stop the beep-beeps after that. This man, finkfull, said he could hear *dum dum de dum dum* good enough by ear'n'stethoscope without getting him going to all the trouble of hooking me up to the ultra-sound. Him with his perfect-pitch n' all. Yeah, pull this one. But was that the end of the ultra-sound sessions? Yeah, like pigs can fly. He didn't have to bother to turn up anymore but me, I still had to front up in that room here next door, go in and get laid out on the slab again next to the ultrasound screen and lay there staring at the black blank screen. I did! There I was... instead of watching my little coming Bubba and me splashing around in the ghost of me wide open-arms, I had to gawk at only the negative of me reflected alone and unloved, like... although, once, he had put on a training video on the seven ages of pregnancy. After that one, when he finally fitted me in at the end of his rounds, he really got up my nose with his supercilious right out of the fink manual: '*Such inspiration is enema-making?*'

While we're on hair etc hygiene and potty training in this vacuum, it's hard to get past his toilet rolls when I look at the fink. The only major renovation he made to the whole house after we bought it was to get twin toilet rollers installed. Suddenly, there's another PostIt staring at you: *Mine to the right; yours to the left.* It's all about greasy spots. It is. Apparently you find a greasy spot on the toilet roll that you know you haven't done, and you have to unwittingly suffer the image of the person you love with unwiped fingers. It seems this is not only a question of hygiene, but goes to the heart of eschatology itself. It's an imposition of the disgusting factions of having to live in the material world that are otherwise best separated from one human being to the other. PostIt put it like this: *Please keep these things to your side of the bog.* If you want to know more, please write to him direct. I tuned out after that. He even got the toilet exhaust fan attached to a pinewood spray can pointed at his side. Where else? But don't ask me why; the fink thing never worked; he was always too busy to refill it, he said.

Wow how now brown cow in my toiletry
Make a stink and end up sub-PostIt-ory
It's sad, so sad and more than absurd
That 'shitty' ends up the final sung word

So, if you missed any of this, what I'm saying is this finko creature before you now, he only sticks one of those pink fink PostIts on the top wire of that ultrasound machine on the last of my last two goes in front of it. It stayed there, a limp flag for the whole Maternity wing to see, for months. *Beware the ghost in the machine. Consult Levi-Strauss or keep your jeans up.* Well, he had to spread it across two PostIts, but, one or two, it was there to humiliate me. I know that now. The true meaning comes out at you from the mist. I mean, when you've been killed by a fink called a husband, it all swims into view, you know?

Yknow whatablow one-two
Living is easy with eyes closed, misunderstanding all you see.
It's getting hard to be someone but it all works out, it doesn't matter much to me.
Lah-di-dah-doh-so-fah, none of that rhymes so blow me down.

Yeah, and as the months wore on, as they say outside this vacuum, this bloody man used to declare out loud how he was so-ooo proud of me. He started chuckling up at plunging neck-line nursie as he probed and squeezed down on little coming Bubba's little fingers. Coochy coo. This man pretended he could tickle her little feet. This man pretended he could wiggle her little coming toes, oh. He threw his arms up oh-boy oh-boy when he felt my coming little Bubba's first little kick, he said. This man, a real fink. How big, he clowned to the bum-wagging nursie, is this woman going to grow to, drum drum a-dum drum? This bloody man blew down into my belly button – not the greatest sight in the world, I admit – and he goes, fink-style: *Come out wherever you are.* Hey, you mind?, that's the centre of my universe and he did that thinking he's so clever kidding around in public. Always this fink thinks he's so great. No, I mean it. One time he stuck on a Groucho Marx's moustache when he got to what he claimed was his world-wide birthing innovation -- vaginal temperature maintenance. When he opened me up for it... his own wife, supposed to be the dignity of the family name and all that... you know what he did? He wolf whistled! He did. A cartoon one. He pretended to take a cigar out of his fink's mouth of rubber of his and kill-ash it, then gawped up at the ring of med students gawking away, only at the nakedness of his own wife, going: '*How's this for a gap your books don't describe, ha ha!*' Real charming. And don't tell me I was only imagining it. When he finished, he'd come up to some surface doing a charade of some kind of air-guitar breast-stroke.

You ask why I was just sitting back and taking all this? I wasn't. Around that time, even in the privacy of our own home, I was starting to get the same feeling of being invisible as I have now. I should have been more suspicious, I know. Perhaps it was my fault. As my little coming Bubba pushed out her petals inside of me and little me growing with her too, I seemed soaked in warm lappy milk. It was yummy. I knew I glowed so. I was life surge. The Show-Wonder show. But maybe, just maybe, I should have given a thought he might have started feeling a bit rejected. You know? You do? Oh, well, boo hoo to you too.

And pee all over what he was thinking too, lah de dah da. Put soft lips on this petal, doo dah.

One two onetwothree
Always, no sometimes, I think it's me, riddly-ree
But don't you know you know I know when it's a dream?
Let me take you down, 'cause I'm going to strawberry fields.
Strub-berry fields forebber.

I mean, in this vacuum of my death'n'dying, will you look at him! With looks like that, you'd think he'd turn a blind eye to the bedroom. Fact is, the bedroom isn't far behind the bathroom for PostIts, either. On his socks' drawer, I once found *No pantyhose*. On one of his shoes, once, a *A reminder...* but it finished in mid-air. I think the double bed lasted for half a year, then the two singles appeared one fine day. He had them delivered when he was away at work, with a delivery note saying we'd talk about what to do with the double bed sheets later but did I know where the scissors were? After that we slept across the great divide, but never again head-to-head. He set the space between the beds ('*ideally*' he goes) at half the width of one of the beds. It was relayed after a week of doing it that heads-to-toes sleeping positions had dual functions: avoidance of gusts of gassy emissions sleep is prone to give even the best of us, and an greater space between the snore (me) and the snorer (him). Then one night he fell out of his half of the bed. He didn't exactly blame me, but a replacement double bed reappeared that same afternoon... only wider than the one before. King size like. *Get the double bed sheets out again,* his delivery note said this time. '*Bubble proof*', he explained. But I never knew what was bubble proof or the type of bubbles he was talking about. Pardon me. I didn't think in this vacuum things were supposed to hot up, but I'm starting to really boil up now...

Pow foul bastard pal when a fink's dipped in ink

Look at those beef-jerky lips of his. Dining rooms are a bit different from the rest of the happy marital nest, because you can't quite quantify the doings of eating and drinking with PostIts in dining rooms like you can elsewhere. How do you write down the prohibition that he does not want you, no sir, to chew lustily when he is not eating himself, like the smacking of someone else masticating can apparently drive one mad according to the finks' grand scheme of things? It puts the thought of living with this person eating her food like that apparently right *off* and, as such, is an invasion of one's rightful expectation of a safe conjugal harbour in the marital nest. Finkwart stormed away from the table one time. On the top of The *Age* he had written *Divorces are made of this. Mouths are made to be closed.* I didn't have a clue what he was on about. I mean, shit, who would? It turned out the way I chewed made the great man think of cows and cuds. I was mortified. He forgave me. I quote the fink: '*We should not have to be reminded of the bovine in the Divine Canon*'. On the other hand, he kept on the dining sideboard one of his mother's framed embroideries which went: *Don't talk or you'll miss a mouthful.* So who can figure and who the frig cares anyway?

It was only last week… although what's time in a vacuum of your own annihilation when you think about it?... we are talking maybe ten days before my little coming Bubba's petal-show Time. I looked up from the telly and there he was in the doorway, all impatient like I've forgotten I'm supposed to be a mind-reader like. He's got me packed up overnight and he's got me admitted for '*a bit of building up*'. Look at him; he should talk. If he's an example of a real man, they need to replace the powder in the powder keg. From that night on, I never got out of Maternity. I did not. I might fiddle the occasional waddle down the corridor going pardon me but with my little coming Bubba's Show-Wonder stretching from one of my horizons to the other, they ought to build these corridors wider. Other than that it wasn't being allowed out of bed for me. *Hold her down*, he told that bum bouncer of a nursie, *throwing free jumps like that what got her into that condition, ha ha.* Yeah, real funny. What's a wonderful pregnant belly without a full Show-Wonder, you tell me? No, tell that fink. And they're holding me down from getting up while he's got that supercilious grin of his on that fink moosh of his, and I suppose that was supposed to show everybody he's some sort of happy about how things were going along, or something. How was I to know how much the hospital staff was all believing him? *Example of the perks*, he whispered to me but loud enough for the interns to hear. What else? They're kids; they're interns, but he's big-timing over my tied-down-in-bed half-nakedness going: *The train's a-chugging*, and then gave all them interns gawking over me a bongo recital on my little coming Bubba's and my belly. *Ensure she eats her greens*, I saw on my chart.

Chart heart all apart

Was the murdering fink finished? No way! *What's Time, when you think about it, but a yodel down the fallopian?*, he asked no-knickers nursie. I didn't disagree, strapped in there. I was starting to feel my little coming Bubba's and my impatience to spread quarters, to render hocks. She and me were getting insistent against this dam wall. I have seen great swells of cyclones on the television; I knew what to expect. It doan't come a-easy. And so, thank God, the labour pains began, almost tingly at first. We begin as drips. We drip as being dropped cha cha cha. I nodded, yes, yes I know to him, this fink of a man, this so-called husband of mine, this 'caring' gynaecologist of mine, this murderer of mine. *Bubba blubber ahoy!*, he penned.

Those dirty filthy PostIts.

But, suddenly, as I swear this vacuum is as in vacates, this man I could spit on before I do more than that to him, he had nothing to do with us anymore. You think I'm joking? I am *not* joking. One day he walked out of this vacuum's door and suddenly it was only my little coming Bubba as me and me in she. My life coming up ours.. Hers as mine. Bubba Above-a! I feel top rate, I yelled out to his back. Up yours! But he was gone, left, departed.

Carted
off
tra rah ra and lah-de-fah cut 'em off

He had left me flowers and has left me flowers. White and red roses. On the card repeated is and was: *I've heard you look u-beaut but still don't wait for me.*

So you would forgive my surprise when I hear this drip fink of a man has left me another message on the Night Nurse's roster. It said I should let nursie slip these new tablets down me to make it all easier and not to worry; they've been doing it since Caesar wanted to come into the world so it can't be too bad. So what else can I do but scoff them down? These new tablets, that night. All I know is, when I opened my eyes next time, all I knew was I was a mother come up at last. I was! Oh.

Who can describe the thrill, the trill, the trillfeel of it? My little Bubba come!

But you know how you go... at first I daren't move. Something made me lie there and listen carefully. I was mugged by the touch of life. Maybe all of us new mums do that when it hits us. It might be like knowing the state you're in is not the stasis you were in. Mine was so quiet, so night, so right. My heart seemed locked into the e.c.g.; my breasts gave up suck gladly to its pads. The ceiling was half in, half out, of light and shade like a no-brainer Rembrandt painting, and full, full to a most wonderful sky full of flurry angel hair breaths. The beeps, the bops, the bopbop pops. Lah-de-lah-alah-de-dah! I remember how my stomach hurt so very deliciously when I saw how my arms were being held out to receive my come-up little Bubba come at last finally at me. Oh.

But then you stop, don't you? I mean, who wouldn't? I could just feel how everything was all too quiet. Far too quiet. Oh so quiet. I was alone. There were no camp tents anywhere near that I could hear. All the calling buttons I tried to press.

Press ess yes
All the hail buttons I tried to press
All those hello anyone out there's
Hoy hoy hey hey who who's spares?

78

In this vacuum, in this nothingness, yes, let's indulge one more circle around him the fink. The brazen murderer, chop chop. I can pretend I'm stalking him. No, I am stalking him and let it be for this one more time. It wasn't even my kitchen. He has a white bread board there and a set of matching knives. For example, you might go for a certain stiletto kind of one, a real flesh slicer, and get a PostIt going: *Don't even think about it*. This fink and how he thinks he can control you even when he's not there and how he knows you only want to slice him when he is. Don't Doberman pinscher it, PostIt. Don't lie doggo, lap it like labia.

Like a complete bone-dry
Like a rolling stone
Like an I-spy in the complete I-die

This man. This murderer. This rat fink. Here follows my testimony of the first few minutes of my being a new mum – finally, finally, getting there with my little Bubba at-last come. Here follows my manifesto from the dock before I do him.

'*Congratulations, aren't you the clever one?*', she, another gynaecologist like fink himself and supposed to be one of my friends, was saying to me as she reckoned she could as this best friend we were both supposed to have going for us, and she's going: '*That busy busy busy man of yours said to tell you he's trying to get to the stage that his presence at the seminar was not so terribly vital for hundreds of people compared to you being just one in number. What a silly billy.*'

I suppose you blinked just then. I know I blinked back then. Did it take time for you to hear that, like it took time for it to sink into me? Out my little coming Bubba come for all to see as the miracle it was of me... come as all the joy of Show-Wonder of your whole life... and you have to listen to what ends in '*silly billy*'. You hearing right?

Rill oh really?
Silly bill of billy?
Hum-de-hum himmy-da-humpetty
I am pregnant my mother said to me
Open your arms and let the cradle be

I didn't know how I'd gotten from the bed to the intensive-care unit. I supposed, yes, I blinked and there I was in intensive-care. Isn't that how it was supposed to go when there's that talk of Caesar? The voice of the Other Woman had gone. The silly billy one. I don't know how long ago. I wasn't in intensive-care at all, you see. I was in Premature. How was this? How was that? How could that be? Premature. Why Premature?, when I had gone full term and never, never once did I let any nerve-thrombics stop me from my little Bubba come. And she was back again, the Other Woman, this fink-sent 'best friend of a colleague', and she was going don't be Premature-ward alarmed; it is only a Premature routine precaution we're taking Prematurely.

Don't be a silly billy, she says to me
You might still feel full without the filling
Oh lah oh de it was better than drilling

And still I can see back that I still supposed that was sort of all right. Fink Himself, having taken over all the 'duties' of me, not there even at our delivery, I suppose that was all right too.

Please bring my little come Bubba to me, to me

But in this vacuum, in this hospital, in this Premature place, you know how the silences go. Don't we all? There is truly no one else. My little Bubba come in petal finally and so don't I reach out to that crib there... so near, I see, next to my bed, to me all the time, silly billy me... wrapped all swaddly in swaddling. I shook my head it's all right, my little Bubba mine, what we'll do is leave *him* a PostIt that the deed's come and gone, and we have bloomed a whole sweet petal's-worth

and we have bloomered
Bubba Bubba bloomfuls of be

and I swung my legs out and I'm putting my arms into those rubber arms of the premature thing of a crib thing there and I am reaching have reached out to touch the me and my little Bubba finally come to me. So fine al lee. They say joy. Full lee. Oh, they are right. They say bundled-up joy. Oh, they are right.

hummmm.

This was a time before this vacuum time now.

ommmmm

and I am hearing that Other Woman's voice come again near then: *'That darling man of you, makes you so luck-eeee, he said make sure you take deep breaths and it won't seem so bad when we all think about it. At the seminar he couldn't get away from, he's messaged they're even discussing it in class in the context of your thrombic nerves'.* She said in Premature.

She said she said she said she said

And in this selfsame vacuum here where this fink has killed me I watch her fink-sent hands take the place of my own and I watch watched did watch, watching was, I see them pick away at the bundle of my little Bubba come at last. No swaddling. Oh, no. No swaddling; it wasn't. Only hospital towels wound around and around each other pretending contents. Full-size bundle, full-size joy. Full lee. I unwound and unwound. She unwound and unwound. I unwound a-unwounding went did she for my little Bubba come to me out of the yellow brick road and watch watched did watch, watching was, her rolling it unwinding it even further until I could roll it no further. Or she, Nor me. See. You see? See, I couldn't understand.

See, how, see there was this thing at the centre of all the world's swaddle there. At the centre of that bundle of hospital towels there was this something black, and something so tiny and something grotesque as, surely, a cinder. Some unshape burnt, fried, sizzled, some shape of something of some other thing. Oh. Some putrefied foetus thing. Oh.

oh-oh
Hey jude, don't make it bad
Take a sad song and make it better
The Great Show-Wonder is under asunder your skin
Na na na, na-nuh-na na...

I am silly billy. I am the walrus. Even I could see it would have died even before even the first ultrasound he gave me. This is my little Bubba supposed to come to me. This is me. Time is a traveller. So blackened, so withered, so devil, she. A something gone to rot in my womb while this rat fink fuck here watched in on the screen, pit-a-patting tunes out on my Wonder-Show naked belly to get a laugh all intern round. See? You see?

I know I have nearly finished my final circle around fink here. There so smug. There so smirk. There so self-righteous. Now you know why he only bothered with those last two goes at the ultrasound and then didn't bother after that, not even with the stethoscope. At my little coming Bubba's first two months; oh, I know, I know now. Now you know why he was pretending happy clap hands while I carried this *thing,* this charred Incarnate full term full term full term. Oh, full term of the months going

hello in there hello
Your father knows
He is getting a laugh drumming ponst my making the wind
Pphhisss, he's going, all piss'n'windy-whoosh

And putting his finger over his mouth going *Ssh she mustn't know the can't-abort for the health of the mother.* I have been one big tortured *fart.* Now do you see? Did you hear this so-called best friend of mine of an Other Woman gynaecologist at my bedrise with all that laid-down bedside manner going:

'Not only is that man of yours good in the cot, but we can all take comfort how hard he tried to get away from his seminar to be here, hmm? He stresses upon you that all this is simply the natural result of the decision he had to make re your welfare against aborting at necrosis at five weeks. Yuk, erky. Let the body do its natural full term thing. For the sake of your health, what's a little enduring a teensie smelly lump for a few short months? Still, my advice is you give it a name before they open the fire doors. Those boys down in Furnace are so right on top of things. Clang bang and all gone! Say, why don't you throw in those thrombic nerves of yours while they're at it, ha ha?

82

She said he said. This fuckwit fink down there, this dirty thing right here, said by proxy. Tom-tomming on tummy-tum all those months to her pulse. There had never been any pulse. Him coochy-cooing and paddy-whacking and using my little Bubba and mine belly button to butt his Groucho Marx cigar out into for a big intern laugh... knowing what's dead, oh. And, see how there were never any little hands and toes, not even stubs? See how there were no little Bubba kicks hello-I'm-coming? See how there was none of my water breaking, only me seeping? So this fink says. I don't think so. I know what murder is.

He, this fink, this murderer of all of me. Look at him. Look. He had finally got away from his seminar and come to pay a visit.

I hate this man. This judas the fink. I loathe him. I want to slap a PostIt on that fink slunk of a forehead saying: *On always for putrefaction.*

I'm going to leave this vacuum and I'm going to come back from the dead and my little Bubba who was coming at last and me... why, we're going right back to screaming at him.

You just wait. I can't.

na na na nad da na na
hey, Jude, how's your iscariot...
gone to rot?
na na na-na-na nod

The old salt lands in the library

The old salt

The old salt was chuckling away on the bench in Pioneer's Park in Dandenong, across from the back of the RSL, where his heart and his focus were.

Still, in that bright wind-of-chill day, quite a few did chuckle with him, or rather over him, as he sat there chuckling in short sleeves, hatless and quite happy while there they were hurrying by with their house or car keys at the ready.

The old salt nodded absently to each, acknowledging how each of them must surely think him RSL and able to show off any old day his service medals in a proper Anzac-Day setting. Bumpf went the chill wind gusts around him. Bumpf-bumpf went the quarterdeck battery of the *Queenborough* in '57 and '59 Malaya above him his head.

And he also was nodding yes to them. Yes, I am an old salt. Yes, call me an old matelot. They used to call me pussers to me face.

He knew very well why he kept chuckling. Why get collared with reality, when you've got creative writing?

A man doesn't have to take going broke looking after his loony old mother for twelve years after she has been deserted overseas in Sri Lanka by the third stepfather she lumbered him and ended up in a wheelchair with no health insurance. And he doesn't have to take getting snared over there just like her and finally winding up himself with four operations there on one dead eye and a dead creek bed of a heart vein – when he had no health insurance either like his mother. Hear all the dollars go running down the old gangway.

But now, no way to all that, the old man is chuckling to himself, yes. A man only has to get on the old creative-writing tramcar and he can have a sexy wife and a beaut dog called Rocky and a house and home waiting for him up there in big-view Hong Kong.

It's all chuckle, this writing stuff.

Well, he thought he was thinking that.

This day, then, the old salt sat there opposite the Dandenong RSL, observed and observing, snapping his mental creative-writing fingers against the wind-as-chill, and he continued to gaze down at what was in his hands.

Funny how he couldn't remember writing the ending to his story. Yet he knew it was the ending to his story come at last into his hands because if he knew he had written his story then he must have put in an ending.

The old salt didn't read his ending in case it wasn't there.

Instead, he put his writing of his story in the sorely-secondhand envelope he somehow had and addressed it:

'Miss Isabella Lily Rose, Library'.

With her, he knew, you could go to the library anytime and borrow out his story. No one in the world need miss out.

The envelope fell from his hands.

Well, it felt like he had delivered it to Miss Isabella Lily Rose, Library.

Rose, Librarian
She was the librarian and her name, as flung around, was Rose. She had no idea why the old salt always called her Miss Isabella Lily Rose, but she loved it. There was, still, the whiff of an old romantic sparking up his one good, his blue, eye. It had the touch of a good romantic class.

It was more out of doing something for the more unfortunate that she started out typing the old salt's story as scrappily scribbled during her Sunday mornings on. The old boy had come up with the first of his weekly shaggy pieces of paper and wanted to pay for a typing service. A dollar fifty, she had joked, and he had solemnly asked if he could have it on the cuff. The cuff. Ha, ha. What could a gal do?

Rose, Librarian, had just turned thirty; she had a little boy of two years; she had no partner; she was half-prim, half-perky, all-contentment, totally continent, with half a snowy smile and half a smile of slow melting of reluctance. Her upbringing was one big purr under family guardianship. Deep in her make-up, she was an old salt's pushover.

One hundred percent of her, though, was pedant librarian. Before she could seriously give of het time, she had to be satisfied he was right about the regulations of the DVA and Medicare he had in his short story. She webbed to the sites.

She found him right and felt her heart being sorry.

So, she started typing and did so free of charge.

The trouble was the old salt had stopped coming in. What made that worse was she just knew he was near to the story's end.

It wasn't much better when it was left to someone handing in the old envelope, but no ending, that a biting south-easterly had landed up against the library's doors.

His story she had typed up to then:
'Fifteen years having the island off Manila from the veranda of his house; twelve years of a Chinese wife in the near distance, eleven years of only staying on there to look after first his old mother and then his ageing dog Rocky. He could wish he could write down how much fifteen years of that cost, then getting a bit ill with no health insurance.

'Never mind, he was back in his Australia again. Home. These feet on Tullarmarine, would you believe it? Nearby his Williamstown boyhood, his Port Melbourne footy ground somewhere around, his gallopings and hoonings around the old wharves. Too long ago. Not long ago. Nearby, Crib Point naval base where life started and the bell bottoms creased into seven creases for the seven seas he later managed to visit and survive.

'The old man greeted as magic the new look notes of Australia-of-now. While others cried out in the glad-greeting of others, he painstakingly re-calculated his six months' budget left. Before it ran out, his Manila lawyer would sell the house and ship out his dog, money and wife in that order of importance.

'The faith in a six months' budget got as far as the $100 taxi fare to get to the Old Mariner's Hostel. He had budgeted that taxi to be $15, max. Then he looked it wasn't even called the Old Mariners' anymore and it was $150 a night when he had penciled in $35 full board, max.

'Yet he was no decrepit old defeatist, never had been. He hadn't even laid his headache down on that coffin-wide bed before realizing his survival until the Philippine house was sold would rely on getting a Rental Property, capital letters, for himself here in Melbourne.

'So the next morning, he began The Search in The Rental Market, don't you know, and in capital letters too.

'It wasn't so much that he was aged. Being limpy, dandruffy, scruffy, daggy, sorry, over-eagery didn't help. Having no current employment, no referees in family or friends in Oz weren't great saving graces either.

'After two weeks of hot daily street-aches and lukewarm inspections far too late anyway, the only thing the Rental Market was opening up to him for was a collective sort of:

'Excoose me, but this is what we now call after 1900 a real estate office, not a free-shade zone. Try the Salvos; they still exist'.

It mattered naught that there he was, up to his knees in the capitalised Rental Market, feverishly touching his forelock, laying on thick kowtows, lacing his voice with the most educated of vowels.

'Even if he managed to find something to his liking, there had to come, didn't there?, the Lease Application of bigger capital letters. State residence over the last two years; no. Where else in Australia?; none. Referees, two or more. Contact address; if not permanent then why not? Current employer; none. Australian? History of any mental illness towards landlords or nice interior decors?

'So it came to pass in another morning that even he could see it had to be the arch identity identifier Medicare first, the no-plastic-no-pleas Rental Market second.

'And there, the very next morning, he was, bright-eyed and bushy-tailed, fronted up at the front counter in Medicare on Collins Street, and he found that he was listening to:

"Health coverage? No problem, sir or so. We are completely universal here. Well, we would be, if you were *proper*. But you are not *proper* at all, are you? Is this really your Australian passport? Well, if it is, do we ever have a regulation for *you*. NO STAYING AWAY FROM AUSTRALIA FOR MORE THAN FIVE YEARS!"

"I'm sorry I've made you shout, miss."

"Sir, that's all right, sir. Some of us get easily provoked. Now, if you knew what a computer was you'd see not being home here for five years means you must prove you're back here to stay. It's no good you shaking all that dandruff off. If you could see this screen more closely, you'd see you've been *wiped*, good and proper. You just can't come *bouncing back here.*"

"I just thought forty or so years I paid tax before I left....?"

"That's nothing. Some people haven't even paid a day's worth and they've been *wiped* good and proper. We don't know if you've come back to rip us off; we can only guess that's precisely what you're trying to do. Honestly...", she called to the rest of the office, then leant forward kindly, "You're old and sick; I have a silly old bugger at home, too. Come back with proof you're back here permanently and I'll see if you can twist my arm."

"With a Rental Property Lease, like?"

"If you mean a proper one with capital letters, that would be nice. Bye, and you have a healthy day, but don't blame us if you don't."

'And so it further was that the old man got further along the cycle of proving he existed he was started to realise certain people required certain bits of plastic with a certain name embossed thereon to be pushed across the counter at them.

'As an old old salt, he was not without thinking resources. Around the dormitory traps, he had already heard about the Senior Citizen Card. It was a give-me, no real questions asked. You add to that, it had discount horizons with shopping vistas. It came in a full-colour plastic with your name impressed upon it, no sweat.

'So, the very next other morning, he found himself looking across at surely a soft touch in the Seniors Information office off Elizabeth and he wasn't fiddling but deadly serious. Application form, thankee ma'am. No, I don't have my over-sixty birth certificate with me right now but surely the skin on the backs of me hands will do rightio instead.

"Yes, it will. Just apply for an application form. Try the internet."

"Can't I just take one?" He pointed to a nearby pile of application forms under *Please take one*.

"Did I say the internet or did I forget? You have to apply for an application form. We are a free service but we are not that free."

"One of those?" He pointed to the *Please take one* again.

'If you're old, best to try to look stubborn.

"Try Medicare." Her lips were pursed.

"I tried Medicare."

"Try getting a Rental Property Lease."

"I tried getting a Rental Property Lease."

"Then try us. No, don't try us. Try Veterans' Affairs. They have been known to suggest a thing or two."

'Of course!

'DVA. RSL. His service medals, where lay true homecoming, yet to come. How could he have forgotten where the best lest-we-forgets reside? Don't you go all forgetful in your old age? Must be the panic on the rising swells.

'So, one of those fewer next mornings, he found himself at the counter of comfort in the Department high up on Latrobe supposedly full of those who look after you've shipped out of the Service. There were smiles up at that fourteenth floor you just knew would be warm in winter and the voice was sheer roasted chestnuts:

"Sir, you only have to prove you intend to stay at least a year, you know. That should be dead easy, I imagine. Although don't take that as a confirmation or a denial one would have to deny. You look like you need a cup of tea. So would I but they tell me out there the machine's run out sad to say. Still, thanks vee much. Oo-roo."

"Any chance of a bit of plastic with my name on it so I can get a capital letter Lease, miss?"

"Your affairs, you see. Your welfare. But not your peace of mind. Sorry. Try Medicare."

"I tried Medicare."

"Try Senior Citizens."

"I tried Senior Citizens. They said you."

"Cheeky bs. Proof of residency means *that* way," she smiled her smile towards the future, "not *that* way"; she was smiling into the past. "What you don't want to do is take so long with giving us proof of a year's staying here that it might take us more than a year of you being here to decide that any proof of intended residency for at least one year was insufficient proof anyway. We can't be keeping a lid on this pension forever, you know."

"Please, Miss. Say I leave here, like, and, whack!, a bus knocks me flat in the street outside? What's going to happen to me without a bit of plastic with my name on it when they go through me pockets?"

'This truly alarmed her, this Department lass. She scrambled around in his papers before, god love her, she could return to him with a new batch of warming chestnuts on the fire:

"We recommend our veterans take deep breaths, Mr … er… VKM5709. We are certainly authorized to remind anyone there is an autumn to all life, although that can't be confirmed. Look, I'll see what can be done. In fact, even if it takes twelve months to process you, you just come back in the next twelve months with proof that you intend to stay the twelve months you already have. Or did. Or might be halfway through or suchlike. It's simple, really."

"What about a letter or something?"

"I'm sorry you had to ask that in a paperless office. People listen, you know. Look, maybe I shouldn't say this, but praps you should rethink your attitude to the real-estate industry, a *truly* Australian institution that you almost gave up your life for in that, ha ha, funny little war of yours. We cannot recommend individual estate agents but we can commend the industry to you."

'Well, you could have knocked the old salt down with a lanyard! You didn't have to be a super-sleeved Admiral to read her lines as really semaphoring: hey forget trying to keep to the fairy-tale six months' budget and then, six months to the day, the gutter, broke. Get back to the Rental Market and apply for the best rat hole you can find not the worst rat hole you can find. Who worries about identity plastic proofs for the top goers? Nix and nobody, nobody and nix.

'And so it happened even further down the line that the old salt stepped back into the Rental Market, the one with real capital letters written all over it. He did so with a spring to his step and a real mariner's roll to his gait. With his the-sky's-the-limit attitude, the real estate offices were full of toothy smiles and really nice cleavages not bothered to be covered. His money was wanted and he did not let them down… for, didn't he inspect only those Rental Property rat holes expensive enough to warrant a rat's bum of his new high-rolling intentions and who cared about him answering a few questions if they were beneath him? Should maybe get a better tailor though.

'Within two days, the old salt handed over a contract application to someone called Ray White. It was with rich gusto that he did so, and it was accepted with a gusto even richer.

'It was for a townhouse out in Springvale at $30000 a month.

'Okay, wasn't that more than he could afford?

'You bet it was!

'For, along that path the true pieces of plastic resurrection lay.

'By the next morning of those other next mornings, he was back in to Medicare on Collins. He was back in Senior Citizens off Elizabeth. He was back into Veteran Affairs on high-old Latrobe.

'Oh, smiles, smiles.

'For, you see, he had finally been discovered back in his Australia again. That he might even have had every right to be back there.

"Ask me no more questions," he smiled back to the lovely smile who handed back a full Rental Property Lease that would bring lotsa identifying plastics, "until I ever sink back into the unrisen dead again."

'All right, as a reader and a library member, you ask how could the old salt do this on a six-month budget?

'It was very simple. He lied.

'He lied about his bank balance. He lied with a capital letter in every box he had to fill in. He lied about having friends, family, current employer, current five-figure salary, referees (from the Yellow Pages under *Medical Consultants*). He lied about a current five-star hotel stop-gap. He even spruced himself up. It was like wearing shore-leave gear again.

'How come, you ask?

'Well, as Vet Affairs hinted, all on board might get the same questions, but only the lower deck get their answers checked up.

'And so it was the old salt was soon flashing a card wallet full of plastic with his name all over the flash.

'He was a living and breathing human being once more. And he simply like saying:

"You want proof? No worries."'

She waited and waited
Miss Isabella Lily Rose, librarian, waited and waited with the old envelope the old salt had addressed to her.

But the old salt never returned to the library. She nearly informed the police. She nearly took time off to read all the local papers. At lunchtimes and other times she walked around keeping a lookout, or nearly often did.

She had no idea what he wanted her to do with his story. For one thing, the scraps. For the other thing, and mostly, no ending.

She just, finally, typed in his ending as she hoped he had wished.

Rose, librarian, typed what she thought
'One next morning, he looked around the empty shell of his Rental

Property. No six months' budget did he have money for anymore. It was a pity he never could afford furniture or any of those white goods you could plug in. In the drawer behind him there was cutlery of a knife and fork and a desert spoon and a teaspoon, and a saucepan for one... as good as it would get. Of plates'n'things, he had four.

'So he decided the constructive thing to do was to sit down and wait for his wife to fly in from Manila with the money from the sale of his beaut near-beach house.

'The old salt probably never heard how his signature had already been forged to sell the house in her own name. Nor maybe he didn't hear how she ran off with his lawyer who had done the forging and the selling and the banking, or how they had put down his beloved dog Rocky because the little fellow didn't fit into her plans anymore.

'Where he sat waiting was on a bench in Pioneer Park by the Dandenong Library.

'From there, the old salt watched the comings and goings of the RSL that he never did get to join, so he never did get to wear in a proper Anzac-Day setting the medals he never did get around to apply for, which meant at least he hadn't lost them or had them stolen. His old shipmates coming and going, in and out, all in the other ship's cutter called the RSL over there.

All drifting away.'

Within the library being annoyed
Rose, librarian, was annoyed with herself for never asking the old salt's name. She was more annoyed with her fellow library staffers when they confessed to never even noticing him and certainly no salty old brown foolscap envelope. What a kidder she was. What a kidder you are Rose.

They just said it was the best short story they had read of hers so far.

The magical purple potato fisherman

And then Leading-Seaman Cornell's newborn...
They might say he never heard the bomb that broke the ship's back because he'd been hiding his growing deafness long before that morning of 9 April 1942. Four days after that, they laid him to rest in the Batticaloa convent in the presence of two Belgian Sisters of Mercy and a little girl. From his sorry shirt's name-tag, they had his name, but not his date-of-birth for their simple cross. They didn't even know he was from HMAS *Vampire*, let alone he was its ninth crew member to perish, because the hospital ship *Vita* had taken the 590 other survivors to Colombo on the other side of the island of then-Ceylon. They were nuns anyway; they didn't want to hear how the Japanese 'Pearl-Harbour' fleet had also sunk the warships *Hermes* and *Vampire* not ten nautical miles away from where they stood graveside then.

A couple of times Ginger Cornell had sprung into consciousness with a startled opening of his blue eyes, gulped for breath, then settled back to sleep as though he only wanted to verify the little dark angel was still by his side. Her name was Ranee, and she was a Tamil girl of thirteen, still angelic, but really a poor-family ward of the convent, and she would never know he was actually trying to warn her about the circling sharks.

Despite his terrible injuries, the nuns had great trouble unclenching the vice-like grip he had on ten ten-pound notes. The girl learnt she could quieten his shaking by guiding his hand under the pillow where the nuns had stowed the cash; after that, she could carry on giving him sips of sugar water or sponging off his sweat. The nuns also never learnt that his grip on the pound-notes was only because the Japanese caught him right in the middle of the one time he'd ever won at cards in any bonanza way. If he had any fame other than his red hair, it was because Ginger Cornell was so bloody-minded.

The moment before he passed away and exactly when the nuns' backs were turned, Ginger Cornell, stoker, fiery-haired, blue-eyed, still freckled and all bloody-mindedness, clawed his way upwards, grabbed his money, lifted up the girl's leg and shoved the money into her sock.

'Ssssshhh', he said. Or it might have been the escaping of the air from his lungs. Or it might have been the only way he could say *give this to my newborn boy.*

but the fisherman...

Ranjith Sathianathan knew Ginger Cornell was one who hadn't been picked up by the *Vita*. It was during a blinding sunset on the evening of the sinking and on the first day Ranjith had ever put to sea. He was a dirt farmer, very sea sick, just there helping out his brother-in-law while visiting his daughter in the convent on the coast. He proved a useful look-out, if nothing else. He beat his brother-in-law to spot the smoke from the stricken warships, then to spot the Zero nose-diving straight at him. Why the smoke on the horizon or why they seem to anger some fighter-plane, like the nuns, he nor his brother-in-law there knew. They were just villagers who had no idea about the Japanese pillage of shipping all over the Indian Ocean then, let alone what red circles on wings meant. They didn't even imagine how lucky they were when the Imperial Navy's pilot suddenly got bored with so many easy pickings day-after-day and contented himself with merely buzzing them. He waved back.

Ranjith Sathianathan, man of the soil, also saw the floating purplish bloom first. His heart jumped. His Bible told of the deep-sea shoals that gave themselves up to the nets of the blest. Then, up closer, it seemed as if 10000 coconuts were quietly bobbing their lazy ways around some palm frond at their centre. But why was the sea churning so at its edges or what palm frond would trail such crimson dye?

About then, the first fin he'd ever seen sliced the surface. In fearful shock, he frantically signalled his brother-in-law to veer away, but the old outrigger had its own headstrong weigh-on and it slid, as if drawn, into the strange sanctuary within. Beneath him, mere feet away, was not one but a nightmare of sharks in frenzy, maddened at being repulsed by the purplish floating stain. And, even though he knew they were not coconuts, it was the first time he'd seen what bobbed, what materialised the magic circle. Even so, as soon as he heard from his brother-in-law there that the English tea-planters called them potatoes, Ranjith Sathianathan knew these strange vegetables must be the secret of the planters' wondrous prosperous bellies… for what else but miraculous powers could protect the life of a man when Death was in fin frenzy all around?

Ranjith Sathianathan simply took this as the revelation of his life. His miracle purple potatoes could never be so mundane as to have been weirdly showered from the ready-use locker behind the *Vampire*'s bridge that the Catering Officer had commandeered. He could plainly see, even as they hauled Ginger Cornell in, what he was ordained to do with the as-many of them as he could stuff down his banyan. See how all he scooped up had already begun spouting roots of Ascension.

They carted Ginger Cornell as gently as the ruts would allow to the convent where surely the residues of miracles all reside. At its gate, Ranjith took charge due to the boss-position of having a daughter at school in this solemn place. He called, as loudly as reverence would allow: *Ranee, Ranee!* She would tell the nuns who it was and they would come, dark or not. It was even fitting to the miracle that his own painfully-shy child boldly took the foreigner's hand without a second thought, and kept a tight hold of it as they hurried the cart to the infirmary.

Ranjith Sathianathan didn't go back to sea. That was not ordained anyway. He waited outside the convent for the next four days, sure there was to be another sign. At the end of that time, his little Ranee came out to him. She was in tears and looked exhausted. But then that was as should be with the tasks that miracles bring.

He knew what was ordained for the £100 fortune in brutalised notes she handed to him. Before he turned to return to his farm up-country, he wiped her teary cheek and he said, *No, little girl, we don't have to give it back. You listen at Mass how that's the way it is with miracles.*

and so the potato farm…
They arose mightily out of the frosts, when perhaps they shouldn't have. High above Kandy, city of ancient kings and imperious saffron robes, the once-only potato fisherman used English pounds to buy new land to cope with all the propagations of his miracle potatoes come from the sea. They were the biggest, the crispest, and, yes, not even the

frosts of his high-domed valley could seem to bruise them.

There was at first the Allied headquarters in Kandy to supply, then the garrisons on the east and west coasts. Post-war followed the eager commercial outlets to feed the new Westernised diets as Ceylon became Sri Lanka. Then came his audacity of exporting potatoes back to India and winning hugely. Far from the sea, he anglicised his brand into Seaview, and never explained why.

Through all of this, Ranjith Sathianathan never doubted to increase his land, his cultivation. This was ordained.

He began to believe his line wended itself back through the landed potentates of the Ceylonese, back through the maharajahs of India, back, yes, into time. Yet this remained his only conceit. His proudly-grimy hands remained proof he was chosen as son of the soil, even in the highest of society he was party to now. Always, always, his daughter Ranee would remember his favoured and wistful warning for all occasions: *Be kind; the sharks are circling.*

It was one of the last things he warned her about as he sent her off to Australia with her mother, promising to follow when he sold up properly. Of course, he never did, and she knew it was because he was such a religious man he couldn't bring himself to leave his beloved magical purple potatoes.

so, Ranee, the little Charity Lady…
Actually, she never did marry, though she continued to nurse enough men that they held no mystery to her. It wasn't that she lost any of her get-up-and-go. Faced with a good eyeful, she could still go all flirty and it wasn't the last time someone would call her a dark angel. She just told herself *enough* one day to end her nursing career at Dandenong General, and simply left to open her second-hand bric-a-brac shop in Lonsdale Street because somehow she needed to be kinder.

Be kind; the sharks are circling.

Not that she was any reclusey type or some poor old maid -- and no

100

way any schoolkid would ever yahoo at her going: *old retard.* The fact was she was tiny-strong and strong-tiny and as swarthy as all get-out, and she had become over the forty-plus years of migrating as Aussie jaw-jutting as they come.

As her father's imprint faded somewhat with time, Ranee held onto two things about him as clearly as she remembered a dying sailor once clutching a great wad of pound notes in her childhood convent. First was her father's delight in shouting, *she was born on the back of a spud,* which she always used when anyone asked where she was from. Second was one of the last instructions he gave to her; it was: *Remember to pay it back.*

Over the years, both of those assertions became so intertwined that they became one and the same. From time to time, some of her closest friends would see her suddenly giggle out aloud: *I was born on a spud and I'm remember to pay it back but I don't know what, ha ha!*

She did pay a lot back as well, did the daughter of the purple potato fisherman, and way beyond paid-nursing. Her bric-a-brac shop looked so op-shoppy and thus so regularly had bags of used clothing and whatnot left outside on the footpath during the night that she began to kit out all in need who wandered in, then, inevitably, all who came knowing she was a giving pushover. Among the beads, books, china and porcelain, wood sculptures, Christian votives, art-deco shades, hand-painted settings, herb sachets, felty-and -sequin'd-and-silky doilies and cushions... the trumpetings of the small and the trumpetings of the trivia... she always, always, had ready her first-aid kit for the unfortunates' pains and coffee-and-tea they could help themselves to anytime.

In Dandenong, they still call her the Charity Lady.

But, this time, the hands held out before her were frightening. They were not the lovely grimy things of her father and they were not held out weakly for the charity, but ones smeared unhealthily with filth, as though the man's overwhelming stench actually rose from them. This stranger, come in for help yet suddenly at the point of killing her, was not old and not large, and his eyes were so black they held no emotion but a shark's intent. For some reason, all she could think of was how the tip of his knife at her heart looked like a shark fin slicing through the water. And for the first time in her life she experienced what it must be like to actually be no more.

Strange, then, how it was clearly one of her brass candlesticks in a slow arc coming from the direction of the front door and how it connected almost gracefully to the side of the black eyes exploding and how she then so clearly heard from nearby a triumphant cry of:

'Bullseye!'

Sure, her rescuer might have skedaddled before the police arrested Shark-eyes, but she knew he would come back sometime because you don't walk out on a minor miracle of a candlestick bullseye. Soon, also, after he surely did come sheepishly back, she came to find him not dirty so much as, like her father, nobly in-dirt. He was, she thought, as purple-hued as the inside of a potato sack and he came to laugh very gummily when she told him. His response was a very surprisingly high-pitched *I'm too young for youse,* then a chuckle very contrastingly low, and so she could also tuck away the knowledge that he had a sense of humour, even though his hands shook holding the one coffee he would let her give him. *You are,* she thought, *too street-hurt and -low.* And he wore his battered baseball hat at the back of his head just as she'd seen young sailors in old photographs. And, romantic pushover that she was, her heart soon came to missing beats, even at the sorry sight of him.

Now at last the daughter of the magical purple potato fisherman truly learnt how the right giving only comes from the given-over heart. She waited in her little shop every Thursday for him to come in, as he said, *to chew the fat, skip* -- and they did that as easy as pie, and she didn't want to even think he might call anyone else 'skip' because it was her name of salvation, and it sounded just as she remembered, in the convent, her dying sailor had gone *ssssshh* in the only other truly-romantic time of her life, and was she flirting? *Can you say I'm flirting at my age?*

Oh, their head-to-heads weren't deep as any ocean, but the weather was

102

enough and shop talk was enough and that he'd only take garments'n'things for '*me street mob, skip*' was enough. But when she tried to find out whether he was ever in the navy because he called her 'Skip', he looked like he wanted to escape. Once she tried craftiness: *Long time ago when a navy-man died my father said I was born on the back of a spud.* He didn't react as any miracle-bearer might but, the thing was, he never showed any surprise either. And so, Ranee began to more than suspect Fate.

'It wouldn't kill me to know your name, y'know.'

'John.'

'John who?'

'John.'

'How to get you on your feet without a second name?'

'Nothing wrong with me, skip.'

She never let on she knew navy men used skip as short for skipper. She just, yes, waited for him every Thursday, had the best civvies (he called them) put aside for him. He would nod thanks and toss his red-hot hair in a curious gesture of self-amused humility that she knew did not belong in the gutter, then always took them only, she knew, to pass on to his street mob.

One Thursday he didn't come and she came to understand she was about to cry the bitter-most.

yet, the one-on-top, one-below grave
They like to get the paupers out of the way before the paying funerals are due to start. In the Destitute's section, there can be up to six to a grave just dug down an extra yard for each body, but it is usually only three. Henry Jeffries, owner of All Rites Funerals with the government contract for burying paupers, looked at what was before his team. This day there was only two, so his grave-diggers were getting off light, since there would also be no crosses, no headstones, but only earth-

103

unto-dust then a quick shovel-over for the second poor sod.

Henry Jeffries actually felt best in his pauper undertaking. Over forty years, these men (never a woman, yet) he'd laid in the Paupers' ground meant more to him than all his paying clients. *It's getting on m'self*, but he still thought of himself as the last boatman left to row them across, help them on and off the final ferry, nod *she's right mate* to their last look behind. With his own arthritis starting to hew him down, he knew he stood by the shore longer and longer watching them go on. To his longtime mate, the Reverend Peter Jones, who hadn't missed turning up to give a lone-one a prayer in all the years, Henry started to say as he always started to say… that it can't be right to lay a man down looking up the bum of another. But as usual he stopped himself because the Reverend had commenced reading from the first of the two slips in his hand that day:

'This service is for the late John…'

There was no last name, and anyway the Charity Lady had shouted to stop. She came on waving flowers and she was clearly disturbed. *That*, she uttered when she caught up, *is my John, well, sort of, no he is!* She stopped unsteadily atop the clod mound as if height alone could express her shock. *Please!*, she thought she added inappropriately. But Henry Jeffries thought nothing of it; he just thought *thank God one of us gets a mourning.*

'He shouldn't… you know... go with no one.'

Her panda eyes were mightily pooled.

'No he shouldn't, miss,' Henry Jeffries said.

They came to a quick agreement after she made him understand she'd have to pay for two separate burials because her John wouldn't come at one of his street mob being left alone down there on his account. Henry Jeffries threw in two real-pine coffins, side-by-side plots amongst the Baptists, equally-dignified simple services, brass name-plate for each man…. £1400 all-up.

It wasn't a bad rate, given that a lot say £100 during WW2 was about equivalent to £1400 today, give or take the rate of extinctions.

The next day, she stood there over John's grave, at once heart-broken and joyful. *Thank you for the miracles*, she said to him and his sailor-man father she was now positive she had nursed too. *Father, I have paid it back.* And though she stood there the longest time, she never did feel the need to look at the nameplate over the other man she had rescued from that pauper's grave and given his own separate one.

It read, 'Bill Cornell 1942-2007'

Even if she had looked, she would not have recognised the surname or what a newborn son he would have been four days after the sinking of the *Vampire* on the morning of 9 April 1942 off the coast where miracles were wanted.

I don't know what to do with you

[short play, 1]

(Rachel feels best feeling lonely. Her mother, proud from the dervish tribes of old Persia, used to say, 'You are lost only if the sun finds you out'.

Six times most days, people bustle her, but they are just tourists to the museum after all, not hot invaders her mother warned her about. Either way, they are as the deserts, or she is. It doesn't matter. She knows the oasis of daily routine cools her from their comings-and-goings.

Already, the tourists are leaving her kiosk for the bus. She moves safely towards her routine: first, clean the coffee-machine. This is when she becomes aware of him at the counter, his presence but a flutter.)

-- Yep?

-- Is that coffee, please?

(He is long, tall, sky-scrapper, looking down perplexed, softly:)

-- Take-away?

-- I don't want to break anything.

-- There's only paper-cups.

-- Coffee in a paper-cup, please.

(His hands hang by his side.)

-- Milk?

-- What do other people do?

-- They take milk.

--. Milk, please.

-- Sugar's there.

(The man stares blankly way down to the bowl of sugar lumps. He is not moving. Rachel feels hot irritability.)

-- They take one or two lumps.

-- One or two lumps, please.

-- You can have more.

-- Three, please.

-- Help yourself! Sorry, sorry. Working. You can sit over there.

(So sadly hunched into himself, the man carries his coffee like an offering and moves precisely to the precise bench she pointed to. This is not helping her much. He is halting her from sheltering in her routine. She has to watch him putting the sugar in the coffee with the paper-wrapping still on. He stirs it with his finger but it gets too hot.)

-- No need a finger!

-- I washed it first.

-- You're supposed to take off the paper.

-- Oh.

-- Look, it's your coffee.

-- It's good coffee.

-- You left your free biscuit.

(He blinks at her. She has to pick up, hold up, a biscuit. She feels how the shade can slide away and the sun could find you.)

-- Why did I leave it?

-- It's okay. You don't have to take a biscuit.

-- I can get the papers back real soon.

(The man is using her table and his hand to iron out the sodden sugar paper. Rachel blessedly forces herself back to cleaning the coffee-maker. But the man is standing at the counter again.)

-- What!?

-- I enjoyed the coffee.

-- You didn't touch it.

-- It was good.

-- Look, you on the bus?

-- We're on a day trip.

-- Who're you with?

(He shrugs, looks around the empty kiosk. The way he does so reminds her of how her mother scanned any horizon, squinting so hard in concentration, wary of where the sun might be.)

-- You can wait here until the bus goes.

-- How do other people know when the bus goes?

-- Just keep your eye on the driver there.

(With huge relief that it's now up to the driver, Rachel can turn back to the coffee-maker again. She barely hears the driver's familiar bark.

109

She hardly registers the usual horn for the usual stragglers, the crunch of the tyres on the gravel. She lets it all go, as routine must.

As sands shift softly underfoot, the man is still seated there, alone.

He has watched the bus leaving.)

-- You've missed it!

-- Is it going without me?

(Rachel scrambles in her own purse for her own mobile phone. The bus company asks her to wait. She can't stand how the man continues to stare so dumbly at where the bus had been. She hurries outside for breeze. The sun cruelly picks her out. Exposed to it against all her nature, she listens to the bus-company, then shouts to the man.)

-- *They don't even know how you got on!*

(The man stares at her with such utter dependency that she burns now with the despair she remembers in her own mother's voice.)

-- Did you stir your coffee?

-- Did I?

(Rachel reaches down to stir his coffee for him, stops, herself confused, did I do this already? She hears herself cry out:)

-- I DON'T KNOW WHAT TO DO WITH YOU!

(The man covers his face with a great shame. She thinks she has fled back to the oasis of her routine, but finds she is sitting beside him.

Silence has come as heavy as the sun of her childhood sand burns. It flares and grips their hands together.)

I know
[short play, 2]

He's A.

She's B.

(B. stands stoically before him, while:.)

A:
I haven't got a wink of shut-eye over this.

B:
I know.

A:
I'm not burning my bum just because of you catching me in the sack with someone who doesn't rasp sensitive skin tissue like some sandpaper I know, you-whistle-I'll-point!

B:
I know.

A:
She might be a slag but she used to be my wife! Who said you had a right to come barging into my family home that used to be my family home?

B:
I know.

A:
What was that: 'Do I turn on the flash or will it come out all right?' crap? How the hell would I know if it'd come out all right? I don't care how it comes out! It's your camera! You're standing in the doorway of my used-to-be bedroom, I'm not!

111

B:

I know.

A:

I'm not tying anything in a knot! Nuts here, lady, nuts here, not knots!

B:

I know.

A:

Yeah, and you think I'm as shallow as that too. Hey, who turned off the tap on a little jiggy-jiggy in the first place? Did you bother asking me 'do you mind if I turn off the tap?' Oh, no. You just turn off the tap and I get the disuse in the goolies!

B:

I know.

A:

Get your mind off the tap. You're obsessed with the tap. Don't think any lack of tap's automatically turns me dry too!

B:

I know.

A:

How can any tap turn on anyway, the way you snore?

B:

I know, I know.

A:

Whatareya? A man goes to the fridge and it's *Kindly close the door* on a fucking magnet. Up your rubber seal!

B:

I know.

A:

There you go again! Insinuations. Always boring in with the insinus. Everything's got to be insinu'd, niggle bloody niggle. What's this *my flannel, your flannel* bullshit Postit note in the bog? Jesus.

B:

I know.

A:

Vegemite! Is it before the United Nations' Security Council for boycotting? It's vegemite. It made my bones! It's only national building, that's all! All I'm trying to do is have a bit of toast and veggie and you're over there making faces and going puke-puke?

B:

I know.

A:

It's the money! It's that purse thing from out of your granny's bum or somewhere, picking out five cents with your picky-picky little fingers pickitty-pick while the whole world's waiting in line looking dagger at me like it's my fault while the checkout sort's silently screaming her head..,
     (draws breath)
  off.

B:

I know.

A:

Spend something! Do a dollar without SMSing the World Bank! What did you donate to that Happy Babies of Sudan or whatever it was? I tell you what you donated. You donated my name. Jesus. Who told you I wanted to donate anything?

B:

I know.

A:

How would you know? It's called talking! What's wrong with a little 'good-morning'? What's wrong with how's-it-hanging once in a while instead of the bottom lip hoovering up the carpet? Stuff it! I'm an architect! They wrote in on my degree a little morning conversation is alright for architects. Show me where it says stay mute or die!

B:
I know.

A:
Driving! Drive, shisssake! I have to be sober watching you get pissed and rolling on the floor. Me going to AA, suffering feeling like the Sahara Desert, but oh no, you don't drive. You go by train? You bother bussing? You get seen walking? Oh no, it's always got to be getting on my wheels!

B:
I know.

A:
You fluff! Always those squeaky little secretive things!

B:
I know.

A:
Fart! Here, I'll show you a proper fart!
    (tries but can't)

B:
I know.

A:
Nibbling. Nibble-nibble, nibble-nibble. *Eat*! Whack it right it into your guts! Whatareya, cwuddly wabbit?

B:
I know.

114

A:

Hey, big deal catching me and my ex in the sack! What's this standing in the doorway saying kindly don't go messing up the sheets? Whose sheets are they? I used to own those sheets. Those sheets are still half mine! But oh no, belittling. All the time you go the belittles. What's that mad moll of an ex-wife of mine supposed to think when some mad moll's standing there in the doorway saying watch out messing up
  (draws breath)
the sheets?

B:

I know.

A

A big fat whopping great greasy big Mac! I'll eat it if I want. Up nibbling on your lettuce leaves!

B:

I know, I know.

A:

Dandruff! Shoot me for having it! Draw and quarter me. You, you think what's on you is just the ski season? And another thing...
  (struggles to bring anything else to mind)
and...
  (sudden re-thought)
Hair hanging outa your ears! Hairy lip! Jesus, who has to pluck between their toes?!

B:

I know.

A:

Great hairy thighs! Great hairy armpits! Somebody get onto Melbourne Zoo! Shaving your fanny? It's like trying to squeeze moisture out of a porcupine!

B:

I know.

115

A:
Pimples! Jesus, who has to go the squeeze anymore like you gotta? Ping, against the bathroom mirror! Choice!

B:
I know.

A:
You keep aspirin. You keep paracetamol. You keep naproxen. You keep ibuprofen. You keep Tums. You keep Lomotil.

B:
I know.

A:
You keep Oxazepam. You keep acetaminophen. You keep prozac. You keep dematol. You keep…

B:
I know.

A:
… I haven't finished! You keep… pacerone! You keep halotussin. You keep tadafil. You keep… that… zanamirlalalala thing. What am I supposed to be, a chemist?!

B:
I know.

A:
YOU LEAK!

B:
I know.

A:
'*I know*'?!

116

B:
I know, I know.

A:
'*I know, I know*'?!

B
I know, I know, I know.

A
THAT'S IT. I'M SO OUTA HERE, I'M HALFWAY TO CHINA!

(He storms out.

She is left looking after him. He doesn't come back. From the longest silence possible, it is obvious he isn't coming back, either.

She turns to an audience in her mind. She appeals powerlessly to it:)

B:
I know that, but…
(pause for one-liner effect, then fires at audience:)
WHY HE WANTS TO LEAVE ME, I'LL NEVER KNOW!

(She stays a moment for any reaction from the audience, then turns and departs)

The can't-seem sea horses

[Mother Swensen, 1]

Though he ought to be too young to, Mahood feels he is dying but they have called it watchfully waiting. And that is all right because he has always felt he was waiting and watchful. What is new here beyond the person he feels he is now? He says maybe to nobody, maybe to somebody watchfully-waited for too, going:

'I know the tides'.

He knows they know he knows the tides but he doesn't know how it is he is so small, left at the tide's ring, now. How did he come to be alone?

Mahood lays his head on top of, he thinks, his father's hand and his head was and is still greasy and sweaty for the boy that he is – past into the present, yes. And he feels the slide, as came the dream of the can't-seem sea horses, as he with his people, giddy at first, then in swirl sweeps down the Malabar coast, the inlets and outlets, from the desert-hupped straits of Oman down the mighty-main'd trade tides of the Arabee Sea brunting against the Indian seaboard sea fords sea wards – the Laccadive, the Lakshadeepas, the Colchins – Malabars, Malabars -- until he with them is swagging around Galle in olde Serendip, haunch to that mighty Fort, the outlets and inlets yes... and, yes, there runs still the ways of the tides, there streams there the means, there waves there the course and the compass of the stars. Of Mahood the Moor, of the Mahoods the Moors, who bore him along with their nods, in their coming eyes too, in their visions of the sea lines ahead. Mahood knows, becalming now, that this is and was of his father and his father's father's father. At prow, at prowl. Of there's the tides, and those, the can't-seem singing sea horses.

Mahood is still surprised; he once didn't know. It is after all his father's hand there or maybe just the side of their old boat, his own head as the thinly-beached watchfully-waiting boy or man, he-Mahood, resting upon himself or his father or their old boat, reliant on the tide, the only thing he knows. Except that he is still a lad, was left lone.

And Mahood can't seem to be able think how come this old boat is all his own now, along the blue strip of his father's boat which is can't-seem, can't-seem to get any brighter no matter how he scrubs, how he lays new paint. It is the same with its orange and yellow bands; the scrapings and the buffing that can't-seem to be. He wishes he wasn't alone. He can't-seem to be lone. He wishes his mother hadn't left with his father, one of them, even, come back from the accident. He bows his head to the feeling he has of them still, closes his eyes.

Dream't, Mahood the lad can't-seem to feel anything but tired now, against his-now boat on the little beach and its thin beaching he and his people brought him to, when?, now or long off then, it can't-seem to matter. This beach the Mahoods beached themselves on under the great Fort ending their black-flag jaunts, saying here's now home, look lively and about... this beach shrunk now to be a few metres wide, lappy where once snorted the great breaking waves, the beach mushed-up now with common domestic trash, the only two other fishing boats husks half skeletons three parts gone to the land. Mahood feels he must have caused all this, not knowing enough. You've got to see, listen more.

Mahood knows this as he sits on the dirty shale but can't-seem to heft his legs, mired to the knees, out of the mud. His crippled, crippling hip hurts so badly, he cannot seem to understand what it is there for either.

Around him are his fish whenever he caught them – a mullet, a guppy, a baby eel. They are sinking too in the mud and can't seem to be sold. Above, up over the vandalised grass verge and across the moulting road the old Orient Hotel stands can-do-can-seem stern over the Fort's great walls, over the great harbour itself. Taprobane, Serendip, the Portuguese cock their *galle*. Is he the last, and is this the last?

Mahood thinks that. It is hardly a dream. Tides of pain in his hip seem to have come a long way. What he will do, the one can-seem... what he will do, yes... is feed his can't-seem sea horses, in the pool to his left, under the rock, where it has always been deep in shade enough for them, where it has always been sheltered enough for them, where nobody else can see them because even he can-seem only to see them not actually see them. The shadows they trot in, buck to.

He doesn't know what he feeds them. From the time of the first Mahood come beached there it can-seem enough to stick his finger in their pool and keep it there until they nudge and nozzle enough and go lightly away, only they.

And if he has made them bellyful enough perchance they will sing. It is a trade zephyr of a song, a tide riverling of a song. It is a whibbling in come back to us and come on to us; here the course and here the shore.

'See, learn' it hushes.

He used to hear, but there was never anyone else there, since he was the last Mahood of his people, he thinks in can't-seem, and, apart from the sweet dyning in his own ears from the sea horses neighing the ages, in song anyway, he only watches and waits.

Mahood moves his eyes. He sees and hears that the day is the fish cart's day for the grand hotel, so close to his own fish, yet can't-seem. This brightens him up. It's, yes, the fish cart day and *Ooday-today* of the grand old lady's cry and though it is not his fish, that cart of someone else's today means life can-seem to rise up again in joy for a lad. The jingles in its bells and the bullocks' clob-clobs, the taste of the trade winds and the odour of its fare it brings.

It is the fish cart of his early times and ever, and it will stop outside the grand hotel and quiver and all seems can-do, and all can-seem, to quiver with it. She, the lady of legend, the owner forever, Mother Swensen, will come out this day, as she rarely ever comes out, and she will emerge on her part of the great hotel's veranda to pageant the cart's coming again, and she will smile as wide as the great fortress's harbour she looks out to and she will raise her hands in the delight the fish cart brings, going in her belling voice that strikes the harbour, calling out her scowling cook waiting sourly in the sulks of the entrance, the known ritual between her and her lout of the kitchen as though she didn't know he would always be lurking in the shades below, going:

'Ooday, Ooday
It's the fish provender today!'

And the lad Mahood claps a can't-seem to clap with them, even though he is so near and his own caught fish can't seem to be sold when they should so near to the great hotel. It is the life he knew before the ever pain of his hip, its crushing in return, yet maybe never did. He closes his eyes and dreams as part of it, dreams of what he really doesn't know about the grand old lady of Galle. Mother Swensen. All he knows is you take a fixture and she is it.

As she occasionally stands on the second floor veranda there, her apartment behind where the pot plants are, and as Mother Swensen stares down at the lad Mahood by his poor boat, by his poor catch, at his poor hip, there, as she does and how it forever rings in his mind, going still:

'Ooday, Ooday
It's the fish provender today!'

And the black-eyed cook, Ooday, scowling, the lout, yes, unseen beneath her upbrights, scowling down at Mahood you-dare-fish-here-dipshit, whatever he is really challenging Mahood about. Why-ever. Mahood doesn't know.

That Ooday lout. You wouldn't think, two hundred years ago, or nigh of that, Mahood used to watch the Governor of Galle living up there on his part of the veranda too and the officers of his garrison on the floor below; fifty great rooms reeking unimaginable riches for him of Dutch and English furnishings snuffing out the languid pleasures of the military elite clattering down its vast jac-wood corridors with their riding boots and crofts. For fifty years, he has watched and not seen now how the great chandeliers of the ballroom have not been lit for the dance. The outer walls of the old Orient peeling away as if like the once-grand and his enfeebled little boat are of the same face. Perhaps they are. And its shutters present as eye patches against the scratching claws of the sun. The tides Mahood have watched, now can't-seem to.

Now, too, Mahood watches Mother Swensen as Mahoods have for generations and sees again for himself how the grand old lady is still yet'n'always sandy-haired, bready-white, whippy-stepped, as proud as Mahood's own sea horses' prances, from the wheat fields of Australia to feed the stale Swensen Dutch-burgher stock with their desperate need for fresh strong strains. Certainly they needed better ears. And she would laugh, a dry-land's laugh in watering.

She had looked at that Swensen male they offered and she took her time... the shreds of her wheat fields, could she bend him up?, could he be winnowed?... before she nodded okay to him and went:

'I'll stay, and I've said it.'

She did. In the of-all-time, for all those fifty years, she had been there she had never gone back. Back at the wheat fields it was suspected there was less harvesting without her. She took the energy of their sun and did not give it back; how could it have been otherwise?

But the tides change, undercurrents. None of her children have survived, and none of her husband's descendants either, such that she might still be called Mother Swensen if people had memories or homage to spare like Mahood. This woman of unchange, more singular now than ever.

From where his head lies against his fishing boat, from where he can't seem to move out of the bog, Mahood asks in his mind for the sea horses to sing again. They do not, or if they are he knows he is in can't-seem and can't see to hear them. It is hard to look sideways yet the overhanging rock is so deep of shadow over the rock pool that he can't-seem to see his sea horses there. He closes his eyes; this time maybe the paint needs to be allowed just to peel from his people's boat. He wishes he had seen better. He wishes he had learnt better.

Even so, there comes the time he hears the provender's great fish cart come again to the grand old hotel, as it has come overplaying him and his father and his father's father, as if it was on a higher can-seem plain to him all his life, he thinks. He can-seem to see, even so, how there will be another boy way, way other than himself, the lad's barely soiled sarong too shortened to half-thigh mimicking his father's, perched above his father's huge bullocks, and the great cart, paint-bright, its red and yellow paint-trusts as gay as his now-boat used to be, the breath of the oxen and the swingeing of the bell. The black-eyed cook Ooday already ready to come with his hand out when it should have money in it instead but chary of being seen by the grand old lady Mother Swensen on the veranda above going for always at a time:

'Ooday Ooday
It's the fish provender today!'

clapping as she alarmingly giggles never-endingly. And he too, this lad as Mahood might have been otherwise had the beach not thinned, forever of the skinny arms and the bony shoulders too, shorn against the fish nets too, his father's kindly demon betelnut smile too... from the big fish cart, yes... this bright-lad's face full of briding teeth ... when he would leap down as Mahood seeing wanted to and join the young Swensen when he was alive, crashing'n'dashing together as Mahood so wished too into the great inn's courtyard to tease the young monkey or to the rocking horse where they would charge their elephants at tigers.

But not Mahood on the thin beach. The fish he has just caught at his feet now are stinking as they can-seem and can't-seem to be. No singing of the sea horse. With the great fish cart gone, has all gone now?

And, yes, there is perhaps no cry for Ooday from Mother Swensen this time or any time Mahood waits to hear her these times on his tiny beach below. Even so, as hard as his hip makes it to do, Mahood moves his thick eyes a little opened. He hardly dare look to see why he has done so, yet as much as he averts his face, he still knows there are steps upon his thin beach not much more than a few paces away, as if it can-seem to be so. And he knows, he knows, they are Mother Swensen's own steps come so far of the world, come to him, come in can-seem on the nearby of him for ever the first time. And when he makes himself see they are grand old lady's feet, those... of the texture of see-through jellyfish flesh and shipped out in great fluffed slippers no one had ever told him about. These things it could can-seem or can't-seem to be.

And from his thin beach the boy Mahood heard going:

'I will take one of those and one of those.'

Her voice was shale whispers with tide and he knows it. And he knowing it can't-seem to be that she is ordering from him not from the great provender's fish cart this time one handful of tunnies, one snapper, one grunt, one skate, one immature tuna (tch-tching), three blueys, a guppy or two (thrown in), a squid, and all that he has fished with his own hands and:

'And one of those little darlings in a plastic bag with water, and no mucking around'.

Mother Swensen is seeming to be pointing to the now sparklingly clear, chippy and whippy, pool where his sea horses jordle and sing perhaps, it seems in can-seem, in ways she might be able to hear with him. Clear as bells, and she the only one of ever.

And while he can't-seem to still, Mahood serves her quickly, and the rough hands of the scowling lout Ooday unwillingly taken her place is doing all her taking the money from him and paying out and short-changing him loutishly, yes. Mahood manages a hard smile at him. Now he is beginning to see the can-seem. It is just a glimmer, but it is a start if only he felt better. As small as whatever the glimmer is, the lout

Ooday has shown him, Mahood knows he is old enough and should have learnt it by now. But it is all too much can't-seem, all too older than him, all too healthier than his poorly hip.

He still lives, though. And still yet the fish he has caught kick and bash at his feet and Mahood is proud of them, how they represented him to Mother Swensen, some of his sea horses gone to her. His boat momentarily leans brightly drunkenly, filled in its duty far from the Malabar. Behind the lout Ooday is waiting, not just inquisitive or seeming to be, and other louts like him, whom the Mahood has watched every day doing their cons, free-booting on better people, they too are watching him with sneers on their faces as the lout Ooday does. A boy, a lad, who doesn't know what. What? What? Mahood just doesn't know. The feeling of usefulness seeps away with the tide he is supposed to know and he hates how he hurts and he hates how he is so childish as to forget this is the time his father's boat's paint is peeling and that he has let some of his people's sea horses go to Mother Swensen, away from the rock pool, where they might not sing much anymore.

Yet in the same moment, then, as it can-seem, Mahood looks up to see Mother Swensen back on her veranda and he can see she is beckoning him to come up hurry hurry. For the next he closes his eyes and can't-seem to be able to open them again. But yet that is all right.

When he opens his life again, he is standing in the doorway of Mother Swensen's rooms up so high veranda'd. He hopes his skin gone to jaundice somehow doesn't seem too invading to her. It is just that his sea horses can-seem to have stopped singing; it is just that he can't-seem to feel well much anymore. His hair is set flat to his skull and neck, stickily, his eyes smarting to flinching as he tries to focus on her. I hope, Mahood is thinking to her, you have not made me come here to kill me.

'Where you been, boy?'

Her voice has sung it, in the spun-somes of his sea steeds, his one thing. He doesn't know what she means and answers, going:

126

'Out'

but it comes out as weakly as he feels dizzy-weak, and he knows she can't seem to hear but that is all right too, because she is a visit given unto him like it came to that other boy in the great provender's fish cart, a blessing in it, energies as soft as he feels they might be seemly to be. The can-seem-to-do-it. Yet for all of this, he pitches on his knees before her, rocking as forcefully as a pendulum, and still he can't-seem to be able to say sorry.

'Poor you, Mr Mahoo yoo hoo.'

Sweet. But his skin is her contrast. It feels like a lizard's, crisp, ugly, burnt to black. Lifeless. Yet still that is all right because there is the strange green light of blinds permanently drawn. There is a softness hymning. There is something like his sea horses humming which he has so wanted to hear before.

When he can seem to open his lives again, he has found his arms stretched out along the arms of an old-fashion cane commode. His lap has been covered with a blanket, tucked in strongly beneath his knees. Swaddling his pain of always.

'Ow do oo?'

Again Mother Swensen is going from her twin chair by him, her finger circling the air as though stirring pots, stirring places, mixing things up, merry to the round as the tide comes and the tide can-seem to go.

Mahood can-seem to nod back at her, can-seem there at home.

'Ow do oo?'

he simply goes back, and then explains because he simply can-seem to go in English too, as easily plying as the wheat fields go:

'See, it was all in the tides you know, you know.'

Oh yes, and then a swun't sleep of can-seem comes in

127

washwooshwish ways all the way over him. He has known all along... what? What glimmer back there? It slips on a tide back away from him. Yet he knows, even as a young lad, this is only on this, the first day of those forty days'n'nights wrapped in Mother Swensen as she does – or at least it can-seem so long so.

Then and on, on the last day of those forty days'n'nights or at least as they can-seem so, when he opens up his existence again he is still rugged up in the commode next to her and she looks the most exquisite thing he has seen. She is sleek now, Mother Swensen, in the creamiest of tans. The seaswum lights gives her a look of softness of the early years, the wide unfurrowed fields open to her, her wave-mane'd hair washing beneath the high arches to come by her.

He feels wonderful, how it is to be pain free. This is no time to move. Mahood can feel how it is to can-seem to stay still and look around. In all the twelve generations he has been beached up below on his thin beach he has never been in the hotel, let alone the famous lady's room. But, like for all the other tellings of it, that is all right; if he knew he would have seen none of the furniture seems to have changed. Everywhere are still her rose-and-pink antimacassars and, there, maybe her husband's red-velvet burgomaster's chair, yes, by the pearl-inlaid side table from where the valve radio used to squeal so high. The three great teak bookcases rise like ranges above them, one book enough for him as high altar. There, too, the same walnut couches, the satinwood settee, the mahogany chair, the sandalwood Chinese chest with its mazes of gilded drawers, yes and yes. And among these marvellous things the lad can see as high-born furniture and its soft-warming tones, Mother Swensen is awake as though it is the dawn of the first day of those days'n'nights can-seemed to have numbered forty of the boy's sanctuary there, and she is saying – to him -- in all the perfected languages of the world, going:

'I have said this recently to another special guest like you, Mr Mahoo, and I'll say it again. What we need are parties and soirees and dances and things, Mr Mahoo, and oo must 'elp, I promise! Now, before we jump up with a rocket up our behinds, here's a bit of a cracking bit from one of my admirers once, a one priestly type called Mr Bood Dah whoosit, as I told the other gent here recently, and, dye know?, that slaphappy little Mr Bood Dah, bit of a dingo really, why, he asked me to make sure I read this little message to you too, same as the one other special guest. Are you pouting sweetly and sitting comfortably, Mr Mahoo, yoo? Here goes with what Mr Bood Dah said, gawd luvya: *"These flowers, bright and beautiful, fragrant and good-smelling, handsome and well-formed, soon indeed discoloured, ill-smelling and ugly they become. This very body, beautiful, fragrant and well-formed, soon indeed discoloured, ill-smelling and ugly it becomes".* ... Isn't that a bit nutty? Thank you for the lovely flowers and fishies and the little singing ones, and thanks for emptying my potty... I prefer doing it in the garden more than in the potty, yoo know. But, wait on, that's not what I meant to tell you, special like, not all that Mr Bood Dah yak-yak. It was... yoo listening, Mr Mahoo?...'

Mahood waves his arms in stark wake-up. They wave as if a million frivolous seaweed fronds. He sees he is doing so to tell her he is listening, he is listening, he is listening and readied, yes, but knows now why – that what she is about to say is certainly what his father wanted to say and, yes, he is listening and readied as she goes into it, singingly, singing can-seem going:

'... Yours to net men, not fish, boy, and you keep them where you can watch them, ooo see'.

Mahood nods. He knew already in fact the moment he woke up. He rises now and dares to kiss Mother Swensen on the top of the head. She is lavender and he shouldn't be touching her, but can-seem to. He finds he has cleaned up her apartment and must have moved freely, has emptied and polished her potty, yes, has corrected her lean, straightened her dear lopsided mouth, has straightened her prints.

Now, he knows he must walk and he knows it is not enough to walk but to see around, head not high, it doesn't have to be high, but to see, *look*, learn – his eyes and how they can't-seem to miss a beat now.

As he reaches the shore on his beaching the surf is rolling in high-hocked and wide now. Where it was his thin beach, now there is a broad horizon beneath the cawling gulls which the Mahoods of the trade routes might have yearned to broach, but not now, not from this landing anew, keel'd-in from here on. Mahood's new eyes sees his bay back to being as broad as his people's plans for their people, as sunbright as their dreams. It is picture perfect. As paint-startled as all their hundreds of brightsmaid boats there, net and painter spritely. And there is no hip to it, as thin as it still might be.

Can-seem now, Mahood hurries along the long churns of the clutching tide to the end of bay, to his rock pool. Standing on the overhang, scowled and arms folded boss-cockey, is the lout Ooday the cook and, yes, loutishly. His shadow is fallen over the rock pool, yes, and can-seem to do because there are no sea horses to sing for lorncast sailors anymore, and the lout ugly to imagine is going with smirks:

'I ate 'em. I like a bit of a batter on the ponies now'n'then, dipshit.'

Who knows what the earlier lad Mahood of plangent pain would have done? It would not have been what this Mahood now does, who now has seen, *looked*, learned, does look smiling but with eyes glinting with men-to-be-netted. This lout, as any of all the louts, can't-seem to know how the sea horses thrum and hum, always yet, back in the grand place's old lady's room as ever somewhere. And this now-Mahood sidles'n'sibilates, signs'n'insinuates, and pulls Ooday aside, pretending to be one of the lout's clap-back mates, off and of the streets too, mockingly going lip-twistedly:

'Ooday, Ooday, you've got shafted today,'

Ooday stops startled. The lout knows he can't-seem to learn how to cock his ears to listen for the singing but he knows some can, some can-seem. But how can he, the lout, or his types, the louts, even sleigh to the sea horses of the true seafarers, quivering Mahood's people on, each and all, down the ages, down each port on their great migration, yes, from the desert-hupped straits of Oman down the mighty-main'd trade tides of the Arabee Sea, yes, yes, brunting against the Indian seaboard sea fords sea wards – the Laccadive, the Lakshadeepas, the Colchins – Malabars, Malabars! – oh yes, as it is always repeated as already been told?

No, can't-seem. And now this no-mere-boy Mahood now is whispering in craft to the lout there are always the eyes of the singing of the sea horses, the singing in their eyes, he should listen to, and it is always over the louts-Ooday, even right now, from the can't-seem sea horses' keepsake with the grand old lady, from their safe-keeping, over, yes, his all-liars and his all-cheats and his'n'their un-toll'd spoils.

And this now-Mahood is sssshissing to Ooday to beware: should the singing stop, then mightn't the can't-seem sea horses start singing for others, some more brutal louts-Ooday netters, brutes after the whole spoils not just the lion's share? If Ooday can't-seem to hear the singing, he should listen to that and be afraid of what might can-seem.

But that can-seem to be all right too, Mahood of now is hishing to Ooday there, for the spoils are easy; spoils are can-seem easily split, and none the wiser. Wink, wink, bob's your uncle. Ooday needs only nod he hears, he hears, and the sea horses will sing of him only very softly so others won't hear and try to move in on his lout's racket of cheating the old lady. Any why, you ask, you Ooday you? Because I am of the netters of men and the see-ers and I can tap the side of my nose on your racket for a small commission.

From the slithers of the shades, from the sloops of the shallows. From the thin beach. From the shadows the singing sea horses trot in.

It's all in the way of the tides, this now-Mahood tells Ooday, for even an ever-lout knows the way of that, the can and the can't seem of what may seem, as the lout Ooday grizzles but nods, oh nods:

'You lascar buggers, sitting there, pretending with your nets, looking, looking. Orright, how much, dipshit?'

It is a mere five percent, of course. Hasn't it always been all down the long lines of aged coasts? All so fixed?

Now is, too, Mother Swensen standing on her veranda picking and being picked at by what heads off the sea. She sees how the now-Mahood now sees he should have been seeing, *looking*, learning and seeing... seeing like his father and his father before that and how his sons will see as they keep the bad things that must happen under the

131

control of can-seem. She is so old, now, Mother Swensen, and she waves to Mahood with a hand with its liver spots, smuchas to say:

'It's about time, boy'.

If, soon, the great provender's fish cart comes back, she might get to see it again. If the horse-drawn carriages come clipping back or the clashing of the new crass horns and, say, some hear her
'Ooday, Ooday
it's the tourist bus today!'
Mother Swensen might see it all again, yes, and her Mahoods down there on the thin beach might smile up again to her, each with his money-eyes, the money-eyes come through the ages. And that would be all right by her by what is only right.

Mahood, the eyes-money man of his people's long tradition of being the eyes-money men, sits there by his paint-flaky boat with his eye on what can-seem or can't-seem, *looking*, providing the spoils are shared by five percent and providing no one is hurt, no one is in the pain he still so much feels.

He won't usually come to you but just watches. You can go down the untidy, rubbishy path to his thin beach; you can go to him, or he might even occasionally come to you. Either way he will shrug and say he is only mending the nets as some lout of a cook told him once. But his thin beach will always be in your shade if you are can-seem.

... And it's best to say going:

'That your sea horses singing?'

and if one of those Mahoods looks up to you from seeing all around you, *looking*, and says, going:

'Dream away'

then the racket you might have in mind can-seem. Or it might be can't-seem. But that will be all right too, because it will depend on which side of the rock pool the shade is, under which rock the can't-seem sea horses are. Anyway, the once-lad, that Mahood, if it be he and not one of his sons, will tell you straight. Past his eyes, his smile is of the wheat fields.

And if you're lucky, or unlucky, he might venture to you that it might be thin, this place where he has been beached, but he keeps it a lot cleaner than it could be. You can't ask for more than that.

And never mind his sons. Mahood has many sons. It seems every time he says, going:

'Ow do?'

to the tide, another one of them comes floating in. These spoils from the wide, oh wide!, line of Mahoods' seas.

The angel of enormous nuzzle

[Mother Swensen, 2]

Detective-sergeant Brian Lee Chou sat on the upright chair that was sticky with leather. The Auxiliary Bishop of Cairns sat at his desk in an upright chair that looked sticky with leather. Even the desk looked wet and sticky. All was melty.

'It's the mugginess normally, but there's no mugginess today,' the Bishop commented then, or ages before, before passing across the desk, as an act of ecclesiastic mercy, a stingingly-starched pristine handkerchief.

Chou managed to register he must have finished his business with the Bishop, whatever business that was given that he couldn't remember momentarily, nor mattered much, and saw the handkerchief had now suddenly become a soggy blackish mass that he was trying to hand back. But the Bishop's walnut of an adam's apple obviously hadn't finished, its bobbing quickening for suddenly noticing Chou as a customer perhaps in need of a new body, if not a dehydration of the soul. Whichever, he wasn't touching it, sweating profusely like that. He held up ecclesiastic hands against the re-coming of the handkerchief, going:

'Perhaps you might manage a little boiling water and lots of disinfectant first…? No tongs here, you see.'

It was pretty much about that time Chou decided he'd better just drop down on the cathedral steps outside and close his eyes and take a long holiday.

As it was, he found himself swaying at some desk almost as suddenly before him in a wide-eyed disorientation. The Detective-sergeant gripped its rutted edge like a man about to spew everything up at sea and not being able to do anything about knowing he was facing directly into a pretty strong wind. If he hadn't been naturally pigmented, he would have presented jaundice itself to the manager somewhere behind the desk... or maybe the manger since the brass tag on the counter had it as 'Manger' and he just couldn't work out why, unless it meant 'cot', which was precisely what he would give his eye tooth for.

But the Detective-sergeant knew exactly what this was really. Does the mind's-eye, not seeing too well, lie? This is just maybe the police department's Entitlements and all I have to do is get in here like Flynn for my retirement benefits before the Police Integrity Commission comes to sink the boot into me, but what's with the 'manger'? What's manager or manger got to do with his corruption being caught out?

The next morning, he would hardly be able to remember signing in under the searchlights some hotel manager guy seemed to have strapped to his glasses. He would remember looking up at the staircase he had to climb to get into a bed, and only making it halfway before he decided he couldn't make it even halfway to infinity. He let himself slip back down so his head could rest on the cool wood of the bottommost step.

While he experienced vomiting, he would remember thinking he was spitting out never re-attainable pieces of himself. Some watchfully waiting this was. What's a prostate if it's the most impatient prostate in the world and can't wait or watch a moment, it seems, in time? Breakfast, lunch and dinner are coming up and I'm on the bottom step on the look-out for something higher, chwissakes. Tell that to the Department's Rehab but for chwissakes don't breathe a word to them about it.

At least he had got onto the first step of a crawl to a heaven's cot. Last legs just have to get going, if only they could be materialised.

But even before he thought he remembered sinking back onto heavenly-sent cot as high up as he could possibly go, he decided he would raise himself from his desk at work to start the day when and if he could get through the spasm of pain that began again to slice through to the core of his very manhood. Easy enough. Just get as they said and wait-in-watch, watchfully waiting. He reached for one of the morphines and one of the bicalutamides, bitter things to swallow.

Detective-sergeant Chou shook his head on himself, even if it hurt. No, he was right for the pills; bring on the pills, any pills. He was right for the watchful waiting. It was right the plumbing was leaking like a sieve. Chwissakes, all I don't deserve is crying over having to watchfully wait over a bunch of cells with their knickers in a mushy knot hard up against my jewels. I could cry about how yellow cake I look. Call me uranium. Don't mind me, just mine me. Come, scoop it out and slag-heap me.

But what he did know was he had been visited by the girl. She said her name was Kyrie Mozetich... but he knew right off she was an angel, even if they must be running short of inspiring angels' names. Only angels drum so playfully on a door, turn the great brass handle, come into the room where you've finally taken to your heaven-sent cot, and know she's so beautiful she has the right to just float right on in. Like anything freely volunteered, she came with two harps on a full set of heart strings.

Of course she was the most exquisite thing he had seen. She was mink sleek in the creamiest of tans. It gave her a look of excruciating softness, excruciatingly forbidden, yet quite possible to touch. Her ebony hair arched in a curve that demanded stroking, arched surely for purring. See how angels have China-bone cheeks, lips pouted and pesky-wise. Angels smell somehow newborn. Never mind wings, latch onto their Benares-silk saris

137

of light blues and stinging greys clung to oh-so-strokable breasts, naked kid-skinned bellies, sweeping hips. High of hock she looked and was or is and natefully proud. And what he stared feverishly-fired up to comprised her mandalas in the blue of mountains swirling into the agates of other mighty dawns. The essence of her danced noonlight azures at him, and he felt how his hair was stuck by sweat to the rude skull of his coarse Mongolian ancestors and how raw-meat and unwashed his wringing sweat would be.

'Hello, Mr You.'

Her voice had sung it. He could hardly open his eyes, yet she was rainbows of soft energies. He nodded that he knew at last she had come to take him away. It was the hardest thing to have ever gotten to his feet. Foot after foot, arms ungainly. Until he pitched on his knees before her, rocking like a pendulum, his rotted lump throbbing viciously in a lower band of himself somewhere in some other realm that shouldn't even be approximate to her.

'Poor you, Mr You. Poor thing.'

No one saw them. The angel shouldered her Mr You down the ghost-flibberting corridors, down stairs, beyond a courtyard of garden under a cooling frangipani tree, up stairs more, to the old lady's room. His feet never touched the ground but that was only because it just had to be.

If not his own mother, why else, he pondered, would he remember word-for-word his Incident Report on first interviewing the old lady there in this other land than his Cairns, than his Australia, as he thought it went maybe in holiday?:

"My instinct for evidence told me she was a wheat person, probably my own mother. She is renowned as the woman who came and stuck to Ceylon, never returning to wheat fields of her childhood in the fifty years of being in this joint -- a bit kooky or what? They said once she digs her toes in, they're in. How more telltale as a West Australian can you get? But then, you have to think: in whatever part of the world she has come from, will they ever learn of her beaching, so far gone?"

On her piano, fingers still deft, she is playing 'Waltzing Matilda' thousands of kilometres away from where it was born, as she always would.

" 'Where...', her gravelly voice was as if it flowed over fine sand and her hair was as wet sand burnishing still, swept back to nip at the nape of her neck, a Forties belle, a war bride, one full of the fruct, come to be harvested and gathered in her own full intent, '... you been, boy?'

With a cry, the Detective-sergeant opened his hands as for a crucifixion, and didn't care why.

'You poor little b.'

And he rejoined his family, as it could have well been, the place perhaps he should have never left, crusty with the self-sufficiency of holding on to perhaps too much emotion. There had to be a small admonition from her major obsession first:

'No way you're playing for the mighty Blues looking scruffy like that.'

None of the furniture seemed to have changed. Everywhere were still her rose-and-pink antimacassars and, there, maybe his own father's red-velvet burgomaster's chair by the pearl-inlaid side table from where the valve radio used to squeal so high. The three great teak bookcases rose in the mist of filtered light, still as imposing to him as high altars. There, too, the same walnut couches, the satinwood settee, the mahogany chair, the sandalwood Chinese chest with its maze, and secret maze, of gilded drawers. She was tapping now the framed photograph that stood on the tip of the upright Krieger piano. It was a faded memory of Sir Robert Menzies as Warden of the Cinque Ports from out almost the dawn of Australian time.

"If good old Oz ever needs a King, he is *it*."

She nodded at the walls as if by explanation. Detective-Sergeant Chou just knew: gone were the English sporting prints and the scenes of olde China that might have been before him of her room. Now were parts of the sports pages from the The *Age* that he must have sent either recently or decades ago, but how would have that been? They were mostly of the mighty Carlton's almost Flag wins, but also the criers of the great moments of Australian sports: Murray Rose World Title, Sir Don Not Out; Our Dawn Ploughs Away; America's Cup Bondie You Beauty; Our Own Golden Girl Shirl!; Kathy's Gold! Gold! Gold!, and miniature plastic Australian buntings... these things of his own long watchfully-waiting time he knew he should have been more precious about. In her hand garden secateurs appeared. Still the tennis court at the centre of the garden, still just as weedy as ever, still shoved brutishly by the roots of the great frangipani and the bamboos, the ferns, the wattles, and all the hidden places he had not known as a child he was peeking out from behind as though all had been his. Could it have been mine?

There were powders. There were her heavy scents. There was the strange green light of blinds permanently drawn. There was a waiting room here that held no terrors needing watching.

When Chou could bear opening his eyes again, he had found his arms stretched out along the arms of an old-fashion cane commode. His lap had been covered with a blanket, tucked in strongly beneath his knees. Surely this was true.

'Park your Harvester.'

Detective-sergeant Brian-Lee Chou had known that came from the old lady seated in a cane commode perfectly side-to-side with his unto touching. She had the knowing white hair of centuries and the clear blue eyes of ages. These things he thought. It was all the same as the things he knew. He simply nodded and thought he had better explain:

'See, it was all as they knew I'd corruptly turn out to be.'

His pain left with the confession or perhaps with her nod. A wondrous need to sleep came all the way over him. He slept in the bosom of her room for two whole days, as though he had known that time all along... that it was there he had had to come.

In the first moment of that time, he saw a state that was either vision or reality. He heard the bedside-mannered voice so smooth that it lubricated no argument, that it demanded its own paragraph in his head. It was all-hospital and going:

'So, Detective-sergeant, I know it's a bit of a bugger but I wouldn't cut it out. Why don't you just try to nurture it? Gather the growth unto yourself, ha ha. Nowadays it's called watchfully waiting. Some have to just watch grass grow. They call it cancer of the prostate. Prostate's a laugh. It ain't prostrated, only sounds like it; common grammatical mistake and amusing. Now it's up on its hind claws tearing the heart out of a man's sperm count, which regrettably means you'.

On the fringe of the Cairns-side corals now then and there, Detective-sergeant Chou was sitting on what would be his corrupt veranda of his corrupt house when they finished building with his corrupt cash. It was the warm and soft evening of all his beloved hotlands. Still, he was sweating and smelling of it. The world croaked lazily. On the plan the architect had coloured in the lawn-to-be with lime Gloliter. It ran down to the creek's edge where, sketched, was a little ill-gotten jetty for a little ill-gotten yacht or maybe even two. One day he would tell Evie and the kids he was going to live up here outside of Cairns, Kuranda actually, after they found out how he turned out to corruptly be, and she upped and left him. Collect a few things and camp out here among the half walls and half timbers and do the frog and toad and cricket and cicada thing. Do as the surgeon said. Watchfully wait. Low thunder from the northwest made his mood even heavier. The builder's mud at his feet smelt as rancid as he knew he would when they sliced him open. But then that would only be as they always knew him to, yes, corruptly be.

It was then that the first state of that time which was either dream or reality simply went away

'It was just in the roll of the vice, you know,' he explained to its back

Yet, wasn't back there a time somewhere the old lady's blanket still tucked right up to his neck, and couldn't he still snuggle down further into the swaddling of it? There, he could see a grace and he could hope for a compassion and at least he could follow a way he might better want to be going. He hoped the little angel calling herself Kyrie Mozetich would come again.

In this, then, last moment of that time that was either vision or reality, the angel Kyrie Mozetich came back to him in all things angelic:

In the mirror of the Dutch dresser, she needed nothing to have her eyes sparkle back in cats-eye. What a watch! What a wait! She had worked in a facial of glycerine-and-honeysuckle until it gave her cheeks a gleam to her natural honey; to her lips, lightly, citrus oil. She pirouetted with her reflection. The figure she watched spun through quoins of busts and bellies, broad hips and curved lower backs, coster buttocks and hints of beckoning clefts under flowing silk. She was

142

winsome with it to him too, or so he had it that she had to be:

"We need parties and soirees and dances and things, Mr You. There's the passions of me and my funny little sisters at naughty fingertips to be got at. We'll get shot of my monthly roses and all your horrid smelly voices and dreams, I promise!'

Chou's heart leapt with joy. He longed to take her up, swing her in circles with the same delight as when he just knew how this old lady beside him in the commode used to once shout her strange private joke whenever the fish man came along with his cart:

'Ooday! Ooday!
It's the provender today!'

and how they were the happiest of times. When the father of some boy he just seemed to know would punch him gently on the shoulder; okay work's over, piss off and go kick a footy around in, weren't they?, these same great caves of rooms he knew he was dreaming in.

Yet Detective-sergeant Chou knew all too well how ungrateful he must look, since it was his nature to detest any beauty he could have very little ownership of. Still, he understood the need to apologise for some rudeness or other:

'Don't mind me. I'm from Australia"

Yet huge in her aureole the little angel Kyrie Mozetich was still angelically giggling. He squinted, trying to follow her spinning up into the spun light. Tingly do the trumpets go:

'I like mirrors, Mr You know. Oh, the good friend of the Bishop of Cairns, a one Mr Bood Da, slaphappy little chap, asked me to read this little message to you. Are you pouting sweetly and sitting comfortably, Mr You?: *"These flowers, bright and beautiful, fragrant and good-smelling, handsome and well-formed, soon indeed discoloured, ill-smelling and ugly they become. This very body, beautiful, fragrant and well-formed, soon indeed discoloured, ill-smelling and ugly it becomes".'*

'Yes!'

He cried out meaning come back; there are healing glows. And, for his pains, she returned the glory of a simple heaven-sent smile, and.

'Don't forget your naughty hots for me, will Mr You?'

Chou waved his arms in warmed joy. They waved like a million frivolous heads in the wheat fields of the old lady-next-to-him's sun land of the wheatfields of Australia. He rose now golden-brown and moved to the old lady's commode next to him, where he kissed her on the top of the head, and called her mother. He found he had cleaned up her apartment this time, had emptied and polished her potty, had corrected her lean, had straightened her dear lopsided mouth, had made square-hanging the Sir Donald Bradman and the Carlton Football Club frames. His matching blanket draped from its armrest to trail untidily on the floor behind him but that was all fine, because he just knew how his Mother Swensen wanted to reach up and hold her boy's hands again. This was, he knew she knew, just another punctuation in life as it is written.

Did Brian-Lee Chou kiss probably his mother on the top of her head for the first time at that moment, or again, or just said he would if it ever happened? He folded the blanket and carefully replaced it on the sick chair where he was not then or now.

There, his hand went out his bicalutamide pills for the first time in a whole dreamtime, but he did so only as a rub of the magic lamp. Far better was, he could touch the remission. It was just that he didn't want to scare it away, this fragile, this timid thing. He let it come right up to him and there to nuzzle quiveringly in his hand, like some little angel might, wanting welcome for any more years they could give each other allowance for.

That was the living moment he went straight for the phone. He climbed the great frangipani, up past the old man he used as a boy, he could see by mind's-eye policely-tuned, to see struggling to get out of its trunk. He spoke to his wife Eve, the first in an eternally-long time. He hoped it all went something like this…

'How are you, Evwie?'

'I still remember you.'

'The girls?'

'I think they still remember you too.'

'I've been away overseas, Evwie, I might still be.'

'And before that?'

'The thing is, I've got this lump thing I'm watchfully waiting on.'

'Oh.'

'I love you, see, that's the thing.'

'How bad's that lump thing?'

'A liwtle less wobbly for twalking to you, Evwie.'

'You're doing that thing with your mouth again.'

'Some call it lallation and I don't give a stwuff about it anymore.'

'Good. I've always wuved it.'

'Evwie...?'

'Chewie?'

'See, I've been building this house up Cairns way. Bad money. I'm a corwupt cop, Evwie. What do you reckon?'

'What's that house like?'

'Wright smack on a nice creek. Ferny.'

'I like Cairns way.'

'Come take a look at it, Evwie?'

'As long as no pegging out first. '

'I will watchfully wait here, Evwie.'

From where he stood or could or might have been standing, he watched over the creek at the end of his to-come lawn and how it plays down there, how over nearby bays it tossed its tourmaline sprays with such living sprite. Its yachts metronome'd their tinny disturbances to him in the way that had always called up for him the fairies of the air. Beyond, in the early morning light, clouds now parted for the inflorescences of the reefs below where he and Kyrie Mozetich were floating free, as free as angels. All up and all down the coast as their eyes could see, whole coral gardens were photo-humming with the life of light, leeching into the sea their oils of greens, purples, violets and blues, opals within swirls, brilliant to the eye, glorious patches, impossible to capture and impossible to forget.

Ah, he seemed to float on vast colonies of life throbbing contentedly their shows of vital gilds and limes, as pristine as how the world could never ever have corruptly been. The air, too, quite, quite still. Leaning against a pylon somewhere in Australia, sitting back on the coming veranda of his ill-gotten house, nuzzle in his commode chair a mind's realm off, Detective-sergeant Brian Lee Chou made vows again and so he thought so.

Does quietus come with the watch and the wait?

If so, there is still this he left behind in his own longhand to work out on the steps of a cathedral where he once fell-and-rose beyond the Auxiliary Bishop's office: '*John 12:25:* ... He who loves his life loses it, and he who hates his life in this world will keep it to life eternal'.
It had to be right. If he remembered it right, that bishopric office there was a place where the handkerchiefs remained ironed and folded.

These were examples to be followed in the nuzzle of them.

My cousin Mahood in 6 easy lessons

[Mother Swensen, 3]

I remember putting down the glass when I heard Mahood had been killed. I got up from the table. I was stabbed by guilt, I think, as much as grief. This was Mahood. More. He was my Mahood when I returned to Sri Lanka ten years ago. He was Muslim; he shouldn't have got caught in one of those Singhalese-Tamil temple clash things. What was he doing there?

It was a question, I guess, you always asked about him.

All I have of Mahood are the few scribblings in my notebook. At the very least those now require a little attention, a little ordering. Even the weakest light might halo a shape otherwise to the dark.

I wrote:

Manhood in the centre of his world
To one side of him in my mind's eye, now, the ashtray is so full it is stinking. He coughs and accidentally gorbies on the paper he is writing on and has to wipe it with his sleeve. He is writing 'Mother' to my mother, and is telling her that he is coming down to Australia from Sri Lanka soon to see her after all these twenty-six years.

'I maybe poor man, but heart in here is being rich. Ha ha, Mis'er Gar'l'

didn't he once say to me.

Mahood. Yes. Mahood is not the most splendid specimen of his race. The cabin boys of the early Muslim traders are in his blood. As though he still cannot stand upright on land after centuries, Mahood half trots beside me. No matter what time I leave the hotel, it seems Mahood has known and is already. He hops alongside me now as I walk past the flustered bazaar of roadside boutiques in this, Colombo's biggest slum quarter of Slave Island. This is Mahood's world. He brushes off with contempt the beggars zipping at me and self-importantly casts guttural greetings to the *modalali*, the shanty shopkeepers.

I might be doing the colonial thing of ploughing on willy-nilly, but Mahood swerves and twists, a salmon among his people, fast and slippery despite his injured hip that splays his right leg outward, that pains him constantly, that makes him hop along, the right leg a balance, the left leg a crutch. His eyes are tombowlers.

I might look and smile into his pupils that are brown agates but his gaze is ever caught by the yellow bands, unhealthy and jaundiced, that cross his eyeballs. They are some sort of medical chart that shows how sick he will always be after the police broke his hip and heart during the '89 student uprising, so said. He will never say.

Everyday, Mahood wears the same white shirt and blue trousers to greet me; everyday they are clean and pressed, done to sheen, just like his long black hair, greased as stickily to his skull as it could be and swept back to oily jags at the back of his neck. His face is long and mournful with its gaunt cheeks, high forehead and terse, over-proper lips that seem to verge always on disapproval.

This is Mahood, a survivor of my family roots as they have spread, who has attached himself to me as a pilot fish. I am his; this is known throughout his Slave Island. I am Mahood's catch and business, so that his fellow rip-artists of tourists know to leave me alone.

Mahood has appeared on the very first morning I arrived at the hotel. After a generation, he has simply fallen into step with me, as though our sides of the family have never taken separate paths. I don't recognise him at first. I say, go rip off a real tourist. But Mahood's hand goes to his heart: I no want money. I talk English only want, sir. I learn English I get big job in big hotel. I your family, also.

Mahood never says, and I only learn when I get back to Melbourne, that he is sent as a minder for me. No one in my family here owns up to it. There seems a one wave in our family's ocean that must keep swelling.

I learn that Mahood lives on *aes-karsi*, money-eyes. In his Slave Island, there is no scam he does not get the whisper about, no thievery, no pickpocketing, no skullduggery. In this alone, he is a bigshot. On any scheme he comes to know about, he gets five per cent or the even more corrupt police turn up next day. Yet Mahood is not a stoolie. The *aeskarsi* is an ancient tradition, the eyes-and-ears against outside rackets muscling in on the locals. Mahood carries his responsibility with a nasty dignity and pride. His eyes, he says, can see in the dark.

Now, he is showing me a hovel thatched with weathered-grey palm fronds, one room, cooking fire on rocks outside, water from the street pump along the alley, bare earth and black inside with only a small oil lamp burning there. This is my home, Mis'r Gar'l, he says proudly. I can't tell if he is being facetious. In here, Mahood states factually:

'Me not marreed, two sister, three men, little chil'ren, my parents being with J'sus yours, nay?'

There are eleven in all in this one hovel. I could cry. I am shifting uncomfortably. But Mahood laughs like a horse, throwing his head back, showing surprisingly white unmarred teeth:

'Not big house, Mis'r Gar'l, but very good air condishning, nay?'

He is pointing to the holes between the old palm fronds of the roof and between the wooden packing-case planks that make up the walls.

He nods that it is also illegally there, that someday they will come and pull it down. He excuses himself to piss against the nearby tree.

Here is Mahood, limping in my shadow, or so it seems. He is the poor of my forgotten-past family and the jobs they must do, interwoven together.

If only for that reason, my Mahood is our real hero.

He not only comes everywhere with me Colombo. He comes down south to Galle too, where we both grew up around our old hotel.

151

Mahood in the centre of history

On the parapets now of Galle Fort, Mahood is high up, a small figure from there but now with some sort of the foreign silhouette, and thus is it haughty?

He stands above the main Dutch East Indies Company gate, the carved initials VOC. He is at one to me as a Portuguese pikeman, a Dutch yeoman, a British redcoat, and he looks with wonder at this part of the island of old Serendipity. Down below his rampart, the bikes, the three-wheelers, the old Morris Minors squeezing in through the gate between his booted and buckled feet could all be the bullock carts, the *natame,* the transoms and the palanquins, the creaking hand carts of the ancients.

He is turning now to face into the wind and, just for a moment, I can see again it is my Mahood, for the wind billowing his clothes only make them preen more pressed even from here. There, below him, facing across the fort to the jutland and beyond to the very sea that saints and salts us now, are the pinnacles of the mosques, the stupas, the belltowers. They are the time rods of our joined history.

So that he stands, my Mahood, taking one of the last of the innumerable watches on the parapet, guarding over this mighty fort, more than three-quarters bound with the weight of surf and the steps of the rocky seabed, its field covered by the cannons of the ten mighty bastions. Behind the great walls behind him, are not now the thatchings, but the clay-tiled orange roofs, serrating the skinny lanes, covering the terraced cottages, the ancient warehouses, the creaky hospitals, the dimmed churches and courts, the graved barracks, the never-ending precincts of Buddhism and Islam and Christianity, all and every one intimate at some crisscross. Among all these centuries, as a boy, Mahood would surely have chased me as madly as he could, but sadly I can't remember.

Is Mahood the right man to be standing the last watch on that parapet? In 1505, during dusk on a course they had suffered wind-stirred, the Portuguese first heard the cock, their *gallus,* crow, my Galle, their name, and there Mahood stands as a sentinel of what is left of our family as we flowed from almost that first cock crow. I imagine his eyes look down on the roof of our old hotel not with the hawk eyes of the sentry but with the eyes of soft loss.

The tiny beach and the catamarans with their catches are on our left. I know they have sold to me from the sides of their boats the great seers, herrings, cuttles and crabs. They are washing down the bright patterns of their crafts, mending their nets. They are as poor as Mahood who is looking across the harbour of the fabled safe anchorages of the biblical Tarshish; for thousands of years those fishers have been casting the same small nets, riding on the same smooth swells, teasing their boats where the running surf falls within itself to continue its anger in undercurrents. The crows and the gulls and the cormorants splash their same flashing patterns beneath the ether of the sea eagles. Small same boys as us are jumping from the ancient jetty; same men in tucked sarongs wade with hand nets across the rock shallows, flinging and probing and hoping for something for their same tables tonight. Across the bay, it is still the headland of the sannis, the disease devils. It sparkles tourmaline.

This Mahood I see up there is stooped as he turns, as though his breastplate and plumed helmet has become too heavy in the sun. He leaves the musket and the powder flask leaning against one of the cannons and, heavily, heavily, scuffs along the parapet to the Triton Bastion where the stairs lead him down from our sight.

I know what he's doing. He is wearily climbing down from his post, unbuckling, working towards our hotel for the light of our grandmother.

Our grandmother, yes. The wheat girl, foreign to our paddy fields, and as sandy as the wheat chaff of her Australia. She came out of Australia for godknowswhy and she stayed, as though these walls were all she ever looked for across the vast harvestings. That's all I know, really, except she never returned to Australia, but always eventually received a Monday *The Age* for the footy scores.

From her loins, our mothers would have passed so close. In the nearness I feel of her, Mahood has brought me home. He has brought me home to my own people at last.

Mahood at the centre of the old hotel

We arrive. At long last. We are sitting in the car outside the steps to the hotel. We don't talk. We watch two tourists, a couple, descend and the movement of the van hirers, the three-wheel drivers, the touts and the cane- and lace-doily-sellers. All flutter in anticipation, then settle back in dulled disappointment when the two chose to walk, chose to ignore.

The tourists are young, look German, knobbly white knees, both of them, in ill-used gaudy shorts. These are definitely not five-starers, but cheap-enders. Years ago, we would have seen them as the sailors or Steerage passengers off the great liners. They would pass by the old hotel for something cheaper.

'Mis'r Gar'l,' Mahood whispers so sadly, 'the tourists come again, nay?'

A few of the staff wander along the front veranda; the doorman stops watching the German couple as perhaps the last human beings he will ever see, and sits down sloppily on the top step, legs wide open, correctly knowing no one will care.

One hundred and seventy-five years ago, the Governor of Galle lived up there on the top floor and so did the officers of his garrison on the floor below; fifty great rooms once splendid with Dutch and English furnishings snuffing out the languid pleasures of the military elite clattering down its great beamed corridors with their riding boots and crofts.

For 50 years, the lights of the ballroom have not been lit for the dance.

Its walls are peeling outside like Miss Havisham's make-up. Its shutters are like eye patches against the bruising eye of lost pride.

I can still hear how my grandmother's fingers are still dextrous for her piano. She is playing 'Waltzing Matilda', as she always would.

'Ow do?'

I can hear her gravelly voice clearly by this sea, as though it thrills

154

through fine sands, and her flaxen hair worn back from the burnt-gold but to a fine burnishing still, nip'n'tucked at the nape of her neck, a Forties belle even yet, a war bride managing on her own; she does not turn her head from the piano keys.

'Ow do?'

Her bed has been pushed into a corner. The huge old living room, the parlour of my family's quarters, all changed. But everywhere are still the rose-and-pink antimacassars. Everywhere are still my boyhood caves of corridors. My grandfather's red-velvet ebony burgomaster's chair still sits by the teak inlaid side table from where the valve radio used to whistle so impatiently. The three great nedun almirahs -- the one that carries the many tomes given to Christian purposes; the other, glassed too, that carries the turquoise Delftware and the gold-plated cutlery; the third, wooden-doored, always locked, always magically *1001 Arabian Nights* to my young imagination.

They still shine rose in the filtered light that still needs candles. The same Dutch jac couch, the English satinwood settee, the calamander chair, the mahogany Chinee chest with its fairy-tale maze of secret drawers.

All, yes, smothered with our grandmother's rose-and-pink antimacassars.

All gone. 'Ow do.

Mahood at the centre of religion
I open my eyes groggily and find it hard to believe Mahood is sitting on the beach wall just along from me. He is not taking his oval-wide dark eyes from me, but that has become a sort of comfort by now. How long has he been there, not saying a thing, or has he been talking? He will have been cooing softly if he has. Those eyes that never miss a thing. What are you doing here, Mahood? Sure, I am here, sure, Mis'r Gar'l, is all.

Have a drink, Mahood. I am Muslim, but I will, Mis'r Gar'l. I go to temple, but I believe Jes's. I ask Jes's and he give. In-terr-essing no?

He a poor man like me but good in heart too, nay?

Mahood's hot and curried breath is on my cheek still. He has drawn closer so only I could hear.

Mahood at the centre of reality
A fine pair, me and Mahood, back along the streets of Galle. Shuffling and hobbling. Four eyes shifting this way and that.

It is becoming harder to tell which the *aes-karsi* man and which the foreigner.

And, with the unerring nose of a street wolf, Mahood smells the possibility of the defeat of my refined veneer. My infamous blues. He knows it is time to move towards the postcards. Just as I see myself clearly in the reflection of the lake there, I see he has whipped off a postcard for me.

In the manner of our tidal country, Mahood is taking my hand along as we hop and skip around the streets of his slums.

On the postcard is a picture of some beautiful sunset. I know what it really says. Mahood says it really says: Go home.

Mahood is smiling hugely, smug with the rally he too can feel in me. At once he is bobbing with spritely imbalances beside me once more, and keeps slightly ahead of me for his rightful street respect. How proud of his foreigner he can become again! Is it good being going home, Mis'r Gar'l? Yes, Mahood. *Hondai, hondai*; is good, good.

Mahood at the centre of my leaving
Poor Mahood is bending close to try to hear what I'm saying about having to leave him now. It doesn't matter. He has prepared me enough to leave my childhood behind again.

And Mahood now using the flat of his fingers to wipe my eyes, my mouth in the manner they do there and mutters something I can't understand anymore, a crooning in the language of our youth, as gently as the lullaby of our Galle sea below us, below the rampart. Shhfff.

Whhhhsssstt. Shchfffff. Whhhiisssstttt. The soft and heavy comings. Those soft and heavy goings.

We rise to tread the path down to Sea Street. It winds down those ancient steps, those tiny footholds. It curves around those granite walls that so many hands have slid along, palm to palm with ours. The cock of Galle is already crowing the proudest, the most heaven-sent, the most heaven-spent. It has called like this uncountable times, over untold steps and untold times and untold number, as forever and as quietly as the dawn it calls up. Nodding, yes. We can leave the Watch now.

At the sea line, Mahood holds back for a moment and looks deeply into my eyes. He nods slightly at what he sees there then lets go my hand. He turns away at first slowly hobbling, then is moving to hurry as best he can over the sand. I watch him go. Deeper than I do, he has learnt life is only looking to win your own way.

Mahood must see to himself once more.

'I maybe poor man, but Mis'r Gar'l, but heart in here is being rich.'

These are the steps we must take on our own. Untold paths, and countless:
Come unto these yellow sands
And then take hands
Curtsied when you have and kissed
The wild waves whist.

I should have written more in my notebook.

His name was Mahomed Mahood. It still is.

157

Dandenong ladies and their all

I made the first woman and therefore the first lady of Dandenong, you know. I don't know if I should be boasting about that, and I'm not saying I made her at my smithy in St Joseph's Presbytery since it was before history when even the word presbytery hadn't been born. But if you look real hard for the flying sparks and listen real hard to my anvil rhythms you'll feel how in time all came to be forged. Then again, some say they can't see or hear a thing, but then they wouldn't be you-my-Dandenong.

Call me Wayland or Wayan or Wallanda or Vulcan or Hephaestus or just plain old Bill the Smithy. I'm easy. I float in zero G between you-my-Dandenong and the higher-ups to me when I am not making little horseshoes for schoolkids just to show them I haven't lost the common touch or the humble ways during school trips to the forge.

More important than that cuckolding first *femme fatale*, my masterpieces are my sweetie-pie handmaidens I made for her. Sure, they soon deserted her to run back to me, but that just goes to show they know which side of the forge their butter is on. Ah, they are such lovely and bidden creatures! They are the colours of you all, the hues of you all, they speak all your languages washing around in the glorious tides of you-my-Dandenong.

They are my Shirl, my Virathni, my Mia-Mia and my Maria of all around the world.

It's them you hear in the great gums of St Joseph's when you think all things in your lives are stilled, when you might gain hold of a whisper that is soft as dew but you turn and see nothing. That would be because you just haven't looked high enough. It's them, my Shirl, Virathni, Mia-Mia and Maria, doing wheelies hither and thither, and so zitterishly, on their golden platforms winging and waving their perfumes into your minds and mouths.

Yet, deep down, I confess my favourite is the-he who I modelled first of all. If you don't have the special eyes of you-my-Dandenong, you

159

might know him as the one looking like the old derro who sits in the dirt outside my smithy, staring madly up at any of you. It's only pretend, but of course you give him a wide berth. You're only human; aren't you all? He was as the mould of all, yet you'll be thinking under-trodden; and even I, as I pity him as his Maker, can understand why. Even the shade for him is niggardly from the jarrahs and the verandas of the great house there next to us. Then again, you-my-Dandenong might have seen him shuffling along the bottom end of Langhorne Street, crazily staring into the shops because he desperately needs to be allowed in, or watched him mountainous with flies bending over the bins at the Station.

He is my favourite, yes, but I won't give you his name since you'd never ever think to ask. In actual fact, anyway, he has no name, born of one use. He is one you quicken your pace past, think of substance abuse not the substance, tense in case he erupts abuse at you or, worse, thrusts out at you what looks like an open palm dipped in leprosy not pure iron, demanding some of your hard-earnt.

But this same iron-black man came out of my first ploughshare, my first sword, my first harvester, my first regrettable instrument of torture – and he came out of them before much of time, certainly even before you-my-Dandenong was born. There was no precious stuffing for him like for my Shirl, Virathni, Mia-Mia and Maria. I shaped him in iron rough and ready, black crusty and burnt rusty. I shaped him hard and without mould, and I shaped him with the rawest blows of the hammer. It was only as an afterthought that I decided to give him something extra and made him a him thing by no particularly-special hammer motion. I could admit no special place for him. It was not for his purpose. He was just a try-out. Even today, he thinks now his only job is to clean up around my smithy.

Aside from that, that new young priest of yours is his only concern. I can give you *his* name. It is Father Nyugen, as you-my-Dandenong creatures called Catholic know him to be, and there are first and other foremosts to Father Nyugen.

First, it is my Shirl who paints the colours of your Father Nyugen. It is a painting on the back of that envelope and as huge as a Hoyt's latest.

160

The young priest is at right foreground, where she has most applied her native Australian wattle-brush greens onto the canvas with a thick palate knife. Her opus hangs newly on the wall of his room at his Redemptionist Retreat House in Powers Street. It has been delivered by my crude old man who told them as harshly as the gravel of his voice that it was a special gift for Father Nyugen, before shuffling away mindless of the main road at his feet.

My Shirl's envelope has a paint-corrupted stiffness that won't take its hold off the good Father's hand until it meets its correct wall-space in his room, from where it doesn't seem to be shiftable.

Father Nyugen cannot remember how he secured it up there. He thinks it might have just *stuck*. He sits turned away from his prim-topped desk staring at it. He sees how it evokes him upon the stage in Dandenong Park last Australia Day, and how he is looking impossibly young for his thirty years, even for a novitiate. He looks out with wonder over the crowd on this fining you-my-Dandenong mid-day. It shows how there is in her colours an inverse reflection of his dreadful childhood in Vietnam by contrast to you-my-Dandenong.

And there seems to slide then elide then slide-and-elide across Shirl's canvas these ways of you-my-Dandenong – ways that are the sun-spun of all the colours in your hues, so swatching before your new flag of the southern stars and the deep-ocean blue. See, how you are come and coming-and-going! My Shirl has you-my-Dandenong creamy as mellow gossamer as piquant as buttermilk as cocoa light and cocoa dark as young as old as clapping as cheering as laughing as dancing your jigs of the thousand steps on this, that Australia Day. She renders you, first, as herself-Shirl, golden and bronzed and so Australian amongst her wheat fields, then as Virathni, all sari and lunghi and salwar and sandal from the Indian Himalayas to the coconut palms; then third, Mia-Mia, all Aboriginal, all ochre washed and foot-free blessed to great-coloured serpent of the boab and spinifex plains; and then fourth, Maria, of the embroidered pleats and chemise and tasselled cap and pompom shoe from the pan-piping olive groves of her native Greece. You-my-Dandenong jostle your ways up to the free barbie sausages and you cry out the sheer deliciousness of being able to. You-my-Dandenong are dancing your ways with Thai fingers with African stomp with Zorba's expansive hops with foxtrot and quicksteps. You are spooning your plastic forks into the saffrons of curries, the glumps of stew-and-damper, the souvlakis and baklavas, the soft seeds of the heavy pandanus. Your band of Irishman and Yugoslav and Philippino splurge into your delighting Waltzing Matilda. As once as all the rainbow of children you practise a cow-corner hoick for a six over long-on off someimaginary called Brett Lee simply because you now can. You-my-Dandenong's Australia's day, as where you belong from around, around the world, the world.

All this Father Nyugen can see and hear in my Shirl's painting on the back of the first envelope on his wall there, yes. It swans him and stalls him. He cannot understand how he is depicted staring over at the old man painted in against the farthest back of Dandenong Park there, alone amongst this great day of romp of you-my-Dandenong all, his olden gaze fixed wildly, his olden feet jigging to the bands but as slyly as a wall-flower's. And on her envelope of a canvas Father Nyugen hears his own mother back in old Vietnam seeing him off to his first high school:

'You look for him M he good you'.

But for all his looking the good Father Nyugen still doesn't know who M might be. He looks again but swears the old man in the park of that Australia Day is now gone out of the Shirl's picture on his wall now.

Father Nyugen was ordained deacon in March 2006, awaits ordination as full priest very soon from this. You-my-Dandenong might have forgotten already but yet in the warming resounds of my smithy there is not forgetfulness. He wrote of himself in the Parish News:

'I am Vietnamese. I have 11 brothers and sisters, a cricket team here. In 1975 the Communist took over my village. I saw people killing each other in battle or dying from the Agent Orange. We escaped, but it was hard to survive -- not enough food, medicine or clothes. Life was terrible for us children. I was lucky...'

Even now, though, my Virathni, the second of my four beloved handmaidens, impatiently interrupts his writing. She is swinging a couple of her many arms in the pity and the pleasure of being near him. Already on her centremost palm she has shaped her saffrons and blues for him as the second of my ladies' four paintings. And already Father Nyugen smooths it out upon his sparse desk to gaze again quizzically at this new work of art delivered, he is told, as a special gift by the same old man at the Retreat House's door. He is told again the old man is mindless of the main road at his feet not waiting for a reply.

I think my Virathni is the most intricate of my girls. She perhaps is the blaze that is most of you, you-my-Dandenong. See how her depiction of a checkout in Dandenong Plaza is tonally simple but templar deceptive. See the strokes; the concatenated patterns of the Hindu Kush. She catches the light-bright play on Father Nyugen's receding hairline as he bends to help at the pensioners' trolley. She is not above portraying herself. Is that her pretend Serbian likeness running the register, or her Lebanese self under the burqa over jeans, trolley huge with Economy disposable nappies and 2-litre Cokes as dark-eyed sumptuous as her two toddler girls, or her Samoan profile or her Timorese half-smile or her Sri-Lankan panda-eyes on this palm? Or is it her pretend Scottish scowl or her Bosnian *razngici* belly or her deep Ngaatjatjarra patience? She as all these are in her scene waiting at the check-out down at the Plaza, yes. And down those Dandenong Plaza aisles, Father Nyugen discerns other nationalities of you, picking and being chosen...Chaldeans Eritreans Irish Maoris Papuans Afghans Thais Tamils Chinese and all humming kind in the way of your shopping trolleys from all around, around the world, the world.

Yet it is not only that of the second painting. It is what Father Nyugen cannot think he sees there seated in his own room, again in the background but further back, but further forward. It is the same old man hunched over a brilliant-red shopping basket back among the fruit stalls, hunched to breaking, cowled to fawning, being pushed at by two security men with their sleeves rolled up on him. Citizen watches are on special down the corridors of your-Dandenong time there. All can be brightly Dandenong borrowed, oiled or massaged in. Yet the old man is being turfed out of the Plaza again and you-my-Dandenong cannot tell if he is just resigned to it or if it is you who are resigned to it. Again, Father Nyugen hears his old mother of his old Vietnam, this time as she sees him off to high school:

163

'You look for him M he good you'

But he still can't see who M might be from the second painting from my maidens.

Time is it. True is it. These are forged by the drawing of the iron and the slew of my hammer's pein. Easy it is. All returns to the anvil, as you-my-Dandenong know. Father Nyugen continues what he is writing for the Parish News:

'I worked on a farm until one day one of the missionaries asked if I wanted to be a priest. I said 'yes!' and left my village for the seminary. I studied English and religion. In 2001 luckily I was sent here to study theology. With God's blessing, I will be ordained priest in March with my thanksgiving service at St Joseph's. So please pray for me!'

Meanwhile the good Father still sits there against my forge beside the Presbytery, does, as well, the old man in the paintings. If you had pity, he sits so scorched with destitution. Soon I will lay my hammer down and nod so he can enter to clean himself up of the singeing flakes. Soon. It is his way of paying for what he has asked me to make for him finally. He muttered the word 'finally' himself. It is the least I can do, since he is my first, my real one-and-only. This poor lost soul I really shouldn't have forged.

Now it is the turn of my sweet Mia-Mia. She moves as Worora; she moves with the plant beings of her Dreamtime; she moves. She has the simmered grace of the orange and red plains, of the heat of the clays around you-my-Dandenong. Now she is waving her hand from the everlasting waterhole, gorged and rainbow'd. On the back of a St Vincent de Paul's tea towel she has stencilled in the ever-dust the dawn and the sunset and the journey of Father Nyugen. She has him standing next to your Mayor before her immense Australian flag covering the western entrance of the whole of McCrae Street. She has him next to the mayoral great chain of office. It shines in the fluorescents like images of the legendary Wandjina Himself, and this is what my Mia-Mia wants for this Citizen Ceremony Day. On the p.a. squeals Slim Dusty. Around the food halls are, too, your festoons, the strobing of your cameras. More than 130 of you-my-Dandenong, my Mia-Mia stencils in ochres from the ever-dust, are to give the final pledge to your new country. You and your families are filling your mouths again just in case. Father Nyugen looks down from among the VIPs and wonders hopefully what it will be like to give the pledge himself too.

This, the third of my handmaidens' four paintings, is delivered to Retreat House again by the same old man with the main road at his careless feet, as a personal gift to Father Nyugen. Its canvas, the tea towel, hangs as against his shallowy window. The Father has to stop his kneeling to gaze at it. He sees how Mia-Mia's markings in the sands of their ever dreaming time has them flashing the very colours of you-my-Dandenong in your saris your salwars your kuruthas your fustanellas your kimonos your sarongs your tsarouhias your tassels your pompoms your string belts your bells and buhls your vrakas and zakas your paris and piupius your pains and sashes and *u. siiaphuri.ttchiithai i* your peran-n-tunbans your jangles and bangles your ochres and cicatrices your babalyias and shaals your capolanas and the great glass beads your cheongsams your thobes to your 'uds to your bouzoukis to your jews harps to your guitars to your rhythm sticks, and:

From this time forward, I pledge my loyalty to Australia and its people.

And my Mia-Mia has remembered your seasons; your mouths are full of your words in all the flavours of your markets' great food hall of life.
See,
the burger and chips, fetta and taboulis;
zilzil and gormans, gorma and nans;
shakes and squashes, chou-bow and won-tons;
wattapullams and bondas, masala and chatnis;
gado-gado and kacangs; chai and kavas
gohreng and satays; tempura and sushis
miso and wasabis; sauaerkraut and wursts
lemon myrtle rums baba and paperbark oils

and all, each and every one of you-my-Dandenong, suddenly wave your brand new citizenships very gaudily while my Mia-Mia glides as *gwion-gwion* among you all and sings her part of the Song of Galilee

165

only for Father Nyugen and into his ear in his room there:

I feel my spirit called like a stirring deep within
So I leave my boats behind, leave them on familiar shores

Father Nyugen hears this but does not know so, yet stares harder at my Mia-Mia's painting on the tea towel in his room. He sees there, again, this time in middle foreground of Dandenong Park on that Australia Day, the same old man standing out in his spuddy bare feet, his arm up to the armpit in one of the mall's rich trash bins and again he is shown being carted off to one side by men in uniform, thrown out just like in the Plaza. And again the good Father hears his mother's shaky voice in his old war-torn Vietnam as she sees him off, this time to the seminary:

'You look for him M he good you.'

but he doesn't know who M might have been even from the third painting my maidens have done especially for him.

Now, in Father Nyugen's Dandenong time, there comes the fourth painting, this time from my Grecian Maria. She executes it on a piece of paper bark she (always) mistakes for a bark piece of one of her Grecian olive trees. It brings to him her beloved Aegean Sea. When the old man, ever mindless of the main road at his defeated feet, rings the door bell at Retreat House and feels it answered, he customarily does not look up but hands my Maria's images over with his usual, 'Father Nyugen'. Only when he hears back a soft word as to why-me, does he look up to find himself confronted by the good Father himself. His sudden panic answers:

'GIFT, GIFT!'

before he flees mindless of the main road at, yes, his defeated feet. I part the ways.

Back in his room, where the last painting, this time by my Maria, wraps itself around his desk's leg as a bit of wood to a bit of wood, Father Nyugen now wonders about her dream-as-scene. She has her work effused with glazes delicate and transparent, such that the same old

166

man, now standing to attention outside my forge by St Joseph's Presbytery, is depicted with the sharp clarity of an awakening. Her old man stands alone there on the porch of the Presbytery where the good Father feels he himself should be standing. And the old man is as monumental as the two great jarrahs in the driveway by where I work, spotted fiercely by the sun and without shadow, all edges keen as razors. Does Father Nyugen think he sees in the glaze a blur of me out back in the forge, the burst of fierce burning sparks, the leather wristband, the great biceps (if I may say) about to fall? He should so wish. But the same old man seated on the weeds besides my smithy's entrance looks back out at him as eternal as all days that have passed to memory, all clocks draped over time. He sees it is the likeness of the old man who has cried out 'Gift, gift!' to him then fled mindless of the main road under his feet.

Father Nyugen wishes he had said more than the word 'why'. He should have stopped the old man, circled him, until he found out what the paintings are all about. But then he sees in my Maria's oils how he could not do that, because there at his own front door he too is caught in the light, stunned by his own astonishing feeling of gratitude for his life. It is so sudden as to be painful. He wants to cry; his chest still hurting, his old mother from old Vietnam still gripping him, seeing him off now to you-my-Dandenong so far away, saying:

'You watch out for M he good you'.

But even with this, young Nyugen still finds he never knows who M might be, not even from the fourth and last foretelling of my golden maidens.

On the weeds, outside my smithy, with those large, yes, flamed blue eyes, the old man silently pleads with me what he cannot say: that I should make the final thing at last. How can I resist? He is near his end; he is on your corners; he is on your park benches; you always see the back of him gladly; how many time can he be thrown out of the Plaza, out of Australia Days?. He has deserved the final thing... and after all I have loved, and still love, this, the making of him. That I could. He listens to me and my all from the dirt outside amongst the discarded ploughs and has done down the dawns. He is my favoured of all when I stop to think about it, which, forging, happens a lot.

By now, of course, Father Nyugen has left his room. He has left the Redemptionist Retreat in you-my-Dandenong. He has allowed himself to be driven as a now-ordained full priest. It is as he has written in the Parish News – of a miraculous journey for him from the broken walls of his childhood to this day of thanksgiving especially put on for him on this Sunday 22 April 2014 by your Dandenong time.

My Shirl, Virathni, Mia-Mia and Maria are in good voice. They are ready. They are choir as the magpies outside are choralling. They sing in unison the whole of the Song of Galilee before all you-my-Dandenong and Father Nyugen at the altar. He is surrounded by his priestly mentors up there. It is his thanksgiving, yes, and his head is bowed, even cowered, by the same sense of gratitude my Maria has depicted. Now he can nod it, that gratitude. He does so to you-my-Dandenong all congregated there and he does so to his fellow priests all gathered behind him there. Above all, he does so to his old mother and two of his brothers seated there, brought anonymously in for the occasion as somebody's gift to him, other than my ladies' painting which he doesn't understand.

Even now my Shirl, Virathni, Mia-Mia and Maria are completing their recessional hymn before they should, going:

Deep within my heart I feel voices whispering to me
Words I can understand, meanings I cannot clearly hear.

Father Nyugen takes hold of the Eucharist. Those ciborium and chalice he uses are copper gilt. As manufactures or mementoes, I regard as them as barely passable. Even now, as my ladies trill their liturgy:
may Nyugen always see Your hand at work in his life
he raises, yes, the ciborium and distributes the host as solemnly as he newly can. Now is the chalice, the wine. It is in the style of my Maria's painting. There are no shadows, no shades, only the quickening edges of a moment in vacuum. We hush; you-my-Dandenong all bow your heads in blessing as you know how it should be at the end of long and vast migrations that have come to you and ended with you.

But yet, there is some fluttering that now raises your heads. Only my beauties can keep to their humming. For you-my-Dandenong, there is the blur of movement at the edge of your world-won eyes that mars the moment. The same old man's breaths shooffff like the wind of my bellows in urge, his feet mindless, still, of any main road under his feet, and in his hands, procession high, is held the final thing he asked of me. It is a chalice and in this light I remain still proud of it. This is no copper-gilt, no silver pretend. It hums of the same gold from which I wrought the first of you all, the best and the worse of you all. Except the old man, of course.

This the final gift for Father Nyugen, yes. The old man nods to the mother of Father Nyugen, how the long ways of all have led to her. She feels how she has stood like that, watching and waiting, ever since she was with child. He nods as he delivers the chalice not to her son but to her as if by solemn fulfilment, dipping his old head again and again until he is sure she has come to understand. Finally.

'Finally' is the word he used when commissioning me to finish it all.

Ah, like sound corrected, time rings iron again. The old man has gone. My Shirl, my Virathni, my Mia-Mia and my Maria swell into the last recessional line:
In memories I have known how you sent familiar rains.

Clear-as-a-bell comes this to the forge. You-my-Dandenong hush and bow your heads as to how you know the end of long detours should be bestowed.

Father Nyugen has already hurried down to his mother. Already she is reeling him in by the corner of his stole and there-and-then hisses how it was his own grandfather who came home from The Deaths to first say:
'You look him M he good you'
while, now in sure instinct, her hand shakes follow-that-old-man, there is M.

Right there, Father Nyugen looks down at the chalice, finally, passed on. In its scintilla he finds reflected a time before he was, when his

169

grandfather and his friend the young soldier crouched among the bloody paddy vowing to nourish each other beyond any grave in the killing fields there. Beneath the chalice he will see my stamp of 'M', exactly as the old man instructed me, exactly as he once vowed amongst the bloody paddy fields.

And, yes, finally, your new priest nods. It is as if you-my-Dandenong have already infused in him how, underneath each and every paid-for miracle come just rightly-timed at every step of the long journey's way, there is a stamp of M-for-me, a stamp of call-me-old-man, the bearer of gifts along the whole arduous trek of it, the journey. And how, finally, it isn't hard to find.

Nevertheless, the good Father knows the duty of incumbency. He kisses his mother's hair, turns to use his own-now chalice for his first ministration to you-my-Dandenong, even as excitement quickens his pace. After, he lets himself fly from your celebrations and from out of the half-guilts of not, after all, being blessed by blind fate. He is urgent to give homage to the old man M before what he has never realised before slips him by again as it did his father, so giving grief.

There is just the invisible side gate to pass through between St Joseph's and my Presbytery. Father Nyugen takes it as the smallest hurdle. He holds out his now-own chalice to share in the way only a full priest knows how *benedicite vobis* goes. He heads for the forge, for my smithy. He is not the first and won't be the last.

Beneath the sparse comforts of the old jarrah by the once-and-ever maid's quarters of the old priest's house I better remember, Father Nyugen stops before what he is seeing and what he thinks he should see. He feels his mother hug his arm, be still now, leaning her face into his shoulder, meaning that finally *look-you-him* is near enough now to be still now. Somehow she knows he cannot see any old man sitting in the dirt outside my forge, or anything of him. There is only the once old stone horse trough down the driveway and some of my old cast horseshoes beneath the ever-earth at your feet.

Yet if Father Nyugen knows how to look, he might notice the weeds impressed where the old man sits waiting for him to finally come. But of course the new priest doesn't know how to do that. He isn't yet one of you-my-Dandenong, able to fully look in on through your ghostly shades and understand at least a bit of it all.

He'll learn.

Last of her tribe

[Truganinni, 1]

Don't blame me like for the rubbing out of the Tasmanian aborigines. I'm already treated like snot back at the office so it's no big surprise when they-who-pay lumber me with recording these two old-boners down the old-boners home in Truganinni Street there, right? At least Nursie Nice-nough's nice enough to shunt me past the old near-goners watching the box in what could be the morgue waiting room and out through the back where old Tru and Jessie are hunched over the *Sun-Herald*'s giant crossword like they wouldn't care if I'm from the United Nations, so I'm recording straight off, aren't I? Getting in good with they-who-pay, right? If you're like listening to what I'm getting down on memory, old Tru's got the crotchety voice past gappy teeth and Jessie's the dentures with a life of their own.

The time I'm getting all this, Tru's blowing her grey mop over old Jessie's dumb silence over some clue and suddenly screech-like going,
'What's the delay, what's the time lag?'
and Jessie's mistaking that as another clue like altogether going,
'How many letters?'
and old Tru really blowing her stack this time going,
'Dopey old moll!'
and Jessie outraged'n'retorting,
'Who's a dopey old moll?!'
and Tru's with hackles up going;
'You're a dopey old moll!'

In disgust of all, perhaps even of me (and I hadn't even been introduced by then), Tru threw down her pen and poked me in the belly button follow-me, sprung to her feet with surprising agility and had already started to trundle off down the long amber corridor there.

Jessie spurted out her own outrage at being left behind. The trouble was she didn't have the joints to overcome gravity as easily as Tru. When she finally struggled to her feet, her Tru was already metres ahead and gaining speed. In almost panic now, Jessie shoved me out of the way and clambered to fall into line behind. You can hear even me doing my own best to keep up.

'Watchit, up-ahead!' Tru was klaxoning ahead.

'Honk, honk!' Jessie honked emphasis from behind.

'Outa the way, mugs!' Tru beep-beeped, waving as though her arm extended to the staff Moses threatened the Red Sea with. As she ploughed onwards, she careened from side to side pretty alarmingly. Even from back where I was, I thought she might have been staggering, and making even old Jessie go:

'Hey, you stick to the left!'

'Up sticking to the left!', Tru goes back even on tape.

'Hey, you stick to the road rules!'

'Up the road rules!', goes Tru.

By now, old Tru seemed to have gotten up more speed than she could control herself. She took the turn at the end of the corridor by bouncing off the opposite wall and then, doing a wheelie, like, on one foot, was gone from sight. On the tape, even I think I hear the screech of tyres from her.

The prospect of her Tru having a collision she couldn't prevent seemed to spur Jessie on more urgently. Just before she herself screeched around the corner, she shouted out with real alarm:

'Watch out, World, Madam Mountain's coming through!'

So there's the three of us squishing and squelching on the old-bones near-goner lino. As I say, listen on the Replay. Even so, already Jessie's nailed my mike and she'd going on the run nonstop going as she goes nonstop:

What can I say to the waiting public? Choof-choof, always on the choof-choof, isn't she ever. They nicked her trying to run a red light.

Dangerous driving in charge of a wheelchair; what sort of rhubarb is that? You're off the road for keeps, the beak orders her. Oh yeah? Eat this one; it squeaks, she says and gives the beak the right royal digit. She just trades up for a Wheelchairs-R-Us Shag-Magnet 4WD mean machine with ochre-n-black trim and matching muddies and Blackpowers-R-Us pennant flag with tungsten frame, bull bars rhino-strength and hunting lights to freeze a charging buffalo or any bank you know back. Gears? They'd grind away your back teeth and they're driving Bridgestone 275s on Dirty Dog wheel trims, enough to make Everest look an anthill. Anyway, there I am tossed out of another kitchen waiting for any lift I can get on the first road I can make it to and suddenly there's Tru gunning smoke outa twin spoilers as she pulls over on the track out of Hobart. Hop on, she says. No worries, I says. Halfway across Bass Strait I finally get to ask at the top of this big brute of a breaking wave we're zooming over, How come the mainland? She yells back, the only piece of me Tassie's getting is the back of my big black bum.

So, I'm beetling down the corridor behind them too and catching up to them sort of, when suddenly I'm getting introduced to their twin-share suite like the old-boner near-goner brochure says, like if your imagination's on the go. It's like a room with a dunny and a door in and a door out. There's chaos there that'd shame my room and I live in *that* out of real disgust. Like, over the TV there's humungous red satin bloomers Queen Victoria would've played rugby in and they're out drying without shame or something. There's bottles and jars and sticky crunched-up kleenexs that I still don't want to think about. I'm getting to go into asthma distress with a fog of talcs and, you-don't-have-to-be-Einstein, false-teeth glues, probably for fixing wigs on too.

But don't get me like wrong. It's not too bad. In fact it's sort of comfy, like. I had a grandmother too. And outside there's this french door caper onto a real cheery little small garden all mardi gras'd up with flowers and what gardens have. Trouble is this french door isn't open to letting fresh air in; and also there's like this something-else smell not quite right, right? I'm thinking zoos and I'm like thinking lion cages and that blood'n'bone knock-the-nose-over you get there. And I'm watching both of them pulling back the curtain that's around one of the beds like it's Chinese royalty inside and holding out this like long-dead

175

ham sandwich they'd pinched from the lunchtime sitting I guess and Tru's going,

'Ooo's my pretty boy then?'

and Jessie's going,

'Ooo's our own King Billyboy, give's a smack on the lips'

and I'm suddenly looking at this goanna, big mothafrrrukker, dinosaur nightmare come true, right there on the pillow there like it's the Lion King up on the rock posing for publicity stills. But it's wearing this like dog's harness on, all tartan, and there's these red bows around its revolting neck and revolting tail and all these Smiley stickers stuck along its back, I mean really badly.

It looks like its thinking it's surveying all it commands and it's got this upchuckative purple tongue thing lolling out of the side of its upchuckative mouth thing. Meantime old Tru and Jessie, they're pushing this sandwich at it going,

'Ooos'

this and

'Ooos'

that, when all of a sudden-like it like snatches it, raises its revolting head to dragon's heaven or something and swallows the bread to halfway and then stops like a statute of the Lion King somebody's shoved his half-finished sanny into the mouth of in the middle of that publicity shoot. Did I say how it's got these false eyebrows the old girls've eye'liner'd in? Eyes in your ears you could see them, even, if you're listening right.

And I'm there cooling my heels in the doorway when suddenly I'm guessing I must be in like Flynn, like, and old Tru's going to me like I've passed into some secret society,

'Scoffing his greens puts hair on his little chest'

and Jessie nodding you're-family going,

'Call him Billyboy, or your majesty will do'

and if you listen you can just hear I'm nodding away great great, thinking how do you work Godzilla the goanna into oral history to impress those-who-pay?, when Jessie snatched the mike away from me again, going rat-tat nonstop like:

What can I say? We're just past Flinders Island when she cops sight of old Bill Lanne hauling in this whale, bleeding all over the place, both of them. I'm sorry more for the whale in the hands of that big black blowhard m'self because they should've been boiling his blubber down for candles not the whale, but Tru's .coming alongside his ship batting her eyebrows and wriggling her hips and she's calling Ahoy you can come alongside of me anytime, you big one-left hunk you. Hop on Bill, she shouts into the Roaring Forties funnily off Antarctica. No way Ugly, the so-called last of the Tasmanian males, useless as my fanny all of 'em, burps back. But Tru, she was a goner for him right from the start. So we end up choof-choofing around that Bass Strait in the wake of that rotgut of a whaler like a lovesick seagull, her not me. Tru gunned the Shag Magnet down to twenty-five fathoms to rescue his false teeth. She thundered alongside when he threw his breakfast up over the side and bottled it in case he needed it later, never mind poor Shag Magnet's duco. She followed him ashore to Hobart Town, George Town, Queenstown, all the whitie towns before Van Diemen's Land got stuck with Tasmania -- or that's what they told me anyway. Old Bill couldn't stagger out of a Ladies' Lounge without Tru waiting there outside for him and then parading the Shag Magnet before him wherever he staggered like make way for King Bill and showing the black-rights flag in the form of a crayon drawing of what was to become when some mainlander saw the light, and her trumpeting MAKE WAY FOR HIM WHO'S NOW ME ONE'N'ONLY, NO BULL to all and sundry, never mind embarrassing yours truly as snow-white as they come. The pubs closed, there he'd be flaked over the Shag Magnet's handlebars like Lord Muck of the Fowlhouse as though that Sailor's Rest was a palace not a doss-down. Only that time when the real lah-de-dah Prince of Wales bowls up to meet him aboard the real royal yacht do we hang back on the tide. By this time they've all started calling him King Billy too on account he's near enough to being the last of the Tassie mob, as close as Bill Lanne would ever get to this side of the law, and after that all we're doing is dodging paparazzi whatcumcallits and other socialite scumbags while we're propping him up on the floorboards drunk as a skunk and twice as salty as he drunkenly goes dispensing holey dollars like it's confetti they've given him dolled-out charity like. I'm telling you all this cos there was nothing Tru wouldn't do for that man. We rode the whale's back so he wouldn't have to strain his harpoon eye. We towed their carcasses back to the big boat so poor little Billy-willy wouldn't get splinters rowing too hard or had to dirty his hands. Even in the teeth of the Southerly, you could hear them all sniggering, bloody old Bill's got his hooks into a bit of a boongy bint; fate worse than death. And if you listened right you could hear Tru crying out inside, He's me last man, ever, no bull! And me trying to point out, He is the last, Tru, no bull. And she screaming back, what's the diff, dopey? Me, I never could say. What do I know?

And that's just half of it. Back in their room when they were introducing him that time like, what I reckon is you can hear Billyboy give this big burp right then'n'there, like publicity wanted him to say a few words into the mike. And I'm saying to m'self like forget oral histories, what I could be recording is a first of some lizard/goanna monstrosity going burp-wise, and on cue. See?, and back at the office I get to tell how Billyboy's been with the old girls for five years or more, no crap, and like how they'd kept him hidden in the closet of that near-goner's place, don't ask me how. Like, the staff there must've thought those two old girls were just a bit more on the nose than a couple of old ducks ought to be. Anyway burp or not, on cue or not like, when Billyboy does it, they're suddenly two sweet old ladies, sitting all prim like, hands in laps, ankles together, lips going that zipped-up thing. And I'm suddenly thinking would butter melt in their mouths before it went off? They're waiting for me to ask what they-who-pay say I've got to ask, so I ask it: like what would you say to Life Itself?, as if it was a question of life itself, and I'm getting Tru going,
'I'd say suck on this'
and Jessie going,
'I'd go for the crutch with me knee'
and Tru going with her finger,
'I'd say sit on this; I'm sitting on yours'
and Jessie going,
'Hey, droopy-drawers, get back in line with all the other lover boys'.

At this stage, I'm really getting dived-up on this oral-history stuff and needing a bit of fresh air, so I'm pushing my luck with old Tru first going like when were you born? And she's going,
'Born? In 1803 before you ever got flushed out, little fellah'
and I'm like double-taking going,
'1803?'

178

and she going all high-horse,
'Who said 1803? I said thereabouts'.
But oral history's at stake here and making they-who-pay believe what they're listening to, right?, and I'm not letting go going where born like and suddenly Tru's replayable going,
'I was born in a rock pool, in a water pond, in the lilies of a dancing tide, Junior'.
and somehow I'm looking at that wheelchair and thinking she's in this near-goners' joint and she's still sitting in it like it's some, yeah, throne and I'm going sorry-sorry and keeping my mouth clammed. Back at the office they-who-pay are riding me why I gave up at that point, switch the recorder off; it's oral history; it's ours too not just hers stuff nor yours to wonder why, kid. Well, it might be like oral history to them but it's all rubbery to me. I'm just the finger on the button, right?

But even so, like, I've plucked up the fortitude to ask old Jessie too when she was born like, and she's going just as bad as Tru had, going,
'You cheeky b.'
and also going,
'Don't ask me where what do I know?, 'cepting it was close to where the migrant ship left from in Pommyland and when it finally got to dock at that Melbourne wharf there, where didn't I ever stand on that gangplank because nobody's going to throw their leg over me and I yelled down to all those horny Eye-tite men down there on the dockside looking for a bit even if they had to take a bride and I gave them a real cop of an eyeful and then gave it to them straight, "Righto, who's game?"'

This Jessie, she's so skinny, it's like when she clacks those dentures, it's like her bones are breaking. Old Tru's as black as the ace of spade but all shiny like you'd like to dive into her at a beach party when the full moon's going. So this is oral history for real, I'm going to myself and the silence that follows doesn't stop old Jessie nailing my mike again going here we go again:

What can I say you ain't heard? She bawled her eyes out after they found old Bill, big celebrity by then, in the lane and sliced his head open to pinch his skull not an hour onto his death bed. Then after the rotten government mob sawed off his hands and feet so no other buggers would have his whole skeleton to sell, she bawled her eyes out. Then after that, after they robbed what was left him that'd been put in a grave that night, she bawled her little eyes out. What could I do? King Billy gone, then gone into pieces. Tell me lovie I go to her which piece did you love the best and we're go after that, but now they started calling her Queenie, Queen Tru, and I'm spending all my time on Shag Magnet's buckboard trying to sink the boot in keeping them all off from coming at her with callipers trying to measure her konk and which piece of her's going to fit in their jars. Y'wanta know what size she is?, I go. She wears one-size-fits-all New-York-Yankee's baseball cap, I yell out but you don't hear anyone laugh. Meanwhile they've got chocks under the Shag Magnet's Bridgestones. They're asking her all these questions with pens n' notepads n' press passes stuck in their hats and there's whole horizons of them, in white coats n' government ties'n'collars too. Then one day she grabs me and crushes herself into me and I cradle her and she cries out, Don't let them cut me up, she screeches. No way little lady, I go, we're getting out of here! And I shove her into the passenger seat and I took the wheel m'self and I gunned old Shag Magnet down the Derwent and we sailed off high into the sunset and at 110 kilometres I levelled her out and tell her it's all right now Tru, and we put our heads down and we sleep the sleep of the innocent at Zero G for, what?, maybe 10 or 20 or so Ashes series, until one day she moved my over and shooed off the family of wedgetails and put the foot down, right hand down back down to little planet in the big wide universe earth again. Let 'em come, she shouted. Do your worse, she shouted. Up all of youse, she shouted. And we whooped and we waved and we went a bit ratbaggy! We caught this boomer and surfed its dump and slid down its great face and we freestyled right across the beach there at Warrnambool, down Timor Street past the Civic Centre, up north to the Murray through the orchards and onto the Dig tree and a turn or two around Burkie and Willsie's ghosts, hammered along with a wurly-wurly northeast-like to nail the Opera House with a few hoony wheelies, crashed the Dividing Range like piss-all until we laid down rubber along a few of those Barrier reefs off Cairns, no sweat n' bugger the greenies, burned off the crocs at Kakadu, showed them a thing or two, bombed out Broome like they thought the Japs were back with a vengeance, then touched down light as a flibberty feather, three-point job, neat and nice, on the top of Ayers Rock at sunset. Lovely, it was. Uluru, Truggie sighed. Oo-roo to you too, I sighed all giggly.

180

Safe at last. Spot on at last. Ozzies. Basked in ruby. I tell you.

The dud thing with being you-know initiated into the tribe is for the week after that I'm Billyboy's babysitter while them two lovely ladies take off as soon as I front going giggling down the corridor and coming back only when time's-up smelling of like chocolate and gin. If it's not gin, it ain't no roses, either. Me, I'm like only the finger on Play; if it's on it's on, like if it's not, it's not, so what do I know? Fact is, best you fast wind to my fourth or whatever visit and I'm just arriving when the near-goners' place's Manager bad-arse's foghorner voice coming over old Tru's there in her room wailing, like I've walked into something terrible you don't get in your normal oral histories. So, I'm there suddenly stopped in my tracks looking in to their room and old Tru's on her knees with old Jessie's trying to hoist her up into the wheelchair but old Tru's holding Billyboy in her hands and I see he's not moving or even pretending to be the Lion King high up on the cliff that time. His erky tongue's lolling out one side. His red tail bow is like dangling just by a last erky scale. All the Smiley stickers've fallen off on the floor. What can I tell you you can't hear listening closely anyway? His eyeliner eyebrow are all smudged, you know? 'Cepting for her near-retching like sobbing away and the Manager, there seems this soundproofing all over the world, you'd think. That's old Jessie finally getting to help lift Billyboy into her lap and old Tru's cradling his or its, whatever, cheek against her cheek and she's like blowing into his spew-making nostril like she's practicing the tuba or something. I'm thinking a fit coming. But old Jessie's holding both of them sort of from falling over going,
'Ssh ssh'
if you listen real hard and old Tru starts grabbing old Jessie's old hair with her old near-goner left hand and like someone had run her through she's screaming going,
'Don't let them cut me up!'

I'm wanting to do something but I'm stuck there. This is really hurtful I tell they-who-pay but at the office later.

Yet while all this is going on, as I say by tape, there's, like, that Manager bad-arse standing back like King Tut Himself and pontificating on high going with a real mealy-mouth,

181

'We'll find out who did this, trust me on this'.

Dude must've been a politician once. Anyway, Tru and Jessie's giving him the big I for ignore and Tru's lifting Billyboy up to me, like why me?, and her big near-goner eyes are going great crying pools and my own chest's going real tight and then, would you believe like?, she's only crawling to the garden outside those french windows on her knees, outside to their garden thingo out there, yes, right? And Jessie she's with Tru and on her knees too. And they're both suddenly on all fours clawing the little earth in that little garden and going all hysterical and you can even hear them digging that grave for Billyboy with their own bare hands. Jesus H. (I hope you didn't hear me going that cos they-who-pay-me don't like that sort of thing around the office.)

Then all I'm hearing is bad-arse Manager King Tut tutt-tutting and he's not coming with any sympathy at all at any of this being done in his heavenly empire, even if it's full of near-goners, and going
'You can't do that without permission!'
and when the old Tru and Jessie take no notice, like who'd expect them to?, he's only turning to me 'stho I'm guilty of going two bare handed too with his heaven-on-earth too, and he's going.
'Nobody's allowed to say we allow that around here!'

Now, I don't know much but I know this ain't right, not even for they-who-pay. I'm thinking oral history's got oral in it, but not gut-bustingness for the near-goners, far as I can see, right?, so I make to slip off'n'out sayonara bad-arsed Manager but, yeah, old Jessie's somehow done the genie thing despite the bad-arse dude, and she's here-not-there collaring the mike again and she's gasping-crying-whispering-going like I thought I was going to be a near-goner myself:

What can I say but you should've copped a load of the two of us up there on the Rock, on top of, oh, Oz world and didn't all those daylets set on the daylight let! Not an inch of the Shag-Magnet's treads moved from there, yet we spun in the swoon of the great rock's eve-tiding, its amethyst in-swathed. When the great dog hooted at the drunken bo'sun moon, we lay the evening of our lives down in it and I think I heard my Tru's dreaming of huge snake coilings, immense gorgings of the pig rats, hummings-along in the all-of-times, in the never-never evers of the Ancestors, and there were moanings there and groanings there and the gay-lauds of all the tribes of her there as all sparks flibberted moon-wooed up and flittered over and over and over all. The lair the moon. The carve drawings caved. She softed and I heard. The lair the moon such a big larry, ha ha. She if-ted and I hah-ed. Then she vibrated and shook me and nodded and let off the Shag-Magnet's triple-bypass, chip-on-board hand brakes, and there we were back in present time and don't we ever lazily roll down in rivulets to the floor of the great rock, paddling across the soft Gibson, bird-tracking the Diamantina-ville with the dreamed Spirit, creaking at Coopers and buzz the bejesus out of the termites in the black stump where Tru says, Got here finally, and I say, Where?, and she just points down and says and said at n' to my Billyboy, where else, dopey?. You can believe this or not. And all she had to do was lean out over the driver's side and there he was, proud as punch, his widdle neck already cocked for the scratchies chooy-coo and his tail going swish on the wag and swoosh on the wag, and she clucking, That's my widdle Billyboy; that's oo you are. What's that?, I ask and who wouldn't?. But Tru, she says, Hey, dopey, d'you think we mob put all our eggs in one whaling basket they could dig up and chop to pieces? As long as he's the last this time, I pretend to growl. He's me one'n'only and very last, no bull, she says. From the first and last Billyboy, he always rode on my lap. What a lovey-dovey! I have a good lap, always did. A real man deserves nothing less than that, see.

The next time, the next morning and I'm already on Record coming down the corridor towards their room 'cause like you just know something's bone wrong you-know when you step in the front door. It's that thing you get in the near-goners' air. All the other old boners on their last legs are sitting around like zombs. Not even the box is on. Well, it's on but no sound, right? So you, like, start creeping on by with your finger pressing Record.

Then you get to Tru-and-Jessie's and like big surprise there's bad-arse snot-ridden Manager King Tut trying to get up on his high chariot again but you can see he's sort of stuck in the doorway of their room there like nobody gives a rat's bum about him and when I show he's suddenly taking it out on me, oh *right sure pick on me*, going, 'She's not allowed to die all over here; no she's not!'

Then he like storms out. He's not happy. You think he might have had a little bad publicity on his mind? Duh. And you can hear him going back where he thinks he can still come back at a few near-goners, going:
'We have walking tours and the shopping buses here! We have music hour! We have Snakes & Ladders and the daily rags! Nobody goes ratty here, all right?'

See, like the thing is, there's old Tru parked out on the floor in the corner of the room and I'm thinking rag doll all flopped out and her poor old head, that's dropped onto her chest and if she's making any sound I'm not picking it up. And old Jessie's by her side, where else?, and she's prodding this cup of tea at old Tru over and over but like deadpan and dead hopeless and all dead weight to it, going with each prod like:
'Tea. Tea. Tea. Tea. Tea....'

See, the thing was, someone had dug Billyboy back up from where they had buried him with their old own near-goner hands. Someone had chopped off his tail and left it there by the grave they'd dug with their own bare mitts. Someone. Had chopped off his head and left it there by the grave deliberate like, like use this as soup stock you old farts. Someone had lopped off his revolting little legs and left them there by the grave. Someone had left his tartan harness and his red bows lying there. Someone had stuck a couple of those Smiley stickers on the French doors by the grave. No one had left his little torso there. That was gone. Was the main part of Billyboy's body. See, this like trail of blood wound off from his little grave there and disappeared into the grass around the place, and all it's supposed to be is a near-goner place. I'm looking at it and I'm thinking like sinkhole, vanished. And I'm going this is not right.

Someone had left no flowers in their little garden. You can't hear any of that. I got no oral history on any of that, 'cepting Jessie's going, 'Tea. Tea...'.
to poor old comatose Tru and I let my mike likeasif fall back into her going like it was a babble, a bubble, a wind-of-all that would never stop just as it had always been started which is all I can say about it; her going in a rasp, in a whisper, but as hard as iron:

Where was I? Star lines shucked us and we took little Billyboy up pointed at the horizon. Where to now?, I shouted into the slipstream Into the lovely wind in her hair, Tru was laughing at last and I heard fly by Billyboy and me the way she said: ' We're going where we are safe where the ham sandwiches are good'. See?, did you see with us?, how the rainbow serpent, I saw as I've seen, chuckled and swaged in the steeps of the flooding inland sea as we floated by on a carpet a-flowering in neutral. Bloom and blush hush-a-bye Australia's land can. Take tea, I said. Don't let them cut me up too but bury me behind the mountains, she cried. Drink tea, I said. It's only tea. It's free. It'll do you good. Don't let them cut me up, promise again, but bury me behind the mountains, oh. Take tea, I tell her. Tru, drink tea now; it seeps down through the ages-oh. Tru. My Tru. Queenie. My Queen Tru that you are.

It's near the end of what I can away with. You have to turn up for the end, even if it's only a couple of days later, and I'm not speaking of the volume. Manager King Tut and co, they might've been able to coax old Tru out of that corner but no way have they got old Tru any further than that, see I told you, sinkhole of a wheelchair, right? I'm like wanting to do something myself but slurp-kicker Manager Tut's in my face, pushing me back with those tonsils of his going like doomsday bells ding-dong ding-dong red-faced risking apoplexy like, going what-a-putz,
'No dying allowed around here!'

What I could see of poor old Tru, she looked now like a pile of ash against the light of day. Old Jessie's like kneeling down beside her waving us all off and maybe it's the same cup of tea she's pushing and prodding away going,
'Don't cry. Tea. Take tea'
to old Tru's tears sparkling off the light of the day streaming in on everybody there now and I swear likely to melt my recorder. Like, as plain as all day. Don't cry, is what Jessie was going to her friend,
'You hear, Tru? My Tru? Just try'
and she has me by the mike and she has me by the wrist and she is squeezing the life out of all that's dear to her, seems like, going like you have to slow it down to hear right like:

What can I say when I know she is leaving?   I kept saying to Tru Don't cry. And she kept saying, Who's crying. And I kept saying, Tru, don't cry.   And she kept saying, Who's crying? Don't cry, I said. Who's crying, she kept up. Don't cry, I'm going, oh.   Who's crying, she said. Don't cry. Tru. Don't cry...

So I'm figuring somebody who-pays-me back at the office might know more than me but what I'm like wiped out about is they didn't tell me about any Tasmanian Aborigines before they sent me there or how you can like have your finger on the button then suddenly there's like extinction's forever, give or take a day. Extinction all over. And what I reckon about that, listening back on it all now and giving it thought, is Extinction stinks cos it always turns up like a bad penny the next day.

Snapped in two Tasmanians

[Truganinni, 2]

1.

From the photographer's rafter hung the rope hung the Thylacine
by the hinders hung near the hunter human-by
hung by the caption 'Extinction is Forever'
hung on the wall, mount-piece. A frame-up.

'If one dour opens, another ope-eyes'.

But Truganinni has never known what a joke is in English,
what is forever untranslatable.
Maybe a joke is a better fret than this thing they call photograph'd.

Extinction, give or take a day.

Still, the old lady frets the fret as it was and is.
The hung carcass where the hunter's eye glints the lens of forever
as much as to how forever perpetuated is.

The old lady, now, harrows for its uniquity hung to hanging.
She knows in her bones this is the
thin and thane strand of coming to know the hunters
in all their suspensions, their scents, their hell bents.

Night sighted, matt-haired reliquary too, she keens and keened oh
'Don't let them cut me up!' They did.
Fleshed her out. Strung her bones. Dangled public display.
Hung upon a post and psst and ssh-shooting-here. Do you mind?

Extinction goes on and on.

2.

The Tasmanian tiger lopes boldly where
humans track on and the moon can candle.
It brings not slink now but is unto the aromas of the sweet earths,

the long earths, the ever-bless. Strobes
are its outline as much as the warm mulcts feather its pads
as much is.

Stretches its shoulders, its hips, for this is the night
it has come from for countless generations. Round and rounds.
Momentum bounds. No studio affix'd.

The tiger the wolf breaks from wood to clearing
as the moon so candles, gambolling thrall'd
above the ever-lair; higher beyond the strange snowlining,
and yoops and yoops down the timelong corridors,
ringing back out the reveilles from all nonhumankinds.

As much as it will come as much is.
The shot too rings out a round and round and round.
Flanked and quivering, it. Hung for the exposures
unending. It ends.

In mind's eye the old lady groans'n'greets at herself
crumpling as well as well is, never understanding:

'Unique forms togetherness form ha ha. You are
the saltpetre of my soul. Simon says peter out'
the hunter jokes or how

extinction goes on and on ever the day

3.
In the photographic studio, snap,
the wolf the tiger frozen in divebomb hung.
The hunter frozen in esteem.
Still life, rafter-strumped forever.
By the side of a plant stand intimating leaves,
by the side of a weary way, lay-thy-lairy-head,
is borne the light of the extinguishing flames.

Such another thing rung out.

She might not know a joke when she sees it but
old Truganinni there stets how it is the hunters hunt
for the forever of it, for the beaters
she knows are coming over the hill for her too
and yet
cold and yet uncovered there
did she lay down adoring alone in the alley outside
and sighed aside as much as a dying whimper is...

The joke she would never get was she'd
taken too many pots, shots, and just Schnapps'd

Outside, just beyond, she was, sure, but extinction's at full pelt
They caption'd her Queen.
They caption'd it Thylacine.

But the flashbulb is forever. Exposure; over.
Shot, the days, as much are.

No better than the kids

'I not only write books. I am this book. The actual person or persons.'

Edward Nugent, the old ex-serviceman, writes that to me.

It was 1979. The blurb on the book jacket read: 'After a flash flood in 1965, an elderly man became trapped down a Sydney parkland storm drain. Children discovered him but did not tell their parents. Instead they fed him a biscuit and a bottle of water once a day for three weeks. When he was eventually rescued, the flesh on his legs had become putrescent. He did not know how long he had been down there because his mind had been wandering. In his latest novel, Bill Reed extends this situation to explore the interaction of innocence and inhumanity that is so prevalent in these days of motiveless violence.'

Elsewhere, the blurb also states: 'The author uses Edward Nugent's writings to give an authentic voice to the old man's ramblings... (he has not) altered the spelling, the style or the expressions of his (Edward's) writings.'

And on the jacket's back flap still is: 'Edward Nugent was born in Belfast in March 1900 and migrated to Australia after the second World War. He is at present living in the Salvation Army Eventide Home for Men in Adelaide, and occupies his time reading and writing. About this book Edward wrote to the author, 'I not only write books, I am this book. The actual person or persons.'

The front jacket of the novel read:
Me the Old Man.
A Novel by Bill Reed
with Edward Nugent.'

I didn't get to know Edward as you'd expect between co-authors. I can describe what I observed the four times I met him but wouldn't even begin to know what even his family situation was. I guess bad. On page 30, he writes:
'I married the wrong woman I can tell you. Her illegitimate daughter bought a house... I worked myself into bad health over it. I was nearly

65 years of age then. They threw me out then and I went into hospital (repat). The doctor had plenty to say to this daughter, all unpleasant.'

I am this book.
Whether this book is him, I don't know. If so, surely it was a poor thing for me to represent a life, to speak for his surge-and-urge. How can it be some recompense just to get his name etched in some library's data-base as a one-off Australian author? Had I known what would happen, I would have tried to do it better. I wish I had been a better author.

What drew me to his writing was, despite all the circumstances, his defiant pride and individualism. This is was most evident in remembering how he had done his bit in the wars. Read him for yourself -- page 41 ibid:
'I joined the R.N.A.S. as an Irishman. What made me join I don't know but I thought I'll have a go. I was sent to Codfort. In the morning your breath would come out as steam. Cold fish for breakfast and Maconochie stew for dinner. After all this I was sent up to Roehampton where I was taught about kite balloons. After this training I was sent to Sheerness and was put on a cruiser HMS Mingarry. Supposed to be looking for Subs. Never seen any. This cruiser seemed to want to do to the bottom and stay there. On the move again shortly after that'.

At the time, I already had my own version of 'Me the Old Man' accepted by Rigby Publishing. One of their editors pointed out the coincidence of my theme and receiving (her words, I remember) 'a funny-old' submission from an old man on haggardy scraps of paper... some 30 or so leaves initially, yellowed with sunlight, badly typed on an old typewriter needing cleaning and a new ribbon. Suddenly I was looking at more immediacy, more authenticity of an old man's stream of consciousness than I could ever effect or affect. I hurried to his Eventide Home. I offered him a third share of royalty for about a third of the book, with the promise he would never be made to feel ridiculed. He didn't hesitate. He called out to the 'Sister' (no anti-Irish, anti-Popery rank like a Salvo's Major for him, obviously) reeled her in with small, bone-swollen hands. He declared very loudly so that all in the common-room (who could hear) could hear that I was going 'to do my book'.

I think he became a celebrity from that moment. I hope he did. He had ended up amongst the destitute but, with this, his beloved stop-and-think had finally stood up for him. Look at what he puts down on page 136:
'Without a very active brain, life would seem like hell to me, I appreciate flowers, the perfume, beauty and beautiful flowers. Don't sit there, THINK… (*and on page 25*:) To sit still without thinking would be impossible for me, perhaps I am suffering from an organic disease of the brain'.

Plus, page 42:
'This time Farnborough. Parachute training. Jump out and hope the thing has been carefully packed. Now that I have been trained it's France. Up goes the balloon with camera and then all hell is let loose. The jerries throw everything at us and the Tommies are cursing us to hell for all the disturbance we are causing. I'm not worried about anything but the planes which I know will soon be over with their blasted incendiary's. At last the powers that be decided we had had enough so…. We were carried right through Italy to a place named Taranta. We stopped at different places to use toilet and get tea and the usual maconochie stew. The man machonochie must have made a bloody fortune out of this stew'.

His Salvos room was the usual economic size, but he called it his apartment. It feels important now for me to describe it. In it were a few feet between the small wardrobe and side table on one side and the single bed against the opposite wall. There was just enough room at the foot of his bed for a stool thing or perhaps a coffee table. The window displayed a typically-draining Adelaide baked-earth, cleared-sky scene looking across a crusted driveway, a crusted garden verge, a crusted back road fronting dry scrub, undoubtedly hot property nowadays. Somehow it seemed a desolation that he didn't warrant. I could see how he might want to turn inwards to his books and his fiddle. His half-a-dozen books, all library-borrowed, were arranged over his bed, quite probably (I meanly thought) for my visit. His typewriter was an old portable Adler, reduced to destitution itself; it sat where he typed, halfway along on the bed itself. (Being able to type on them, however crabbily, might be an overlooked use for those rock-hard Salvos mattresses.)　His typing paper comprised an untidy pile on the windowsill in the sun.　And he did, he did call it his fiddle.　Page 28: 'The violin. I prefer to name by the affectionate, Fiddle.　What a swine of an instrument to start on.　NO guide of any kind. Ah but the beauty, Later.　Much later. Then the bow. Something else to learn Staccato. … Pizzicato I used to dread pizzicato'.

Violins all look polished and new to me so I can't say how he had gotten hold of it, or when, or if it was anything special. It occupied an equal pride-of-place to the books, on the foot of his bed and, like the books, he obviously wanted it to define him. When I asked him to play something, he declined, saying it needed 'a good tune'.

Remembering on (page 44):
'We got on a boat at Taranta.　As soon as I sighted de Lessops statue I knew where we were, Port Said.　We were allowed ashore and there I had my first view of the Egyptians.　They didn't seem to like us very much but would sell to us.　Anyway, all the stuff was fakes.　Turn it upside down and it was marked, Made in Birmingham'.

For some reason, I always want to say 'needless to say' whenever I (still) described him as a little scrawn of a man.　He was Irish-pixie. He was imp.　He could be living at the bottom of all our gardens.　But, you see, how much of this is just what remains of what I wanted him to be… some actor fitful to my script of the little old man stuck in a drain? Yet I remember how he did purvey that manic kind of core aggression you associate with driven Irishness.　He was bandy, of course, had wisps of hair stuck across the top of his head, of course; he wore socks gone at the elastic tops showing leg-bone; he rolled his own with gourmandising care of attention; his dentures fitted so badly, of course, they often echoed a word; his eyes were green and shy more than shifty. All, of course. He was and did all of that. And yet, with all this and down-trodden, I felt he wouldn't mind coming out punching. Somehow his name had it all.

Page 120:
'I served in two world wars, R.N.A.S. – R.A.F. France, Egypt.　The suffering I have seen is beyond imagination.　France, spotting from kite balloon behind the lines for artillery, Shot down twice, Bailed out,

194

Powers in charge decided to send us to Egypt, was brought back, Tunic and all clothing taken off and steamed. The rest of us thrown in creosote tank to get rid of lice. Was put on train. Floors covered, carriages were there for horses and smelt like it. Through France and Italy, Stops for food and drink and toilet use, Sailed to Port Said, Escorted by Japan Navy, Egypt shocked me, poverty, Flies, Mosquitoes, Sand all the time, Frozen at night, burnt up through the day, When it rained as it did once a year it never stopped, I was 18 years of age then'.

He hit the sauce a bit. He had a good 'topping', as he put it, if he had something to 'plonk down on the bar'. What with the smokes, Eventide Home, pleasant and caring though I found it, would not have been an easy place for him to live in. But you knew he would have lived in it his way. I think he would have been a bit cute at any telling-off about standards, but it wouldn't have made a blind bit of difference.

And on pages 45/47:
'I was sadly disillusioned by this time. I had had enough of wars, that blasted stew. We were stationed for a while on the other side of the canal. We were here with these blasted kite balloons in the event of any Sub entering the cannel. They asked for an N.C.O. volunteer to escort some top secret stuff from Alexandra to Cairo. I volunteered, I noted the length of the train. I pointed out that one man couldn't look after all this length but all I got was we can't spare any more men. So ON I got. I had plenty of company. (Flies.)
The driver of this train seemed as if he never wanted to get anywhere at this speed. I am a crack shot so I let the driver have a bullet just above his head. I said I want this blasted train stopped every 4 hours to enable me to get some tea. Told him he would get the next bullet where it hurt if he didn't stop. I would run up to the engine and fill my tin up with water from the boiler. On my return to Kantara c/o sent for me. I wondered what the hell have I done. I thought, 'Fanning pain into a tortured death'. It was nothing. The C/O asked me if I would accept a commission. I said no, I want to get back home. This is the end of my exploits in world War one. Or as much as I can remember. FINALE. I will write about world War 2 later'.

God help me, this is about as much as I can do to honestly describe him. Why I didn't take more notice of him I don't know. It wasn't any superiority, believe me. I think it was something about a fear I had – rightful, as it turns out – that the destitute state he had fallen into would one day claim me.

Page 52:
'War; Syphilis. GONORRHEA: LICE. A Parade. Naked. You have one of these complaints, Whose fault? YOURS. You caught it where? The most likely place, Skin St, Marseilles, France. Anyone picking up a woman there was asking for trouble. The medical officer lifts up your penis with a pencil, if you are of these who can't do without a woman and can pray, start praying'.

I enlisted his words to make a novel about an old man kept trapped in a storm drain, dreaming of his life, rotting within a neglect really only shown to the least fit in society. Yet wasn't this precisely what I did to Edward -- trapped him in a book, neglecting to look down more and get to know him? Did he know this of me? After all, hadn't he written to me: 'I not only write books. I am this book. The actual person or persons.' ?

Page 121:
'1939, I was in London then, British asked for men who had been in previous war to give their services again 'Planes this time. France and Egypt again. I made a great mistake when I joined up again. I put my war ribbons on so naturally everyone turned to me as a man of experience. Instead of marching in fours, everyone was marching in threes. I had to learn, quickly, so back to books. Whilst others were out enjoying themselves I was intent on books on movements, guns etc. Books are friends. They teach you how to think quickly you are alert and out think the other fellow'.

There might be another truth in all this: it's a fair bet I might be one of the few to carry around his memory. Who else? Certainly no family, I think, and age would surely bar anyone else associated with the men's hostel of then. I might even be the only person left in whom he can hang on to having lived. It doesn't make me feel any less inadequate. In fact, I feel guilt. It's not just the guilt of not trying enough for someone who shaped me as much as any other in my life. It is of another guilt that came to hit me... some other thing I was left with shame for.

Pages 89/90/91:
'Thoughts on the Futility of war. Helopolis, Egypt. Started off with brand new Wellington. Loaded with fuel, Ammo for Malta. Lovely morning. Give pilot course. Got to Malta. They had to shove some Spits out of the way so we could land. Malta was in a hell of a state. Got the stuff off and started for England. Half way, got a radio message from England. Germans playing hell over Channel and south of England. Plotted new course over Holland, gave it to pilot. Lots of flack over Holland but couldn't touch us. When we got over Dover all hell let loose. Another radio message Gatwick fogged up. I asked how about Biggen hill, No good, fogged up. I asked the pilot if he had enough fuel. Not a chance. Well theres only one thing. Hendon. We get to Hendon and there were planes all over the place. I said to pilot get higher. No reply so I went to see what was the matter. One pilot had incendiary bullet through both legs. There was a hole beside other pilot. It looked as if a cannon shell had knocked him out so I couldn't do for him, I set plane of auto-pilot and had a look at second pilot. He was groaning a lot so I went to first aid box and got a needle and filled him with morphine through the thigh. That quietened him. I took off auto-pilot and go as high as I could. The Spits seeing the danger we were in flew around us to give us some protection. I got on to radio to ground and informed them that I would circle round to use fuel and when I had done so I would bring plane in. There were more excited. When I had used up enough fuel I started for ground as undercarriage had been shot away. I had to side slip a lot to lose speed. Their air gunners seeing that I could use plane had gained some confidence now. The ground staff were excited and I was getting fed up with their chatter. I said for Christ's sake shut up I can manage. I picked out a grassy place and touched down. I didn't do much damage. There was fire and first aid wagons all over the place but I couldn't care less. I had saved crew, plane and most important, Myself. Only the good die young'.

That other guilt I mentioned hit me so simply. I was simply driving home from work listening to the 7 o'clock 5AN news, when I simply heard the lead item which went simply something like this:

'This afternoon, the fire brigade was called to the Eventide men's hostel at Linden Park. Fire fighters found the charred body of a 79-year-old man in a room they believed the fire started in...'

The advance copies of Me the Old Man had come out only a week before. I had sent Edward his by express. A dream of his materialised. Not by hand. Express delivery. I kidded myself I'd pop round later and pop the cork with him. Try excusing that.

Three months earlier, he had written at the end of the book's typesetting-proofs (page 139):
'The old man has gone devoutly to his Creator.'

The new councillor's inaugural speech

[The new councillor, 1]

If you can ever nail down the URL of the Council you've lost the name of, then the following navigation might help you further on the website you can't find:

Home »
    Your Council »
        Media Releases »
            November »

31/04/14 - the Inaugural Speech of Cr. Lisabeth Getem-Kraken: minutes of Council Meeting April 2007 in which you'll find the full text if you're good at site maps:

[transcript]

"On a Whiff'd Prayer:
Gasping the Nettle of Local Development"

Councillor Lisabeth Getem-Kraken brings international expertise to your Council, especially as a conservationist and local-government specialist with The Commonwealth Secretariat.

This expertise came to the fore on the occasion of her maiden speech to the Council, when she tabled the transcript of the speech she gave to the Fifth Commonwealth Local Government Conference, rather than address the Council herself and contribute unnecessarily to the debate on overblown human carbon emissions and whether they were worth having in your face

.

She is married with four children, who were brought up, and pertaining to which plus other things, she says, *on the fundamental human rights principle that a breath gained is a proper airing given. At the Commonwealth Secretariat she had special responsibility for the overall analysis of expiry dates.*

Good afternoon. I have great pleasure in welcoming our conference

199

partners in the Commonwealth Local Government Forum*, especially the Association of Local Governments of Australia which represents all 675 local living-and-breathing councils here and of course to our hosts the Clean Air City of Melbourne**.

(Ed:
   * *please read instead here: 'welcome to my fellow councillors at this April meeting of the Boroondara City Council.*
   ** *please fill in your own area if you have come across an URL that also features this.)*

I would like to commence on a personal note.

Given the global issues of climate change, I am reminded of the late-2013 bushfires which led to a state of emergency in my second cousin's home town of Omeo in the slopes of eastern Victoria. As a result, my family and the whole population of over 263 were held in a breathless state for ten whole days. The fires came within a few hundred metres and, for safety reasons, along with that of the horses and cattle, we moved to the coast where breathing restrictions had not come into place. I observed then at firsthand how communities come together in the face of potential breathing disasters that, in my humble opinion, all branches of science, including shared ethics, ignore at their own peril.

At the time of the fires, I had already spent almost a decade researching rural communities trying to understand why and how they were successful at turning individual breathing into a shared survival. This frontline ability to deal with adversity I call community breathing. It refers to a locally collective reaction that deals with breathing in such a way that any adverse reaction to breathing is minimised until the threat of not breathing is over. Threats can be natural breathing disasters like said bushfires or tornados but they can also be things such as community breathless moments or situations such as mine disasters under which the whole process of breathing can come under strain.

The Morwell mining region had long ago sprang to my mind as an ideal location to study this breathing resiliency. For example, in the long mining history of the region, there have been hundreds of mining accidents in which over 99.99% have resulted in breathing deficiencies that have, in turn, become a major social challenge for the people of

Morwell to face. I began to talk to people there to find out why they thought the community had been able to breathe through all these events. Furthermore, I did control studies with neighbouring communities that had also experienced breathing which might indicate non-mining breathing activity. One of these communities had dealt with the possible development of a large scale breathing learning institute in their vicinity, resulting in a costly ten-year battle with authorities and costing the community a lot of wasted breath. An important point here was that it created tensions between those who wanted the new breathing technosciences and those who wanted to stick to the traditional ways of pulling things in. Other communities between the mining and non-mining sectors talked about the stress they were under due to breathing taking the middle path. They reported being so small they found themselves being starved of oxygen.

So what might we learn from these communities and their breathing experiences? Firstly, community breathing is a process that all communities strive to gain mastery of, and that this aspiration fluctuates over time. Secondly, sometimes communities can handle breathing more successfully than others depending upon outside influences allowing new populations to have breathing space – or, I should add, suffering a net loss due to mortality and youth-depreciation and the like. Thirdly, it is very important that the community develop positive breathing techniques in order to develop a sense of belonging. Fourthly, this leads to creating a sense of community or of sharing a useful activity as a binding activity without lung leakages. Finally, people feel more community-bonded if they are encouraged to help their neighbours during breathing alerts. An common example given to me was to follow what happened on maternity beds.

It is crucial that residents are proactive; anticipating what breath lies ahead of them by preparing themselves for breathing as an inevitable process. I have called this breathing resiliency. Breathing resiliency depends heavily upon having visionary leadership in breathing supported by greater State investment in the area, especially in the aspirations of minority groups. When all this is in place, patterns of breathing should become discernible such that plans can be formulated for early-warning systems to counter Nature's inevitable out-of-breath ructions as a force of gasp we have to suffer. It is also in times like those that we learn how much a community relies on its past breaths, facing the fact that the last one isn't necessarily the last one. This doesn't mean that all residents will be happy with the breath they take. But for the majority, a better breathing process should result in their community being better able to endure through the direct path of their nostrils.

My conclusions posed a core problem for the UN Framework Convention on Climate Change – that is, why is breathing important if it is interfering with the CO_2 emissions? I believe a community with inherent breathing resiliency has a greater chance of sustaining breath in the long run. I also believe there are people we are able to turn to help make this breath happen on a regular basis. Health and social service providers can work with rural residents to help their communities overcome ignorance of breathing. Ways to do this include: developing breathing demonstrations that foster the use of the body's own breathing tube as an aid; building breathing resources and capacities; and working with communities to sort out what they want to accomplish with the breathing they already have. Breathing builds on the strengths of rural communities -- and retaining local residents is its greatest guarantee of being fostering a healthy sector. Sustainable-breathing communities, or SBCs, mean a stronger society. If a future, there lies oxygenation! We have only to turn upon our respirators!

I would now like to turn from the personal to the broader multinational issues of the atmospheres we have to operate in.

In exercising our breathing rights, no country is an eerie. One might speculate that the future of breathing is no longer a case of pie-in-the-sky aeromancy. The United Nations itself, through UNCED, adopted Agenda 21; the UN Framework Convention on Air Climate Change (UNFCACC); the Convention on Breathing Biodiversity (CBB); and a Statement of Principles on the sustainable use and management of lungs and/or chlorophyll systems in the not-so-respiratorial (NSRs). It also set in motion negotiations that led to new agreements on nasal filtration under desertification, migratory air stocks, and the sustainability of so-called de rigueur breathing regimes in small states, starting from what is escaping from the side of mouths in froth-form is often pure oxygen wasted.

Yet many Commonwealth developing countries, especially the Least Aerobic Countries (LACs) less able to cope with the cycle of inflation in and deflation out, inflation in and deflation out etc, lack the capacity to suspire effectively during such negotiations or, indeed, to keep abreast of all the issues nation-building breathing exercises clearly outlined in wall charts in gymnasia all over the world sans borders. You might recognise this as the classic gasp-and-clasp syndrome. The Commonwealth Secretariat provides support to help these countries keep breathing in and out in self-supporting ways. Even so, advisory work on the development of legal and policy guidelines to ensure international agencies get to the bottom of lung capacities at the national level would seem to require, frankly, less throat clearing and more talk. Hot air is a killer of people with hot air in their sinuses.*

(*Ed: *See Fifth Assessment Report (AR5) -- IPCC Working Group II; turn pages until it matters.*)

At all times, I think we should all remind ourselves that there resides an underlying principle for all of us – and that is there can never be any life after breath unless you possess the lung capacity.

Lastly, I would like to touch on the legal and regulatory breathing spaces concerning the obligations of small states under the various environmental conventions to counter oxygen deficiency -- a condition I am wont to call Societal Hypoxyia – and to complement respiration.. The Commonwealth Secretariat also sensitized air-locked and geographically-vacuumed states (Swaziland, December 2004) on the rights accorded them by the 1982 United Nations Convention on the Law of the Air -- especially on access to oxygenic particles, sharing of surplus breathing stockpiles through Exclusive Aeronomic Zones, and maintenance of all deep air recesses. This over-riding Convention encourages those states to enter into buddy-breathing protocols such as that advocated by Dive U.S., with states in oxygen-desperate states given full rights to a good old-fashion suck and keep sucking until someone tells you to stop.

Finally, I think we should all reflect on how one exhalation held off is extinction forever and how we cannot hold our breath while waiting for the future just to blow over us..

I thank you* all very much. And I can tell you the first thing I'm going to do now is find out what Arab walked out of these chambers and left the door open. I am not a fan of draughts.

(Ed: please read here: 'Mr Mayor, Councillors, guests in the public gallery, and all those of Cougham ward who vented for me but still couldn't blow me off track, without their help of which')

The new councillor's in-demand speech
[The new councillor, 2]

The other Councillors broke and, as a result, the Council chamber broke for afternoon tea for the first time ever, since that's what all, other than the new Councillor Lisabeth Getem-Kraken, said they had to desperately go outside to get their hands around. Tea proved hard to find. Not one, other than the new Councillor, made that scheduled evening session.

When they arrived the next day, they found Cr Lisabeth Getem-Kraken had not moved from her place, no sir, nor even, it is said, sat. She understood about the tea but her constituency demanded she made a constituency before she stormed out of the chamber making a rude noise on her constituents' behalf. If her vocal cords had any life left in them, they wouldn't be coming back. It was plain her international experience had better things to do. A morning cup of tea for a start.

Over the next tea break, the recording was compiled and made available. It was also said to have been availed upon the once, or it might have been the twice.

Please note: there are no Ed. Notes to this transcript. The Ed. prefers to let the piece speak for itself.

[transcript]

"Speaking for the lost generations"
Good morning. I will not hum nor ha for I know how important it is to speak plainly on this subject of national importance before the next tea break.

Vocalising abuse and neglect among the human race is not new. In the nineteenth century those advocating for the maltreated were called 'the sound biters'. They tried to help communities change from seeing humans as slugs, snails, and the slimier like who are unable to make any sort of meaningful sound outside of various traction squeaks to fully-formed creatures with sounds to voice and words to give.

Nowadays there are entrenched groups even within us who work on the impulse of admitting words into society, but who still remain the objects of verbal abuse. From our early economic migrants to the first people in Australia who could form the sounds to say 'Aboriginal, bub' – who anthropologists have dubbed 'The Mouthy Australians' -- we are finally learning about the painful experiences of sounds kept warehoused in voice boxes no bigger than a solitary-confinement cell in old Pentridge Gaol where many of those voice boxes unfortunately ended up.

However, the removal policies in relation to such pent-up sound and voices, and perhaps even words of Aboriginal or nonAboriginal descent, remain one of the heaviest calls to arms for our nation, especially in the total lack of such removal policies from a surgical point of view. Very few of us, I venture to say, have witnessed a humanlike sound set free or an unfettered word on the loose.

The State *in loco mentis parenthesis* seems to have nothing but silence to say on this atrocity, though all of us know how many have demanded a simple sound – that is, two sounds -- like sorry, let alone five sounds like I apologise. Without citing words or sighting sounds, we are confined to ask in a terrible vacuum how any State can perform the functions of an encouraging society to rise up against its grip on words. These are not idle words, either. Very recent US research suggests that many voice boxes stolen by society are moved from foster voice boxees to foster voice boxees without a word in edgeways... and most of them do so without a word being said let alone that edgeways, while those left to remain in the familiar circumstances of the one foster family, or voice boxers, have been known to more easily emit sounds that approximate to fully-formed words – and these from between the lips.

Sadly, in some parts of Australia two-thirds of the local population caught trying to form words in articulated sound forms have had four or more placements under Society foster care. Adult fumbling at the runny nose aside, there are over 2,500,0000 children in our community who display the characteristics of fish gobbling for air while stranded in the dumbstruck syndrome. This is an 82% increase in a decade in which the number of muzzle sales declined even after the influx of cheaper Chinese imports sold under the banner of 'Everything under $2'. Clearly, much remains unsung, much remains at throat depth where the bends lurk but not the hand in the pocket.

One would have to maintain that the current system does not speak well of itself. The lost generations of words have been too long eschewed by the voice boxers in favour of the voice boxees. What chance did our indigenous people have? If we could but stop and listen to the deafening silence of our people's screams, we could understand how on the vast scale of one to ten how many human beings are suffering the agony of being rendered soundless. When last was a human presence last heard on the moon? When last has a good word reached the ear of God or any evacuation of wind risen to join the music of the spheres?

When, in 1948, the brilliant Russian-Jewish vocalist Rachaël ('I Hear You') Lemmings proposed her new concept of "vocicide", she took great care to define it broadly so it meant everything. Vocicide signifies a coordinated plan to destroy any meaningful exchange of sounds within and from within a group of people, including indigenes, who are not closely tied to slugs and snails and the slitherier like. Vocicide was defined as reducing words to croaking and then, by both natural and unnatural selection, reducing croaking to corking – commonly known as bunging in the bung. And when the UN Sound Accord followed the Lemmings, whole nations, whole streets suddenly were able to make themselves heard. No longer was the human race going to stand silently by while cultural, political, social, legal, intellectual, spiritual, economic, biological, physiological, psychological, moral, religious and cosmological considerations of the heard-expression type were couched only in nonverbal bugger-yous. Not only is vocicide, for Lemmings, not confined to mass killing of indigenous peoples- though it certainly may include their mass suicides - it is not necessarily any longer directed at the vicious jibe or the jape at the underbelly, eg, 'how's it hangin'?'

I have followed here in the footsteps of Lemmings to illustrate how society once again has the framework, if not the will, to imagine what sounds like human might have been like, before the critical mass of the silent is reached, if it hasn't already been reached -- and, I might add, 'speak easy' becomes just another unspoken word for a place of eating and drinking illegally .

In prohibiting sounds like human, the State has unwittingly championed substance dependence on unarticulated noise, like the current wave of car-horn conversations, bumper-against-bumper road rage, etcetera. No less than one in 20 Australians are now living in households with padded walls. Similarly one in ten Australians cannot even open his or her mouth for fear of being shushed in the cruellest of manners. Not even the privacy of toilets has remained sacrosanct. Everywhere it is no shouting in the library; rather it is oil that tractions like the snail. Those who say with sign-language that this is going too far need only look at the enormous success of Channel 7's 'Look Who Stays Flabbergasted!'. Not one of our indigenous people's stolen generations has been returned during its airing.

With over a quarter of a million notifications of suspected verbalisations per annum, Australia has the second highest notification rate in the world... yet only one in five of these cases comes before a judge. In some Australian States one in seven citizens can now expect to be mouth-gagged, subject to a vocal protection notification by the time they can say 'up youse for the rent'. These people must be fed intravenously, but no one says a word. In Cleveland, Ohio, this has reached the absurd level of one in two African-American born in China and one in five Caucasian children born to Mongoloid parents emerge from the womb with only vestigial vocal cords..

Huge numbers of dumbstruck families are "investigated" but too few receive the help they need. Many parents, mostly low income single mothers, are crying out against such investigations, thus paradoxically increasing the risk of suppression orders to both themselves and their children. Our child insulation systems are placed under enormous vocal strain, making them dangerous places for anyone daring to rail against a system that sticks in the craw like a tuning fork or a stuck pig on a bull-roarer, especially of the China-manufactured kind on the most tenuous dangle.

So what can be done? While we do not know how to prevent all bad people from sneaking up on us, a sound public-health approach which tackles the underlying risk factors of stunting vibrations holds great promise. We should sound out the following possibilities:

1. Address indigenous poverty and poor housing to reduce parental shouting words they regret later
2. Strengthen all vibrating muscles of the body, including sphincters and creaky joints, with concrete health services to support all new indigenous babies, excluding concrete bouncing exercises under five.
3. Provide free, quality elocution lessons for those with the rudiments of talking and encourage talking to spread to neighbouring tribes where any are left.
4. Resource local communities, regions, nations, space programs to encourage sounds like human to mimic what we have come to expect from fire and water, wind and sky and corroborrees where no one gets out of the bus.
5. Improve the knowledge of all professions working with, and teaching of, languages by redefining the shameful and bringing back the outburst, providing no outburst is more than one sound long, that sound to be decided by Government committee.
6. Enhance the capacity of domestic violence, dementia and drug and alcohol dependence to create greater awareness of beneficial effects of making oneself heard while sniffing the double-sounded word petrol.
7. Replace the word 'adjectives' with 'alcohol' in 'Adjectives and Children Don't Mix' advertising campaigns.
8. Throw out the Outback.
9. Overthrow all forms of government, from the smallest council to the highest international forum, that have replaced the gravely voice with the gavel. Support the 'Kill the Murderers of Rhyme and Verse or Any Other Bastard' petition and say the indigenous population started it all.
9. Fart, not to put a too fine a point on it; don't fluff. Practise eating with your mouth open for at least two hours a day. Reward snoring. Talking in one's sleep not recognised.
10. Finally, if you're out in the bush or kicking around Redfern and you come across a lost voice, tread on it and stop the infection in its tracks.

It is time to go beyond a world where only Nature has its say. We are in the 21st Century now, no longer that 20th Century. The human race has a right to its say. One could go on and on about this, but I think it is sufficient to remind you all there was once a thing called literature, you know. It is time to bring it back and then to bring it to Australia which had missed out on it altogether, providing not a word is said about it.

The stolen generations of our indigenous people demand to be heard as really stolen not just said to have been stolen.

Lastly, forgive my throat. It's the frog's fault.

Sticking the boot into Charlie

I ate my first and only rose in the old Drill Hall in Dandenong when it was used by the RSL way back. Charlie was still in uniform, as I remember, and he and Mum were dancing the Pride of Erin or whatever, when I did as big sis dared and gulped down the rose from the flower-setting on the buffet. I didn't chew it; that was my excuse.

I have no idea why I wanted to own up to that now, except that I've always associated doing weird things around Charlie, a man I'd have to say I never ever bothered to get to know despite the fact, I guess, he raised me.

That Mum met Charlie I couldn't deny, since they were together for more than forty years. He sort of just materialised. One day he was not in my life; the next he was not only in my life, *but there was no other life but him*. No announcement of 'my new friend on a little visit' ever came from Mum. He was just there around my fifth year -- and I'm even guessing there.

So, would you expect me to say that he was a real train-wreck of a stepfather? I honestly can't. All I can is he kept driving me up the wall day after day.
\
You ask where did all this wanting to put the boot into Charlie come from? It came via big sis. One day she insisted she'd heard 'undeniably' our real father lived in Adelaide in a big house with its *own* swimming pool. The logic from that was Charlie was keeping us back from our natural birthright, as in our own swimming pool. In its place, he dispensed daily trials-sent-to-try-you, like greasy spikey-hairy pigs-trotters on Saturday nights and those Sunday-night one-for-all baths... take four turns, four added saucepans of hot water – and me always last go. That sort of lack of birthright.

The earliest job I remember Mum doing was at that shoe factory off old Lonsdale Street. They might have met there. Her punching the clock with him in uniform (a private's, what else?) waiting outside on a blind date, maybe. I still hope that it wasn't in the front bar of the old Orient next door to the shoe factory.

211

From a very sorry old wedding certificate, they were married in 1945, 12 April, at St James. Our place was right around the corner, but big sis and I were at home at the time. Suddenly a crowd of rollicking adults stormed in. All I remember was Mum looked nice.

Mum? She moved at her own serene pace, as a one-time third-place Miss Amateur Springvale should. Was there a non-genteel bone in her body? I don't think so. Maybe her: 'he's got a shitty liver' whenever Charlie sulked, as he often did, comprised a kind of, you know, *streak*. But, as for us trying to put the boot into Charlie in front of her, she was all hum, but not hum *for* us. Something somehow would contrive to distract her and she'd start humming. Humming. Not listening. What can you do?

When big sis left to vent her spleen nursing, I was left to fight for *standards* that represented the birthright of our own swimming pool and the like. I couldn't picket my own home with placards, so I decided to plump for brains over brawn and turn to gentle irony to bring his birthright-killingness to the outside world. I forced myself to call him Sir. Not Dad or Charlie or Chook, but a yes-sir-no-sir, two-bags-full type of full-kitbag Sir-gentle-irony.

I thought I was being so crafty.

The snag was he didn't bat an eyelid at Sir. For all those years I tried, Sir just passed over his head. He just seemed to accept it was right me saying it. The more he went on doing so, the more it drove me crazy. And what did I get reciprocated? Never son or Bill, but always, *always*, boofhead, droopy-drawers, stinky, bill-the-dill, buggerlugs -- *and not giving a stuff who was within ear shot to hear it.*

Or you get a load of that punching on my arm... the fist with his forefinger's knuckle protruding and whack!, right on the bone of my upper arm. It hurt. Did that matter? Did he ever change? For years and years there I'd be screaming inside when he guzzled straight from the milk bottle while standing right at the fridge... or let loose wind in that squeaky way then blame the dog. There were those singlets he wore, so half, half-not, over that beer-gut, parading those leaps of skin from

212

suntan to slug-bleached that could never have lounged around one's own swimming pool. And that fag, seam-kakky from spit, nasty-thin and nasty-crooked, stuck on his lip, flapping as he coughed his heart out... it's a public fanfare that he and his owned no swimming pool. And cough? That wasn't coughing. It was cranking up some old buckboard and it bent him over barking to some earthbound fiend to let the last bit of barbed wire out. And would any pool owner sit like that in a TV chair? Forgive me if I don't know who you know, but who else would be stretched back, legs flung out as in pole-axed, bare feet producing some odious kind of air-spray, the dog slurp-slurping between his toes?

Who could blame a kid for turning to invention as an aspro to reality? I started telling my mates that 'Sir' was no mere nightshift casual taxi-driver, but a fleet-owner. Also, he, and therefore me, was the closest relative of that interstate trucking concern of the same surname (far enough away) in Geelong. And our weatherboard, all floors rot-soft, was only temporary until the insurance company finished rebuilding our Mt Dandenong residence following the bushfires. Oh, and the one I really savoured the best to spout: how it might look like his bum was hanging out of his strides, but at home he always insisted on collar-and-tie for dinner.

It was with horror of being caught out then that the next thing I started hearing after he got that new job 'carrying spuds' was something called a suspended one-month sentence. I mean, sure lift a bag as one of the perks, but even a kid my age could see how hard it'd be for anyone to get caught... like, caught *redhanded*... when all he had to do was use a judicious toe-cap, as in oops-did-that-fall-off-and-get-spoiled? But caught red-handed he had to be, didn't he? One month, too. A measly one month. Not even anything you could boast about. I mean, everything had to be a disaster with him.

I didn't start this to give any wrong impression of my stepfather Charlie. As far as I can remember, never in his life did he take even one sickie from work. I know he always turned up at home to fry up those leftover mashed potatoes for my lunch when Mum was at work and I popped home from school to save the lunch money. And if occasionally he'd drink himself a bit silly down the pub, he'd sneak in without saying a word, like a soft brewery breeze, crawl into the cot, turn out the light, and you wouldn't hear boo until next morning. And I won't lie about how he always let Mum dive into his wages every week. Didn't she ever! And I won't go on about how they cut that brute of a tumour out of one of his buttocks... gaping, it was, and deep and bloody, as raw as a shark's attack. And I could go on about never once hearing him complain over the whole six months it sort of, and sort of didn't, take to heal

----

Charlie.

He glided out of a war smelling of sweat-staled khaki serge, and into my life. I wore his slouch hat down to my ears. I wrapped his webbing belt twice around my midriff and managed to clip it. It was the same with his garters; their straps'n'buckles never could be tightened enough. These were too big for me to play war, yet I knew even then they allowed me to make-believe within a mystery of some greatness and some sadness of things other than my own world. Even today, I can still smell him as the soldier he was when he came into our lives. It was as if he had emerged from the war the real deal to be perpetuated, forever shaped and fashioned and sensed in a way that would make him indivisible from anything he would thereafter touch with a full-on world-war's chaos.

And why or how had he appeared out of a furlough? It took me a full thirty years to realize it wasn't for the express torment of me, but simply for the love story of his life.

You see, I had the grief and I had the pain of lifting his bloodied shirt and that one shoe out of the boot of his decrepit Holden HJ. Where I leant against the bumper bar there was where the myocardial infarction would have felled him. It fell to me to take that shirt, that one shoe, inside to Mum. Oh. To her humming, oh.

She was then in her brief remission from the breast cancer. .

It had been the year before that, leaving her back there in the hospital, to fell to my lot to have to tell him:

'Charlie, Mum has cancer'.

He pinned those green eyes on me as though I was physically attacking him... such a big man to step backwards in shock... and he cried out in a way that could well have started the rent in his heart:

'*She is my woman!*'

I knew then. Then I knew how it had been a love story all along -- and how, while I, boofhead, was setting my sights to always try to put the boot into him, he with her and she with him, they had simply always been gliding too high for the likes of me, and from where, it was plain to see, they had a better view of everything, including swimming-pool genes.

Charlie.

He glided, yes, out of a war smelling of unwashed bottle-green serge, and into my life, and what I was was just a witness to his love story. He had come to say:

'*She is my woman!*'

But the whole thing of it, you see, was his old bombs. I couldn't begin to count how many there were of them. One time he boasted he changed cars at least every six months. They talk about compulsive behaviour nowadays, but, if he'd been recorded, he would have had to be some sort of pioneer with it. I know for sure he never had the cash to actually buy any of them outright, but after he'd somehow got the first of them, then the old Fords, and Oldsmobile and Austins and Morrises and Holdens and Falcons, you name them, still came and went as though he had his own production line of old bombs. Somewhere along the line even the old garage at home lost its doors. And I say pioneer, because he rode the new-fangled Hire-Purchase phenomenon even before it was understood, let alone became half-respectable. By playing car-yards against each other, one bomb half paid-for became the deposit for the next waiting H.P. contract. Trade up, trade down, who cares? Just *write the new agreement*.

It wasn't the cars he called 'the old crates' in themselves so much, though. I'm inclined to think his mania for the next-one revolved all around the boot. I reckon the next car was only a mildly-interesting new look built in front of the same old boot. I mean, I never saw him under the bonnet up front, but he was always fiddling away in the boot behind and waving us all away from getting too close. I am not kidding. For example, before getting in the car he'd always walk round to check if the boot was locked. Mum, big sis and I would be seated inside waiting for the earthquake to come when he bullied the boot handle up and down as though the boot could take it even if the rest of the old crate couldn't. At least after that, then we could relax because we knew we'd finally be off soon. If he was near the boot, he wouldn't go direct at it, but do a whole circuit of the car before assaulting that boot handle. The signal of his hand patting the boot on the head meant all's-well-with-the-world, and open road here we come.

It was how he drove too. It seemed to me to be all about what was behind, not what was up ahead. He drove one-handed, with the right arm flopping away outside the driver's window like it was dismembered, even while he changed gears. His head was always tipped outwards as though what he could hear was more important than what he had to look out for. All right, you might want to listen to the engine occasionally or the road hub-bub, but I always felt he was listening more to what was happening behind. Often, often, he'd suddenly jam on the brakes with:

'What's that *banging*?'

meaning out back with the boot, and out he'd get and you'd hear him trudge around to the boot, give its handle a couple of those earth-rocking yanks, then he'd climb back in as though disaster had been averted and take off one-handedly again.

I actually couldn't say if he was a tidy man or an untidy one. All I can say is how it looked. Big sis and I – or anybody – had to share the back seat with the spare tyre, the jack, re-useable fan-belts and all the stuff like tools you'd leave in the boot because you are a normal sort of person. I can honestly say without rancour here that, in this, he wasn't. Most of the time I had to sit on the spare tyre like it was a giant donut cushion because it wasn't lady-like for my sister to be plonked there, or stay where she was plonked. I still cannot look at tyres without thinking of the rashes their rubber so easily drum up on the back of your thighs and calves. The same goes for rims and thinking how nasty on the bum they get on long journeys. When I got too big and my head started hitting the roof, a concession was made and the tyre got slotted behind the front seat, but then there was no room for my legs and I had to sit side-saddle, which was okay because it got to irritate my sister. Even today all car trips smell of hot rubber to me.

As I said, tidy or untidy, I don't really know since I'm trying to be objective here... Charlie never let me close enough to his boots to see what was in there or what state they were in. I just got the fleeting impressions they were all pretty empty and all pretty neat in there but I wouldn't admit it.

Talking about when I got big enough, Charlie was never stingy, you have to give him that. At soon as I turned sixteen, he always let me borrow the car. Okay, I always had to suffer the usual singsong ritual of:

'Boofie wants to prang the charabanc again, bing bang bong!'

But he'd always give me the keys readily enough. I'll rephrase that. One key. The ignition key. He'd take the key to the boot off the key-ring first and put it, for a careless man, terribly carefully in his pocket. Not that I cared a hoot. Who needed a boot? You kept valuables, like the new beer stubbies in those days, in your lap or on the floor under your feet where you could keep an eye on them from thieving mates.

One night there was a real crisis. I pranged the front passenger-side into a no-standing pole while parking one-handed like he did. It was a catastrophe for a teenager, as though that parking sign had been something alive and only there to make me fess up to doing something down to his non-swimming-pool level, and, worse, *in public*. I still remember how this bomb was an old 20-year-old Terraplane, yet it's still hard to own up to something like that to your old man. To say I was just as careless, or maybe accident-prone, as he was. He was on the couch listening to the races. I stepped up to the plate and said,

'Sir, the car got itself a bit bingled.'

He jumped up like he'd been shot and shouted:

'*Where*?!'

'Front mudguard!', I cried out with contagious alarm.

But all he did was giggle and flop back onto the couch.

'Oh, how shitty and stiff titty. Droopy drawers.'

You see how you could really get to know him?

Okay to enter the boot, though, were suitcases and bags and stuff. Anything that represented a bit of a travel was happily hoisted up and gently laid to rest in there. Oh, and picnic things, like blankets and food and those huge early metal eskies... these were fine. Pop, in they'd go as merrily as you'd like. Then slam crash, and the whole car being on rockers while the lock got tested again by what felt like Iron Man again.

There was one time I remember when the lock had obviously 'gone'. The boot handle was tied down to the bumper-bar with more rope than used on Gulliver in *Gulliver's Travels*. I know that particular old crate of his got given a swift replacement, as though he could stand for most things but that was *it*.

Infarction they call it.

Such an ugly word, such a thing. I was around home with Mum when one of his workmates drove the old E.J. back from the market and sheepishly left it in the driveway. It was so painful to see the blood still on the lip of the boot. They said he went quickly, standing there looking into the boot, before just keeling over and hitting his poor head as he went. His gear they put in there. They said that, yes. 'His gear'. And me, I felt bound to go out and collect it before Mum tried to.

As it happened, his gear turned out to be his shirt fullstop. It was torn and bloody. Oh. I rolled it up so Mum wouldn't see that, but she was behind me, watching, standing back reverently, as though not yet invited 'in'. It was her standing back like that which, I think, made me force myself to take my first real look into one of Charlie's boots. At first, nothing apart from that horrid shirt thing... in there all was neat and pristine, *un-violated,* as I think I expected. Yet I felt ambiguous, and I'm sure that must have showed on my face when I turned back to Mum.

'I always thought,' she shrugged terribly, 'he always wanted to be ready to go. Him and his boots.'

And then she said, yes, terribly, pointing towards the back of the boot,

'Don't forget that.'

I hadn't seen it. It was an old Cadbury's Old Gold chocolate box. I dared reach in for it. Now I felt the robber. Very carefully I removed the rubber band that was holding its feeble top on. There were brand-new, yet surely wartime, army-issue underpants and one sock folded neatly on top of his war medals.

In those thirty-some years, I had never seen his medals, never even thought they might exist. I didn't know. I hadn't asked.

There was not one but six of them, all war-service, but one struck me in particular.

On its red-white-and-blue ribbon there was a silver oak leaf clasp.

And also, you see, there I was not three days later in the caretaker's so-called parlour, shown in through heavy curtains that seem to part onto another scale of experience, where formaldehyde was air, and where Charlie was laid out for my formal identification. Without his dentures, he looked so *dehydrated.* I nodded: our Charlie, yes. In there, too, I pointed to his shoulder as if that was the identifier needed. It was dead centre of his left shoulder -- a circular welt, still ruddy, the skin puckered in widening swirls around it. I somehow always thought of time stopping on a stone dropped into a pond. I still do. I must have asked a question.

'Bullet. You wouldn't want that covered up, mate', the caretaker fellow just whispered.

Bullet. I didn't know. I'd stared at it, revolted, for years but I never asked, did I?

You know, this is what the internet can tell you. It can tell you what the oak leaf clasp on his war medal was for. It tells you that it is for being Mentioned in Dispatches for 'bravery or for exemplary service'.

I didn't know. I hadn't asked, had I? And the internet, it tells you where to get a service record and how to see he was a POW and how his oak leaf was for carrying on fighting after he'd managed to escape from the Japanese and into the steaming jungle on the trip between Changi and the monstrous Sandakan POW camp. When the Nips executed the last 21 survivors, on 27 August 1945, 10 days *after* the Japanese formal surrender, only six out of the 2434 men who arrived at Sandakan had managed to escape and survive.

The internet could tell you that. What the internet won't tell you either was what the sheer horror must have been, but would you have bothered to ask?

My mother had said about the boots, 'I always thought he always wanted to be ready to go. Him and his boots.'

As I say, what did I know? I hadn't asked. And, you see... you see... the thing is my Charlie wouldn't have told me anything about the sheer horror either.

That much I do know of him. Now.

critics on Bill Reed

'Bill Reed is a major Australian author... one might find much of his writing Joycean, some of it Kafkaish and mostly all Rabelaisean. Yet it remains uniquely his own very Australian voice... a great writer... a great original'
Nadine Amadio, Arts National

On STIGMATA
'Stigmata is a compelling Australian novel with the kind of piercing emotional power that illuminated Patrick White's writing.'
Review, Sunday Telegraph
'Challenges comparison with Faulkner, not to mention Patrick White.'
Veronica Brady, Australian Book Review
'Bill Reed's characters bear stigmata, like Patrick White's "the burnt ones", but there is nothing derivative about Reed's highly original and forceful style, nor his driven, anguished characters.'
Helen Daniel, the Age

On ME, THE OLD MAN
'Like certain Samuel Beckett novels, it could have left the reader feeling suicidal but in fact the final effect is one of driving elation.'
Jill Neville, Sydney Morning Herald

On IHE
'IHE is a fabulous comic creation.'
Helen Daniel, The Age

On CROOKS
'... totally uninhibited, Rabelasian and inventive'
Elizabeth Riddell, Bulletin Magazine
'Reed has a great comic gift. Crooks is a very funny book. An hilarious and outrageous book.'
Nadine Amadio, Arts National

On TUSK
'A fascinating hybrid of political thriller and metaphysical fable.'
Andrew Riemer, Sydney Morning Herald
'Tusk is one of those rare novels that really deserves an immediate re-reading. It is complex, multi-layered, and a superb psychological puzzle.'
Rosser Street, The Australian